# WIND RIVER LAWMAN

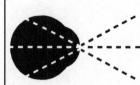

This Large Print Book carries the Seal of Approval of N.A.V.H.

# WIND RIVER LAWMAN

## LINDSAY MCKENNA

**THORNDIKE PRESS**
A part of Gale, a Cengage Company

Farmington Hills, Mich • San Francisco • New York • Waterville, Maine
Meriden, Conn • Mason, Ohio • Chicago

Copyright © 2018 by Nauman Living Trust.
A Wind River Valley Novel.
Thorndike Press, a part of Gale, a Cengage Company.

**LIBRARY OF CONGRESS CIP DATA ON FILE.**
**CATALOGUING IN PUBLICATION FOR THIS BOOK**
**IS AVAILABLE FROM THE LIBRARY OF CONGRESS**

ISBN-13: 978-1-4328-6475-0 (hardcover alk. paper)

Published in 2019 by arrangement with Zebra Books, an imprint of Kensington Publishing Corp.

Printed in Mexico
1 2 3 4 5 6 7 23 22 21 20 19

*To my 2 favorite dentists!*

*Dr. Steve Vergara,*
*Arizona Smile Designs,*
*Cottonwood, Arizona,*

*and*

*Dr. Danny Ripplinger,*
*Las Vegas, Nevada,*
*who saved a very important tooth,*
*working 2.5 hours to do just that.*

*Two great guys, very kind, humorous,*
*and sensitive to a patient's needs.*
*You can't ask for more of a dentist.*
*Now? I don't fear going to one.*

# CHAPTER ONE

*June 1*

Sheriff Sarah Carter didn't know what the hell to do. She stared down at the help wanted ad she was going to place in the Jackson Hole, Wyoming, newspaper. Her finger hovered over the Send button. Had she gotten this right? Had she revealed enough about the person she was looking to hire? Conflicted, feeling as if the devil on her right shoulder was shouting at her to cut out some of the work qualifications she'd put in and the angel on her left, saying it was fine as is, she sat back, frustrated.

Her office was glass-enclosed on three sides, with a red-brick wall behind her squeaky desk chair. Outside, the deputies for Lincoln County were getting ready for a shift change at four p.m. It was the weekend, always a brutal time for drunks on the roadways. Every Saturday during the summer months, she'd assign a small task force to pull over suspected drinkers to give them Breathalyzer tests. The Wind River Valley stretched a hundred miles long, hugging the western border of the state with Idaho and Utah. It was a fifty-mile-wide valley, bracketed by the Wilson Range on the west and the Salt River Mountain on the eastern border.

What to do? What to do? Her red eyebrows bunched as she studied the computer screen.

WANTED: Wrangler with medical background. Further duty to be an assistant to an older woman. Send résumé.

Was that enough of a description? Wrangler and assistant? Actually, she had little hope that any man who applied for the position would meet both criteria. Sarah desperately needed a male wrangler to fill in and help her spry, seventy-five-year-old grandmother, Gertie Carter. She was her father, David's, mother. And the word *spry* was less than what she would use: *rocket* was more like it. Type A, unbound. A go-getter. Or, as Gertie would say, no moss *ever* grew under her feet. No siree Bob!

Her lips twitched. She dearly loved both her grandmothers, Gertie and Nell. Both were intelligent, accomplished business-women, but in completely different ways. On her ranch, Nell sold grass leases to cattlemen from other western states every spring and summer, so they could fatten their cattle on some of the greenest, richest fodder in the US.

Gertie Carter's husband, Isaac, had died a year ago. They'd been married at eighteen, started the Loosey Goosey Ranch and the rest was history. Together, they'd built an organic egg empire with free-range fowl. Today, it was the largest company in the country, providing organic eggs and fryers to all the major grocery chains. Gertie's egg empire was worth three hundred million dollars.

Now, Gertie needed some male help. Isaac had always taken care of the chicken and egg business while she tended the accounting books, the contacts with the grocery stores, orders and such. Without Isaac, and having arthritis in both her wrists, Gertie couldn't possibly fill Isaac's shoes. No, she needed a wrangler. But she also needed a man who had a medical background because Gertie would get sudden, unexpected dizzy spells and lose her balance. She'd fallen many times. And each time, she called Sarah on the cell phone, asking for help instead of dialing 911.

The problem was, Sarah was often involved in law-enforcement situations as the sheriff of the county, and she couldn't just pick up and drive back to the ranch to help her grandmother. Gertie needed help. Desperately. Right now, Sarah's father was filling in, but he couldn't do it forever. No, they had to hire someone much younger.

But who? Who would want to be known as the chicken wrangler of Wind River Valley? Maybe she should tell the prospective applicants they'd be an egg wrangler. Clearly, there was no pride in telling folks you were a chicken wrangler? With a sigh, Sarah put down her private phone number, hit the Send key and prayed for the best, not really expecting anyone to answer the ad.

Dawson Callahan was sitting at a café in Jackson Hole, having just driven to the cow town an hour earlier. He'd come from his parents' Amarillo, Texas, ranch. They'd tried to dissuade him, but he'd always wanted to find out what it would be like to live in Wyoming. No, it didn't have the Alamo. No, it didn't have the history of being the largest state in the union. All those attributes his father, Henry, always talked about, fell on deaf ears.

He'd managed to survive as a Navy combat corpsman assigned to a US Marine Corps company from age eighteen through twenty-nine. When his enlistment was up, he went home to Texas, back to being a wrangler on his father's small ranch, where they raised cattle. But it didn't fulfill him. He was restless. He wanted to strike out on his own. How many times had he dreamed of coming to Wyoming? Too many. Well, this was his chance. And as he read the help wanted ads, one caught his eye: for a wrangler with a medical background. That was him. And because his Grandma Lorena had helped raise him while both his parents worked, Dawson had a soft spot for older men and women, seeing his own grams in all of them.

Okay, he'd answer the ad as soon as he got a big breakfast. He'd find a local motel, use their business computer, fill out his résumé and see if he couldn't get hired.

*June 2*
Sarah's eyes widened. There on her personal computer the next morning was a résumé for the ad she'd placed! She quickly scanned the email.

11

My name is Dawson Callahan. Enclosed is my résumé for your job.

She sat at her desk in her own small home, a block from the courthouse where the sheriff's department was located. It was seven a.m. and she was due to go to work at eight. The only thing good about being the sheriff was that she wasn't on a shift schedule, which she hated but had done for many years earlier in her career. Trying to quell her excitement, she opened up the file that said "Résumé" on it.

Leaning down, looking at her Apple Macintosh laptop screen, she watched the file open. As she rapidly scanned the résumé, her heart beat a little harder in her chest. This man was a Texas-born wrangler, thirty years old, single and had been in the US Navy as a combat corpsman for over ten years before his enlistment was up.

What were the chances? Sarah let a soft sigh escape from between her lips, staring at the résumé, reading it again. Making sure she didn't miss anything. This sounded too good to be true. Was it? In her business as sheriff, she saw the worst of society. Not the best. Without thinking, she touched the screen with her fingertips. Dawson Callahan sounded perfect for the job, but she cautioned herself to be wary.

First, when she got to work she'd run a thorough search on him via law-enforcement channels. There was no way she wanted a felon or someone with a bad background working with her beloved grandmother. No way.

Next, after ruthlessly researching his background for law-breaking issues, Sarah would contact a friend she had at the Pentagon. He would get her the man's DD Form 214, which would fill in any blanks about his entire military service: what kind of discharge he got and if he'd had any issues within that time frame. People lied all the time. Or they told half truths or half lies, thinking that was all right. It wasn't. She wanted to know everything about this Texan — if, indeed, he really had been born in Amarillo — before setting up a meeting with him to pursue the possibility of hiring him as Gertie's assistant.

She wished she had a photo of him. She ran a Google search and came up with nothing. That was strange. Most people nowadays had a social media account, but he had no Facebook page, no Twitter account . . . no . . . nothing. That raised a red flag to a point. He'd been a US Navy medic, a combat-trained one, assigned to a Marine

Corps company. She was intimately familiar with the Corps because she'd joined at age eighteen and left at twenty-two, but not before serving in Afghanistan in Helmand Province, one of the most dangerous places to have a deployment. Every squad in a company had a Navy combat corpsman assigned to them. So that part fit and was likely accurate.

Sitting back, she wiped her face with her hands, feeling the weight and stress on her shoulders. Funny how she could let the stress in her sheriff's role slide off and found it much less troublesome than family stress. Family was as personal as it got, and Sarah understood why it was taking a toll on her. She loved Gertie. And she wanted to protect her and find someone who was damn near an angel in quality and mentality, and very compassionate to aid her. And she knew just how long the odds were of finding a man like that.

Her mind canted to the past, to the Navy corpsman in her squad. He was kind, quiet and listened a lot but didn't say much. Most of the others she'd met in those years in the Corps were like that. They were people you'd want at your side if you were bleeding out, knowing you were going to die. There was a streak of compassion in them, a humanity that Sarah rarely found in fields other than medical first responders — whether EMT, paramedic or combat corpsman. There was no question that those in the medical service field had a certain personality type. She hoped with all her heart Callahan possessed that same kind of personality, but she'd only find out if he passed the first series of rigorous searches. What did he look like? She was dying to find out because she had a knack for reading faces.

## June 3

Dawson looked at his cell phone when he got up at six a.m. The motel where he'd stayed was the cheapest he could find, on the outskirts of the wealthy corporate community. Jackson Hole, he'd found out real quick, wasn't for the poor, the disenfranchised or even the struggling middle class. When he looked at house sales, he realized Palm Springs, a very rich community, had been transplanted here. No one without a lot of money could afford to stay in this town. Himself included.

Rising to his six-foot, two-inch frame, feet bare on the oak floor, he stretched fitfully. The bed was lumpy and not supportive, leaving him with a backache that would probably sort itself out by noon. He ambled over to the desk, where there was a coffee-maker, and made a cup. Turning, he walked to the window, seeing the sky was a pale blue, the sun tipping the horizon, the town just beginning to wake up. He'd left the phone number of his hotel when he sent the résumé. Wanting to hear, he opened his cell phone email. The note was cryptic: I've received your résumé, Mr. Callahan. I'll contact you in two days. Thank you. SC.

Well, he wasn't black ops for nothing. He'd been ordered to Recon Marines, their stealth branch, and served in that capacity for ten years. More than likely? This SC, whoever that was, was checking and vetting him about now. He grinned a little and sipped his coffee, heading to the bathroom to take a hot shower. It didn't bother him that SC was giving him a thorough back-ground check; he had a grandmother, too, and he'd want to protect her from any man who wasn't on the up-and-up. Nowadays, people lied too easily. And fake news was believed, unfortunately. In the world he came from, you didn't lie at all. If you did, you were tossed out with a bad reputation and no one wanted you around them, became a pariah.

His curiosity rose as he wondered if SC

was the individual who'd placed the ad. Man or woman? He didn't know. Finishing off his coffee, he pulled open the shower-stall door.

## June 5

Deciding to take in the scope of Wind River Valley, Dawson had spent the last couple of days nosing around about potential work in the Jackson Hole area. Now, it was time to explore this valley south of the famous town.

The small burg of Wind River had 965 inhabitants, or so the sign read. It was built up on both sides of Route 89 and looked more turn-of-the-century — the twentieth one — to Dawson. He'd gone to the Tucson Wild West show and the OK Corral depiction of that historical shoot-out. This town's footprint building-wise reminded him of that time. The only impressive place was a three-story red-brick building midway down on the right, the courthouse. He saw a number of deputy cruisers on the left side of the large, 1910-style building. The jail was part of the sprawling complex. It had Victorian touches, with white wooden decorations, black, freshly painted wrought-iron fencing around the entire area, plus lots of nicely trimmed bushes and colorful foliage with a rich green lawn in the front.

It was clear to Dawson that this was a ranching town. Coming into the city limits, he'd seen at least four different three-quarter-ton pickup trucks with different ranch names painted on the side doors. There was Charlie Becker's Hay and Feed store, and he swung in and parked because the lot was full and busy with ranchers. He saw a number of men who seemed to be employed either by the ranchers or by the store, hefting hundred-pound sacks of grain or using hay hooks to load alfalfa or timothy hay into the backs of the waiting trucks in line at the two busy docks. This would be a good place to find out if there were any jobs for wranglers in this lush, verdant valley. Climbing out, he saw a sheriff's black Tahoe SUV parked with the other trucks, with gold on the sides: Lincoln County Sheriff.

Dressed in a pair of clean Levi's and a plaid gold, orange and white shirt, the sleeves rolled up, he wore his comfortable, beat-up cowboy boots and settled the tan Stetson on his head as he mounted the long, wide, wooden steps up to the double doors. Men and women were coming and going. They all looked like outdoor types, the men darkly tanned thanks to the coming summer, the women looking fit, firm and confident. Most of them wore their hair in pigtails or ponytails, all sporting either a straw hat or a Stetson. Working ranch women, just like his mother was, among her many other duties.

As he entered, he saw a gent in his sixties behind the counter with silver hair, a pair of bifocals perched on his nose and a canvas apron over his white cotton cowboy shirt and dungarees. He was sitting on a four-legged stool and punching an old-time calculator. But what got Dawson's attention was the tall, statuesque woman standing nearby in a sheriff's uniform. Her ginger-colored hair was caught up in a ponytail and she wore a black baseball cap on her head. He liked the strength of her body purely from a combat standpoint: medium boned, about five foot eight or nine inches tall, shoulders thrown back, and an easy confidence radiated from her. Dawson would swear she'd been in the military. He could only see her profile, but he would bet anything she had a heart-shaped face. From a male point of view, she was the whole package. Long, long legs encased in tan trousers that were pressed to perfection. The huge black leather belt around her waist sported a pistol and several other leather pockets, plus a flashlight, pepper spray and a pair of handcuffs. It blocked his view of her waist and hips. The long-sleeved tan blouse she wore wouldn't stop anyone from realizing she was a woman, however.

"Ha ha!" a woman called as she came in the rear door of the large store. "Here they are, Charlie! Brownies with walnuts! Come and get 'em!" and she placed a huge cookie pan that was covered with foil on the coffee table in the rear.

Charlie grinned and looked up at the sheriff. "There you go, Sarah. I think Pixie made enough for your shift-change people. Grab a box below the table where they're sitting and put one in for each deputy coming on duty, eh?"

Sarah grinned. "You know that's why I dropped by, Charlie," and she laughed huskily, lifted her hand in thanks and swung around the end of the long L-shaped counter, heading for where Pixie was bustling about.

Craning his neck, Dawson saw the huge number of brownies being uncovered by Pixie. His gaze drifted back to the gentle sway of Sarah's hips. He liked her more than he should have. Walking up to the empty counter, Dawson said, "Brownies?"

Charlie grinned. "Hello, stranger. Saw you come in the door. I'm Charlie Becker. Who might you be?" and he thrust his hand across the counter toward him.

"Dawson Callahan, sir. Nice to meet you."

"What can we do for you, Son? Or did you hear that my wife brings baked goods here around this time every day and you'd like to eat some of them?" He grinned and waggled his silver eyebrows.

Releasing the man's paper-thin hand, Dawson said, "No, sir, I'm checking out if there are any wrangling jobs in the valley. I figured a feedstore would know about such things." And then he added with a sliver of a grin, "But those brownies do smell good."

Nodding, Charlie finished adding all the items on his calculator, then ran the tape. Looking up, he said, "Well, Sarah Carter, our sheriff, is lookin' for someone who has a wrangler and medical background. That's the only job I know about right now." He waved his hand toward the rear, where Sarah and Pixie were filling a large cardboard container with enough brownies for the oncoming shift at the sheriff's department. "Might go over and introduce yourself, Son. Sarah doesn't bite," he added, his smile increasing. "And grab one of Pixie's brownies before the horde comes in the door after seeing my wife bringing in all those goodies."

Lips twitching, Dawson said, "I'll do that. Thanks."

So, Sarah Carter was the one who'd put the ad in the paper. The *SC* he'd seen signed on the email clicked. His mind worked at the speed of light — back into combat mode, he supposed — as he slowly approached the two women who were gabbing and laughing with each other. Because of his combat duties, Dawson rarely missed anything. He liked the slender length of Sarah's hand as she daintily chose brownies from the cookie sheet to place in the cardboard box she held in her other hand for her deputies. Pixie, who was very short, in her sixties, was giggling about something the sheriff had whispered to her, helping her pile the gooey, frosted brownies into the container.

It was impossible, even in so-called male clothing and wearing a baseball cap, that he would call Sarah mannish. That just wasn't gonna happen. Sarah wore loose clothing, but not too loose. Nothing was tight or body-fitting. But she sure filled out those pants and shirt nicely. Tucking away his purely sexual reaction to the woman, he saw her briefly glance in his direction, as if sensing him approaching her from the rear.

"Coming for some brownies?" she asked

him, amusement dancing in her green eyes.

Dawson halted and met her teasing grin with one of his own. "Yes, ma'am."

Sarah stepped aside, placing the lid on the box and setting it on the table. "Help yourself. And drop the ma'am. Okay?"

He liked her style, liked her low, husky voice. Turning to Pixie, he said, "Ma'am? May I take one?"

"Of course you can!" she said, pointing a finger at them. "Are you new? I don't recognize you. I'm Pixie, Charlie's wife," and she grabbed his hand, shaking it warmly.

Liking Pixie's warmth, he gently held her small hand in his. "Nice to meet you, ma'am. I'm Dawson Callahan."

"Oh," Pixie muttered, shaking her head, "I'm just like Sarah: don't ma'am me."

Hearing Sarah make an inarticulate sound in the back of her throat, he turned back to her. He extended his hand toward her. "I'm Dawson Callahan."

He saw the shock in her eyes, recognizing his name. And just as quickly, she recovered and extended her hand to him.

"Sarah Carter."

He enjoyed the warm strength of her fingers wrapping around his. Not bone crushing, but a woman who was fully in charge of herself and her life. "I know. I think you're the *SC* I sent my résumé to a few days ago."

She released his hand. "Yes, I am."

Pixie tilted her head. "Oh, I saw that ad, Sarah." She gave Dawson a thorough up-and-down look. "And you're applying for that job with Sarah's grandmother, Mr. Callahan? To be Gertie's assistant?"

"Yes, ma'— I mean, yes, I am."

Sarah gave Pixie an amused look. "I've had his résumé and" — she turned, looking up at him — "was going to contact him via email after the shift change. He beat me to it."

He liked her easygoing style, seeing a faint pink blush across her wide cheekbones. And sure enough, she did have a heart-shaped face. Tendrils of ginger had escaped her ponytail, collecting at each of her temples, emphasizing the light sprinkling of freckles across her nose and cheeks. "I didn't mean to," Dawson said, reaching for a brownie and the paper napkin Pixie gave him. "I've spent the last few days nosing around for any wrangler work up in the Jackson Hole area and decided to drive down here today to scope out the valley."

Sarah nodded. "Kind of synchronistic we met here."

24

The brownie was mouthwateringly sweet as he chewed on it. Pixie was looking up at him expectantly, hands on her hips.

"Well? How's it taste, Mr. Callahan?" she demanded pertly.

With a chuckle, he said, "Best brownie I've ever tasted, Pixie. Thank you for making them for all of us. Do I owe you or the store some money for taking one of them?"

"Oh heavens, no!" Pixie muttered, giving him a dark look. "Anyone who ambles into Charlie's store is welcome to them. There's no charge. I like makin' people happy."

"Thanks," he said between bites. "It's really good." And it was. He could sense Sarah's gaze on him and felt his skin contracting in response. Maybe because of his black ops background, he could always feel the enemy's eyes on him, his skin crawling in warning. But this wasn't about a threat. He inhaled her feminine scent, light and citrusy combined with her own unique fragrance. Sarah didn't wear any perfume, that was for sure, but his nose and ears were supersensitive, honed by years of knowing if he wasn't hyperalert, he could get killed.

Pleased, Pixie patted his arm. "Well, I'll leave you two alone. I'm gonna go up and give Charlie two of these brownies or they'll all be gone before he can walk back here to grab some for himself," she tittered.

Dawson watched the small woman go off with two brownies in hand. He could feel Sarah's intense inspection. She stood about six feet away from him. Turning, he connected with her assessing dark green gaze and said, "I didn't mean to put you on the spot."

Shrugging, Sarah said, "I don't feel like I'm in a spot, Mr. Callahan, so relax."

"Not much gets your dander up," he drawled. "Does it?" Again, he saw those full, well-shaped lips, without lipstick on them, curve faintly upward at the corners.

"Not in my line of work. Doesn't pay to let one's emotions run roughshod on someone else. Never ends up well, and I don't like to see a confrontation escalate."

She'd chosen her words carefully. He wiped the last of the chocolate frosting off the tips of his fingers. "I don't care for them myself."

"No, I can see you don't." She lowered her voice. "I was going to email you later to ask you to meet me at Kassie's Café, across the street, to talk with you about the job possibility."

He stood there listening to the tone of her low voice, understanding this was personal business, not law enforcement, because she was the sheriff. "Sure, that's doable." The corners of his eyes crinkled and he added, "I'm assuming I passed your deep, broad background check on me? Pentagon? Law enforcement?" The corners of her mouth deepened, and he could feel or maybe sense her humor about his knowledgeable comment.

"Yes," she answered coolly, "you did."

"Check out my DD Form 214, did you?" Dawson wanted her to know he realized, as a law enforcement officer, she would do such an investigation on anyone applying for a job with her grandmother. She needed to know he expected such research on her part.

The humor transferred to her eyes. "You were in black ops, Mr. Dawson. I figured you knew I'd be doing something to dig up the dirt on you when you were in the Navy."

A rumble came through his chest. "Indeed, I did, Sheriff."

"Call me Sarah when we're alone," she said.

"Call me Dawson anytime you want."

"I like your style, Dawson."

"And I like yours."

He saw pinkness once more stain her cheeks, realizing she was blushing. She might be all business, cool, calm and collected, but there was a mighty nice personal side to her, too. "We have a good place to start, then." He felt her hesitancy. Worry, maybe? He sensed it, but she had her game face in place. Was she ex-military? He was itching to know. Because she sure as hell fit the image to a tee.

Sarah had opened her mouth to speak when the radio on her left shoulder squawked to life. She held up her finger to him, then devoted her attention to the incoming call from Dispatch.

Dawson listened intently to the short conversation. There was a rollover accident on Route 89, ten miles south from where they were. The only ambulance owned by the Wind River Fire Department, which had paramedics, was twenty miles north at another accident scene, tending victims. He saw darkness come to Sarah's eyes. Then, she glanced over at him.

"Hold," she told the dispatcher, lifting her hand off the radio key. "Mr. Callahan? On your résumé, you said you were a licensed paramedic. I checked that out and verified you're up-to-date and can practice. I need you to come with me right now. Our other two paramedics are north of here and can't make it to the scene."

"I'll come with you." He made a gesture

with his chin toward the door. "I always travel with my paramedic bag. It's in the truck."

"Good. Come with me? We'll grab and go." Sarah was on the radio again, giving the intel to the dispatcher and then signing off. "We're between shifts right now. All my men and women are coming into the court-house as we speak," she said, hurrying toward the door, box of brownies in hand.

Dawson easily swung past her to open the door for her. She looked shocked by his action, but then shook it off, diving out the door and rapidly taking the steps to the gravel parking lot. "Yes, and not all your people coming in are there yet, right?"

"Right. Grab your bag and meet me at my cruiser."

"On it."

Dawson split from her at the bottom of the stairs. It felt good to be needed. He'd always liked being a combat corpsman, and he'd saved many lives with his knowledge. And he already liked Sarah way too much.

Pushing thoughts of her from his mind, he opened the door to the cab, reached in and grabbed the hefty red canvas bag by the wide, thick nylon straps. In moments, he had locked his truck and was trotting toward the Tahoe, which was now in motion, heading in his direction, lights flashing on the bar on top of the black roof.

Without preamble, he pulled open the backseat door, throwing in his paramedic bag. Shutting it, he opened the passenger door, quickly climbing in. She put the pedal to the metal and the Tahoe growled deeply, moving swiftly out onto Route 89. He didn't need to be told to buckle up. All her attention was on driving; they must have hit seventy miles per hour after getting outside the city limits. They were heading down a long, flat expanse now, with few cars on the highway.

"I'm officially deputizing you, Mr. Callahan. I can't have a civilian without a medical license with the state of Wyoming serving as a medic to potential injury victims in that rollover. Lawsuit time if I don't."

"Fine by me. I accept being deputized."

Her lips twisted. "I like your no-nonsense approach."

"Comes with the territory."

"You're okay with this?"

"Absolutely. I feel like I'm back in Afghanistan on a black ops mission," and he tossed her a grin.

She gave a snort. "Good to know."

"Call me Dawson. Okay? I don't stand on ceremony much."

"Okay, Dawson." And then she cast him a warm look. "Thanks for picking up the slack on this. You didn't have to and I know it."

"Glad to help." And he was. She was a nice blend of being businesslike and vulnerable at the same time. That drew Dawson strongly. He didn't see a wedding ring on her left hand, but in law enforcement, just as in the military, she probably didn't wear it for many good reasons. She was in her late twenties, so he would guess she was either engaged or married. Sarah Carter was way too good-looking not to be in a relationship. That saddened him, but he let it go. Since his marriage to Lucia Steward, and their subsequent divorce three years later, he hadn't been interested at all in another relationship.

Until now. What a helluva twist.

# CHAPTER TWO

**June 5**

"Are we the only help on this call?" Dawson asked, looking around. The valley was composed of farms and ranches all the way to the Wilson Range on his right and the Salt River Range on the left. There weren't many cars on the highway this time of morning.

Sarah said, "Shift changes mean people are coming and going in one concentrated area, the courthouse. We aren't out on the county highways patrolling like we should be." Her lips compressed, and she gripped the wheel a bit tighter, pushing the Tahoe to eighty miles an hour down the empty highway. The light bar was flashing, the siren screaming.

"I never thought of it that way," Dawson said, "but you're right. It's sort of like one of our Marine recon squads coming in while the other is going out beyond the wire. The

Taliban would sit for weeks watching our coming and going, keeping tabs and times on us. That's when they'd jump us."

"I was in the Corps, too," Sarah said, wanting to connect with Dawson. For a Texan, he sure seemed laid back, more a type B than a type A, but maybe she was wrong about that. She'd read the unredacted version of his DD Form 214. He'd earned the Bronze Star with a "V" for valor, a Silver Star and three Purple Hearts. He was a true hero. And typical of black ops types, those men and women in combat never pushed their weight around, bragged or boasted of what they'd done to earn those medals. She doubted, once they had time to sit down and talk, that Callahan would admit any of that unless she brought it up first. And even then, he'd probably modestly resist admitting anything.

"I guess I'm not too surprised," Dawson said and gave her a wry look. "I knew you'd been in the military."

"Oh. How?" Sarah was pleased by his insight. The man saw a lot. She needed someone who was observant like that to monitor her grandmother's busy, hectic life, to be a support to her. A mind reader of sorts.

"The way you carried yourself at Charlie's

feedstore. Squaring your shoulders. There's no slouch in your spine, Sheriff." He'd said it lightly, with a teasing note, not wanting to make her feel insulted. Or hit on. The longer he sat in the cab of the SUV, the more she interested him. There wasn't anything to dislike about this woman, he discovered, much to his chagrin. He needed a job. Not a relationship.

Laughing a bit, Sarah said, "You can't take the military out of a person, can you?" Slanting a brief look in his direction, she felt warm all over. The man was tall, ruggedly handsome and a gentleman. The old-fashioned kind, but hey, he was from Texas, and they tended to be that way, from her observations in the past.

"No, you can't."

"We'll have to trade Corps stories when we get off this call," she said. "Are you up for some coffee and chatting at Kassie's? I've read your résumé and it all checks out. And after meeting you in person, I think you might be a good fit for Gertie, my grandmother. But we can talk about that later."

"Yeah. I see a car on the berm about half a mile ahead. I thought you said it was a rollover accident?"

"That's what Dispatch was told by the

driver who called 911." She eased off the accelerator, starting to coast, eyes narrowing. There was a dark burgundy van, an older one, maybe a Toyota at first glance. Frowning, she said, "That van looks to be in perfectly good condition, as if it's never been in an accident."

"That van isn't a rollover. It's got no dents along the side panel nearest the highway and the top isn't crushed in either. And all four tires are still inflated. You wouldn't necessarily see that in a rollover. Usually one or more are blown by the impact."

The hair on her neck stood up. They were within a quarter of a mile of the vehicle.

"The hood is up. Two men are standing on the ditch side, below the berm, but I can barely see them," he added.

She appreciated his attention to detail. "This doesn't feel right," she muttered, starting to brake.

"Why? What's wrong?"

Before Sarah could speak, three men rushed from the hidden side of the van, all sporting AR-15s and firing directly at them. Bullets smashed into the windshield, thunked along the top of the vehicle, ripping and peeling back the metal. Glass shattered into thousands of glittering, sharp pieces, each a slicing projectile. Sarah cursed. She'd taken evasive car training, and she slammed on the brakes, wrenched the wheel, making the Tahoe perform a one-eighty in the middle of the highway, its nose pointed toward Wind River. The smell of burning rubber, the scream of the tires skidding across the asphalt, entered the vehicle, hurting her ears.

She'd ducked her head, but never let go of the wheel. Tiny, hot pinpricks of pain struck her chin and neck. Her mind snapped to survival mode. To getting out of this alive. Worse, she had a civilian in the Tahoe with her. "Get down!" she yelled at Callahan as the gravity hurled her back against the seat, the belt biting hard into her shoulder as they swung around.

There was no way she could take on three heavily armed men with combat rifles. Hell, she had one rifle and a handgun in the SUV and that was it. Worse, a civilian in her Tahoe, and he could be killed. She had to protect him, first, and then herself. They had to escape.

More bullets crashed into the vehicle. Her whole life, her only focus, was getting out of those gun sights. "Cartel!" she yelled to him as he ducked his head below the dashboard. The vehicle anchored after it turned. Stomping on the accelerator, Sarah hunched over as more bullets came slamming through the cabin. The rear window blew outward.

Weaving the cruiser, crushing the accelerator with her foot, she tried to make them less of a target. *Please don't let them hit the tires!* Zigzagging erratically, she tried to avoid the armor-piercing bullets that tore so easily through the metal. If any of those rounds hit, they would destroy a human. Sarah yelled, "Keep down!" She had on a Kevlar vest, but he didn't. She powered the vehicle forward, the engine screaming along with the siren.

*Son of a bitch!* Sarah would bet her paycheck Pablo Gonzalez was behind this hit. He was setting up sex trafficking in Wyoming. Gonzalez was a well-known drug lord from Guatemala who had hired merciless, hardened Central American soldiers to invade Lincoln County.

She jerked a quick glance at Dawson, who had his head and shoulders pressed below the dashboard, hands over his neck to protect it.

"Grab the radio!"

Dawson reached over, unhooking it from the dash, thrusting it in the direction of her open hand.

Taking it from him, Sarah saw that the

37

cartel members had stopped firing at her. They were almost a mile away from them. Instantly, she straightened, one hand on the wheel, the other around the radio, calling Dispatch and giving them the situation and instructions. She tried to keep her voice calm and low. Every few seconds her gaze shot from the rearview mirror to the side mirrors, making sure the men weren't following them in the van.

When she got off the radio, she saw Callahan sit up, his eyes narrowed. She heard him say as he looked behind him, "The van just left in the opposite direction from us. They're heading south on Route 89."

Sarah called Dispatch again, giving them the information. *Damn!* She'd been lured into a trap by Gonzalez. And he'd timed it perfectly. His soldiers would know this was shift-change time, that there was no one who could come to help her, much less tail the van and catch up with it. "They'll take one of many, many dirt roads off 89 and disappear," she growled, hanging up the radio. Glancing over at him, she asked, "Are you all right? Any wounds?" The wind was screaming through the Tahoe, cold and sharp.

"No, I'm fine. You?"

"Pissed, but I'm okay. I'm sorry I got you into this mess."

"Don't be. I'm used to this sort of thing." His mouth twisted. "I thought I'd left this shit behind in Afghanistan."

Snorting, Sarah rasped, "Since Gonzalez, a Guatemalan drug lord, moved into Wyoming last year, it's been an escalating war zone between his soldiers and our law enforcement. Reminds me of Afghanistan, dammit." The explanation came out gritty, filled with disgust. She saw Callahan give her a long, appraising look, but he said nothing more. The man was unfazed by this firefight. If she had any worries about him should Gertie need sudden medical help, this man would be her guardian angel, no question.

"What can you do? It's nearly 0800. Do you have a drone operator? A helo you can put into the air to follow these bastards and bring them in?"

Unhappily, she said, "No. Teton County, north of us, where Jackson Hole is, is the richest county in the state. Lincoln, my county, is the poorest, economically speaking. We couldn't rub two nickels together to make a dime out of them, much less purchase a helo."

"Does Teton County have a helo?"

"Yes, they do. You heard me tell Dispatch to contact Commander Tom Franks at Teton's sheriff's office?"

"Yes."

"I'm going to ask him to spend some of his fuel budget and fly it over here to try to locate that van and follow it."

"Will he do it?"

"Yes, unless they're using it for an emergency somewhere in his own county. Gonzalez is pushing into their turf, too. There's every reason for them to help us out."

Her heart sank as she felt a wheel wobble. It was a tire losing air. "I've got a tire going," she told him. "I'm pulling over." But only after she looked to make sure the van wasn't following them. It wasn't.

"I'll get the spare. You stay on the radio, okay? I'll take care of this for you."

"I can do it," she insisted, throwing the Tahoe into Park, setting the brake. She saw Callahan bail out of the seat and give her a one-eyebrow-raised look.

"You're the leader. You stay in comms while I do the dirty work," he ordered, shutting the door.

Sarah wanted to curse again, but it wouldn't do any good. Callahan worked hard and fast. In no time, he had the cruiser's front end up on the jack and was busy changing the tire.

All the while, Sarah contacted Dispatch, gave their GPS and kept in touch with her deputies. Right now, three Tahoes were headed in their direction at high speed. In about fifteen minutes, they'd arrive. Relief raced through her. Looking at the empty front and rear window, she decided to get out and survey the rest of the damage to the SUV. Those AR-15s had used, she was sure, armor-piercing rounds, because a shell could peel metal off anything.

Unsnapping the safety on her pistol, she warily watched the highway south of them. Gonzalez was a fox, and he was vicious. She wouldn't be surprised if the van turned around and came back to hunt them down. Gazing at her side of the cruiser, there were ten bullet holes — large ones — behind where she'd sat. She'd gotten lucky. Her adrenaline was still pumping and she was hyperalert, as she'd been in combat in Afghanistan. Her hand rested tensely against the butt of the pistol as she walked around the rear.

Callahan was putting the finishing touches on the new tire. The old, deflated one lay beside him, and she examined it. It was a self-sealing tire, but two slugs into it and the poor thing couldn't maintain air.

"That was close," she muttered, leaning down, touching the two holes.

"Yeah," he grunted, lowering the cruiser back to the ground and pulling the jack out from beneath the frame. "See the slugs down the panel?" and he gestured to them.

"Seven slugs," she said, shaking her head.

"I think our guardian angels are both bald about now," he said, hefting the tire, taking it to the rear and opening it up.

"Yeah, both hairless."

He tossed the tire into the back, pushing the rear door shut.

She chuckled. "Oh, mine has been bald since I was in Afghanistan. How about yours?" Glancing over her shoulder, Route 89 was empty. No van in sight. She felt jumpy and wary. Looking north, she wished she could see the three Lincoln cruisers speeding their way. She'd ordered her deputies to pair up, get into Kevlar, and carry rifles as well as their pistols. She wanted them armored as much as possible. Who knew what Gonzalez had up his sleeve today. If he was bold enough to attack a sheriff's cruiser, no telling what he might do next. Sarah knew she'd be calling the FBI as soon as she got back to her office.

Dawson came over to where she stood. "You sure you're okay?" and he pointed to her left upper arm. Her shirt was torn open and stained with blood. "And your face and neck has sustained a number of glass cuts."

Touching her arm, she muttered, "I didn't even feel this."

"Adrenaline's still crashing through your system, that's why." He wrapped his hand gently below the injury. "Come on, get back in the driver's seat. Let me at least put a quick dressing on it until we get back to Wind River, where I can do the job right."

His hand was firm but not overpowering. He stood at least four inches taller than her. She was five foot, ten inches tall. The look on his face was one of genuine concern. Sarah didn't want to like his steadying hand on her arm, but she did. Right now, she was starting to get shaky in the aftermath. It was a normal human response, and law enforcement got those symptoms just like anyone else who had just been caught in a trauma. "Yeah . . . you're right. I'm fine, though."

He fell into step with her. "I know. They all say that."

She managed a short bark of laughter. Before she could open the door, he opened it for her.

"Don't damn me, Sheriff. I'm a Texan. I was taught manners."

Her lips drew into a real smile. He released

43

her, and she climbed in, leaving the door open. "Most Texans I've run into are bona fide Neanderthals by nature," she shot back, watching him open the door behind her and dig into his bright red paramedic bag.

"Naw, we're not *all* like that. Some are, though," he admitted, pulling on a pair of latex gloves, getting out a roll of gauze and some scissors.

Opening the cuff on her shirt, she rolled it up and over the wound. Staring at the cut, which appeared to be from a piece of glass. In fact, she could still see it stuck in her flesh. Callahan came and stood in front of her, blocking the early morning sunlight from the east. Looking up, she drowned in his eyes, noticing the pupils were large and black. And centered wholly on her. His attention felt good, as if a blanket of calm were coming across her. "There's glass in it."

"Yeah, I can see it." He handed her the dressing and tape. "Let me examine it a little closer?"

She sat back, feeling some weakness stealing down her spine, grateful to rest against the seat for a moment. "Sure . . . go ahead."

"Relax," he murmured. "Your people will be here shortly, and I don't think those drug soldiers are going to head back in our direction."

His hand, even in latex, felt warm and comforting as he cupped the area, leaning over, eyes narrowing on the piece of glass sticking out of her flesh. A little sigh escaped from between her tightened lips.

"It's all right," he soothed, sliding his fingers along the one-inch cut. "I'll dig that out of there back at your office. Simple enough. I've got some lidocaine in my pack and I'll numb the area before I do it. Okay?"

She had closed her eyes for just a moment, giving in to her crash, absorbing Callahan's light touch. It crossed her mind that he'd probably be a pretty good lover. That popped her lashes open. Disgusted with herself, she sat up a little. "Yes . . . that would be fine."

"I can save you a trip to ER at that little hospital if you'll let me fix you up at your office. Your call, though."

She liked looking in to his eyes. They were a light gray with a black ring around the outside, telling her he was at ease and feeling calm in the moment. Sarah was sure her pupils were constricted, which was how they got when someone was under threat. "I'm fine with it. You're going to have to stick around anyway."

"Oh?"

With a grimace, she uttered, "You're a civilian I took along with me. You'll have to fill out a report. It's just the regs."

He chuckled and took a square of gauze he'd put some alcohol on, wiping away the blood beneath the cut. "Now I really feel like I'm back with Recons. I always had to fill out a sitrep — situation report — when we returned to base. Never mind I was their medic."

"Yeah, but you were a combat medic and you carried weapons, fighting right alongside them. That's the difference."

He smiled a little, set the bloody gauze back in her hand and took the roll of gauze. "We got in a few of 'em," he offered, quickly and expertly wrapping it around the wound. "There. How does that feel?"

"Okay," she said, glancing over at it. The bleeding had stopped. The white was bright against her skin. "Feels good. Thank you."

Nodding, he took the rest of the items back from her and transferred them to his bag.

Sarah rolled down her sleeve, buttoning it around her wrist. She looked up at the rearview mirror. "Here are my people," she called to him.

Dawson zipped his bag shut and closed

the door just as the three Tahoes rolled up. One parked in front of Sarah's vehicle and two behind. Six deputies bailed out: four men and two women. And they were dressed for a firefight, no question. He stood aside. Sarah quickly introduced him, and he remembered each of their names and shook their hands. They were all grim-looking, and he didn't blame them. This was not only a serious incident, but also an escalation between a drug lord and the law. They were getting ballsy in his opinion. And that was dangerous for everyone in this county.

As he stood back, he watched Sarah lead. She asked a lot of questions, got her people's input and that was good. He also saw the respect they all had for her. They reminded him more of a team out on a mission with a possible firefight than law enforcement per se. They were in their twenties and thirties, he would guess. And there were no prejudicial reactions from the males in the group. They looked to Sarah and respected her, regardless of her gender.

Once she was done speaking to them, a call from Dispatch came in, and she answered it on her shoulder radio. Dawson heard the Teton County helicopter was coming their way. It would set down, pick up Sarah, and the other three Tahoes would follow on the ground, awaiting further instructions should the helo find the escaping van. Once the radio call was completed, Sarah turned to him.

"Would you mind driving this poor old Tahoe back to the courthouse? We have a garage beneath it, and we've got two mechanics who service the vehicles."

"No, I don't mind."

"Good. Do you have a pair of tweezers, Dawson?"

His brows rose. "Yes. Why?"

She pointed to her arm. "That helo will be here in ten minutes. Can you dig that piece of glass out of my arm? When we get back, I'll make sure I get medical attention. Okay?"

He nodded. "Sure. Go sit down." She was a gutsy lady, for sure. Digging into his paramedic bag, he pulled out what he needed. The other deputies went back to their vehicles, preparing to be part of the coming chase.

She rolled up her sleeve, exposing the bandage. "Thanks for doing this. You've been indispensable today. Are you sure you're all right? It isn't every day you get shot at."

Chuckling, he quickly cut the bandage away and swabbed the area with antibacterial liquid. "Over in Afghanistan, it was like this at least two or three times a month for me and my team. It just feels like I'm back in the swing of things."

In no time, he'd given her the lidocaine, pulled out the offending piece of glass and placed a dressing over it. "You need a stitch or two in that, Sarah." He wanted to say her first name because it felt right, felt more intimate. His protective hackles were rising, and the need to be close to her was growing within him. He knew to cool his reaction because she was fully qualified to do her job. She didn't need a protector, as much as part of him wished she did. "There," he said, satisfied. "The only thing I'd watch for is redness or swelling. That means it's infected and your doc should get you on the appropriate antibiotic."

"Gotcha. Thanks," and she quickly pulled down the sleeve. "A shame to have to throw away a perfectly good shirt," she added, scowling at the torn fabric.

"You'd never get the bloodstains out of it anyway."

She smiled at him as he stepped away. "What a mother hen you are."

"Naw, now don't go tellin' anyone," he said in his best Texas drawl. Zipping up the bag, he shut the door. In the distance, he could hear the helicopter blades whapping through the air. Following the black dot in the sky, he turned, holding her warm green gaze. She was a beautiful woman, makeup or not.

"I like your accent, Dawson."

"It's all I got, ma'am." Now he was teasing her.

She stepped out of the Tahoe, handing him the keys. "I want you to fill out that report at our office. After that, you're free to go. Just leave me your motel name, phone number and your personal cell phone number. I was serious about interviewing you for that job with my grams."

"And I'm still interested," he said.

"Good." She reached out, her fingers curving around his lower arm. "Thank you for everything. I'll be in touch with you. . . ."

# CHAPTER THREE

*June 5*

Sarah couldn't sleep. It had been a long, stressful day. They hadn't found the Gonzalez soldiers' van, which left her uneasy and worried. She tried not to go there, but the drug lord was a genuine threat of the worst kind. He was trying to set up shop in her county, understanding, she was sure, that it was the most economically deprived one in the state, which spelled out less law enforcement protection. The county was too poor to pay for the deputies she desperately needed. She'd cut her own salary in half to get another employee on the payroll nearly two years ago, when she was voted in as sheriff.

The worries were so many that if she didn't block them out, she'd lay awake in a half-sleep state and then go to work tomorrow sleep-deprived and irritable. And right now, the most important personal thing on her plate was getting her feisty grandmother an assistant. If she could just offload that responsibility onto someone she could trust, it would help her so much. Her father, who had been Lincoln County's beloved sheriff for thirty years, was behind her idea to hire an assistant for Gertie.

Her small home was a block away from the courthouse, in a quiet, tree-lined neighborhood sprinkled with 1900s' two-story Victorian houses. She turned in her bed, punching the pillow, tightly shutting her eyes. Her hair was shoulder length and curled around her neck and shoulder as she tried to force her mind to something pleasant. If she could just think of something positive, good and healthy, she would fall asleep right away. On most nights that worked.

And then, Dawson Callahan's face gently intruded into her worries. He was an island of calm. Nothing seemed to rattle him. God knows, she'd been shaken up after that battle with the drug soldiers, but she wouldn't show it to anyone, not even him. As sheriff, everyone looked to her to be steady, thinking clearly and knowing what to do next. The Texan's face was oval, with a strong chin. His black hair was cut military short. He had wide cheekbones and a muscular body. He looked like he worked out, but that was conjecture on her part because he wore a long-sleeved shirt, Levi's and cowboy boots. The clothes hid his body from her for the most part. There was a quiet power around him as well. She had seen it while the bullets were flying into the SUV.

It was his eyes. . . . She could drown in them, feel the care radiating out of them toward her. Reaching out to her, the sense of protection embracing her, making her feel safer. Focusing on his medical side, she'd *wanted* to be touched by him. Sarah needed that connection after realizing she'd been injured in the fracas. It was only a piece of embedded glass in her upper arm, but it hurt like hell. She thought she'd left that kind of firefight behind her when she'd been discharged from the Marine Corps, but here it was again. It was a war out here gathering steam in Lincoln County. Rerunning Dawson's voice, remembering how low and steady it was, soothed her fractious mind and roiling emotional state.

She fell into a deep, dreamless sleep.

"Mind if I sit with you and have some coffee?" Sarah asked

Dawson looked up from the booth he'd

just taken at Kassie's Café. It was six a.m., and they'd just opened. Instantly, he was on his feet.

"Sit down," he invited. She was dressed in a pressed tan uniform. Her hair was down, the highlights reddish beneath the lights. There was a slight pink flush to her cheeks as she slid into the booth opposite him, setting her black baseball cap to one side. He could smell a subtle scent of almonds around her and wondered if it was the shampoo she used or the soap from a shower or bath. Didn't matter, really, because she smelled damned good to him. There were shadows beneath her eyes, faint, but telling him yesterday's firefight had taken a toll on her, as it would on anyone. He hadn't exactly looked chipper this morning either as he shaved and glanced into the bathroom mirror, wincing at what he saw reflected there.

The waitress came over and filled a mug of coffee, sliding it in Sarah's direction.

"Thanks," Sarah said.

"The usual?"

"Yep."

"And you, sir? What would you like to order from the menu?"

"What are you having?" he asked Sarah.

"I'd love waffles with bacon."

Dawson looked up at the waitress. "Make it two, please? And give me the check."

Sarah started to protest.

"Yes, sir," and off went the waitress.

"I should be picking up the tab," Sarah said.

"Hmm, must be my Texan ways, then," and he gave her a wry grin, watching a smile come to her green eyes. Dawson felt his whole body go on red-hot alert. Sarah's lips were perfect: full, sculptured and arresting. She wasn't classically beautiful but had a natural attractiveness that made him desire her, as well as intrigue him. He wanted to get to know her as a person.

With a snort, Sarah said, "Last time this happens, Callahan. I don't care if you're from Texas or not. You should let me buy you breakfast because you could have gotten killed out there yesterday morning. A peace offering of sorts."

"You could just as easily have died yourself," he reminded her gently, sliding his hands around the mug of coffee in front of him. "Let's just call this breakfast a celebration of life, okay? I don't do arguments in the morning if I haven't had at least three cups of coffee in me first." He held up his mug in a toast, and then took a sip as her eyes narrowed speculatively on him.

"To life," Sarah agreed, touching his mug.

"Do you come in here often for breakfast?"

"Yes, especially when I oversleep."

"What time did you get off the job yesterday?" he wondered.

"Around midnight."

"Do you normally work such late hours?" He sipped his coffee, watching more patrons moseying into the café looking half awake. This was a happy place, with smiling waitresses who he'd found out were all ex-military. And Kassie had opened the doors at six and welcomed him in even though she didn't know him personally. Her engaging smile, the genuine welcome in her eyes made him feel special. This was a woman who loved her job. Dawson was hoping the lady sheriff was dropping by to speak to him about the job.

"No. But there are days like yesterday that turn into long nights sometimes." She shrugged. "It's just part of being in law enforcement."

"At least you're not bored." A slight smile tugged at his mouth as he watched her grin a little.

"I've always had a low boredom threshold. What about you?"

It was his turn to shrug. "I thought you

got everything you wanted to know about me from that very thorough search you did both in and out of the military."

"It told me some things, not everything."

"Are you thinking I'm a possible fit for the job with your grandmother?"

"Yes," Sarah admitted, "I am. But first, I need to fill you in on exactly what you'll be doing. I don't want to hire someone who isn't fully informed of the expectations."

"I'm a wrangler and a medic, according to the ad you placed." Dawson saw her squirm a bit. Nothing obvious, but it was there. Why?

"My grandmother, Gertie, was married to Isaac Carter from the age of eighteen until he died last year at age seventy-six. Together, they created the largest organic egg and free-range chicken ranch in the country. Gertie is seventy-five and a force of nature. She's independent, runs the company to this day from her home on the ranch, deals with the buyers, the trucking schedules and all the very necessary details to keep cartons of eggs and fryers getting to market on time."

"I'm sorry her husband died. That had to be tough on her."

Sarah compressed her lips. "They had real love. They were so close. She's had a lot of depression and grief since my grandfather passed. I try to get over there as often as I can, but my job keeps me very busy. I need someone who can help Gertie daily when she needs it. Her doctor and dentist are up in Jackson Hole, and that's fifty miles away. She can't drive anymore because of some eye issues. So she relies on me and my father to drive her up there and back. My dad has his own health problems, so it falls mostly on my shoulders. She wants her assistant to live in the house with her."

"Sounds like you were caught between a rock and a hard place."

"You could say that, yes." Sarah took a deep breath and added, "Look, I'm not going to sugarcoat this for you, Dawson. Yes, you'll be a wrangler of sorts, doing odd jobs around Gertie's ranch. She's got twenty-five employees who run the egg and fryer operation. Gertie's the boss. But sometimes, her arthritis, which she has in both wrists, acts up. The pain is severe, and her brain sort of blanks out when it happens out of the blue. She doesn't have dementia or anything like that, but she's forgetful because of the pain."

"Pain will do that and more to you," Dawson agreed. "Is she open to a stranger, a man, being her assistant? Does she have a say in whether I'd be a good fit?"

Giving him a wry look, she offered, "Gertie's well aware I can't continue to do the things I've been doing for her. I can't take time off whenever she has an appointment to go somewhere. That bothers me a lot because I love her so much. She wanted me to pick a candidate I thought would be right for her and then she would interview him herself after I sifted through the wannabes and tried to match the person to her needs. I believe you'll be an excellent fit, but Gertie has the final say."

"Fair enough. I wouldn't want to take a job like this without her being part of the decision-making process. Besides, your duties lie in another direction," he pointed out. "You said the person who's hired will live in her house?"

"Yes. It's a three-story Victorian house, really beautiful. She lives on the first floor, which is the largest space, and where her office is located because she has problems with stair climbing. Her knees are getting a bit arthritic, too. So, whoever is hired would have a second-floor bedroom — it's really a suite — plus a small office. Gertie already has a housemaid, Cece, who is in her forties. She washes her hair, trims her nails and does a lot of the girlie things Gertie needs help with now. You wouldn't be expected to do anything like that. Cece has a room on the second floor, too."

"So? Do I shadow her business activity, then?"

"In a way. She's very sharp, has a degree in accounting. She has a secretary, Ann, who comes in to work six hours a day, Monday through Friday. She assists her in that area."

"Good, because I'm not a numbers guy," and he smiled a little. "I do a lot of things right, but math, aside from figuring out dosages in syringes as a paramedic, is not my strongest suit."

"You would be at her beck and call. There might be days when she needs nothing from you. She might ask you to help with packing egg pallets or something like that down at the truck depot. There's so many different things the business has to attend to. Mostly, it's helping her when she asks for your help."

"I'd be a chicken wrangler, then?" He said it teasingly.

Her grin was sour as she regarded him. "I know it feels like a demotion from being a ranch wrangler with cattle, horses and all."

"Or maybe an egg wrangler sounds better?"

60

Sarah managed a soft laugh. "Take your pick."

"What about medically? Will I be privy to her medical records?"

"Yes, all of them, plus connection with her doctor in Jackson Hole. Gertie is an old-timer who hates drugs, so even if she's in pain with her wrists, she'll never complain, and she's refused any medication from her doctor. I always had a helluva time getting her to take two aspirin to help alleviate some of the pain when it flares up."

"Well, there are a number of alternative medicines that might help her condition. I'd need to meet her, assess her issues and then I could let her know what options might be available to her so she doesn't have to suffer through an episode. Get her doctor on board and in agreement with any alternative medicine approach, too."

"That sounds good," Sarah said. "My dad will pay you twice monthly from Gertie's company banking account. Dad will be giving you your paycheck because he works on Gertie's books with her. He's responsible for paying all the employees. You'll like him a lot."

"I'm sure I will. I'm already impressed by his daughter." Again, that faint pink flush that brought out that nearly invisible coverlet of freckles stained her cheeks. Sarah looked young and free in that moment. Dawson was just now beginning to realize how many other loads she carried. Being in law enforcement was enough. But having to try to pinch-hit with her ailing grandmother and other family demands was railing on her conscience, from what he could see.

Sarah's fingers tightened a bit around her mug. "My grandmother is willing to pay you sixty thousand dollars a year for your services. Plus, full medical and dental insurance, which she'll also pay. You'll get three weeks of vacation a year. She doesn't expect you to work on weekends unless something special comes up. She gets up early, around five a.m., every day and works until about three p.m., when she lays down for a nap. Cece will take care of all your meals, and the house cleaning."

Shock rolled through him. Sixty thousand dollars was a lot of money. Far more than he'd expected. He tried not to convey his surprise. "Sounds like a good package. So? I'll pretty much be a chauffeur for her?"

"Yes, but Gertie is very active. She goes horseback riding two or three times a week when it's nice outside. You'll go with her, get the horses saddled and take care of them after the ride. She has some nice quarter horses."

"Does she need help with the barn and feeding them?"

"Yes, you would certainly help her there, although I know a couple of the guys from the egg side of the business have been donating their time to do it. They're not wranglers like you are. You would be taking over those activities, including daily box-stall cleaning."

"Good, at least I'll get a little bit of ranch life in this," and he smiled a little, seeing the brief anxiety in her eyes. Sarah was wound tight. Dawson thought she was worried he wouldn't like the job, but he did.

"She loves being outdoors. And she attends a lot of functions in the county. She donates money, eggs and fryers to a number of charities all over Wyoming. In Wind River, she works closely with Delos charities, which has a soup kitchen and a food pantry. You'll be busier than you think. No grass grows under her feet. It won't under yours either, so forewarned is forearmed."

"Sounds like she has a soft heart. I like that."

"Oh, she's a handful," Sarah warned. "Gertie has a heart of gold, but she does *not* suffer fools gladly. She's not PC at all.

Diplomacy is not her forte. What you see is what you get, warts and all."

"What does she mean to you as her granddaughter?" he wondered, seeing Sarah's surprise at his personal question.

"Well . . ." Sarah stumbled, "she's always been a part of my life. She and Gram Nell both played a strong part in my growing-up years." Turning away for a moment, she stared out into the café, which was getting busier by the moment. She said, "Let's just say there was a terrible moment in all our lives a long time ago, and it was Gertie and Nell who came to our rescue and pasted our broken family back together again. Gertie, in particular, helped me when I felt so guilt-ridden, blaming myself for what happened," and her voice trailed off to a painful whisper.

Dawson could see the pain in Sarah's eyes, heard it in the whisper of her barely spoken words. Her brows were drawn down, and there was grief in her expression even though she tried to hide it. "I'm sorry. I didn't mean to stir up something so painful for you. I was trying to gauge what Gertie brought to you, why you had such a strong, loving connection with her."

He'd stepped into something emotionally disturbing to her, much to his consternation. Sarah was no longer the sheriff. She had been terribly human in the past few minutes. Wanting to hold her, somehow comfort her because she appeared distraught and shocked by his arrowlike question, he was angry with himself. All people had skeletons in their closet; that was a given. And he'd mistakenly opened one of those doors that held something terrible from the past that she didn't want to discuss with him.

"It's up to Gertie to tell you what happened if she wants to. We never speak about it in the family. It's the elephant in the room, you know? Everyone sees it standing there, but no one is willing to say, 'I see the elephant.' " Rubbing her brow, she shot him a glance. "Every family has heartbreak, Dawson. This particular incident is ours, and it's something we'll all carry to our graves."

"I understand. I'm not going to ask about it again." He wanted to reach out but stopped himself. There was confusion in her gaze, and he sensed she wanted to share more, but now wasn't the place or time.

"What about your family? The good things about them that you could share with me?" she asked.

"My father, Henry, is a wrangler on the

65

Double Circle Ranch near Amarillo. I grew up there. My mother, Donna, is a social worker with the county."

"That's a nice combo of physical work with a mother who probably gave you a pretty good background in psychology and such?" She put her cup aside and folded her hands beneath her chin, studying him.

"Good call," Dawson congratulated her. "Yeah, my medical side definitely came from my mother. And she taught me about people, their actions and reactions. I got interested in it from an early age, but I wanted more excitement and risk taking. That's probably why I joined the Navy and became a combat medic. I saw my mother making people's lives better with her words, her knowledge of human beings, and that was a place I wanted to go, too."

"I know not all Navy medics are able to move into combat medicine. In my experience, they have something more than the usual medic."

He chuckled. "Well, there were times, Sarah, when I questioned the sanity of my choice. I'm sure my DD Form 214 showed you I was assigned to recons, and that everything we did was top secret or above. And we got into some pretty dicey situations from time to time."

"Yes, I did read your DD Form 214." Her voice lowered. "And you need to know that I consider you a genuine hero. You saved men's lives out there. You have three Purple Hearts."

Moving a bit, he shrugged. "They weren't for major injuries, so don't put much by them, okay? I didn't want them and tried to tell my CO I didn't deserve them."

"I see. Well, you can't say the same for a Bronze Star with a 'V' or a Silver Star, Dawson. I don't expect you'll ever want to discuss it with me, and that's okay. I know what those medals mean, and I know they aren't given out 'just because.' So? Are we clear on that point?"

"Clear. If you don't mind me asking, what did you do in the Corps? How long were you in for?"

"My dad had been a Marine for four years when he was young, and I followed in his footsteps. He's always been such a great role model for me. He's a good person, with good morals and values, and his integrity is without question. I wanted to be like him. Once I got into the Corps, I went into the law-enforcement side, as he had. I loved it, and when I got out at twenty-two, I had my law enforcement degree and got a job with the Teton County sheriff's office. I stayed there until two years ago. My father retired, and at his suggestion, I ran for his position to be sheriff here in Lincoln County. I got voted in and so here we are."

"I'll bet your parents are proud of you." He saw her eyes go soft with emotion, and the last of her game face dissolved. These little discoveries were thrilling to Dawson.

"They are. I think, in part, the voters of our county were hoping my dad's way of delivering justice would be similar if I was voted in," and she smiled a little.

"Were you running against a man?"

"Yes. But it wasn't much of a contest. I received eighty-five percent of the votes."

"Were you scared at first, taking on the job?" he wondered.

"Terrified. But I had good training with Commander Tom Franks up at the Teton's department. It's just that I was a woman, only twenty-seven years old when I ran for office. I honestly didn't think I had a chance, but my dad sure did. He stumped around the county for me. I'm not exactly a great speaker, but he coached me, and it worked out."

"So, you're not a very public person?" and his smile widened as her eyes grew amused.

"I'm a Scorpio. I'm a very private, intense, quiet person. My dad is a Libra; and he's a meeter-and-greeter type, very outgoing and an extrovert. I'm a complete introvert, so for me to go out and be a politician was pretty painful. I'm good with one-on-ones, but not a crowd of fifty to a hundred people."

"Funny thing, my mom is a Libra like your dad."

She laughed. "Seriously?"

"Yeah."

"Your birthday is in January. You're a Capricorn."

"Yeah, the old sea goat. My mother always teased me about that."

"What sign is your dad?"

"He's a Sagittarius. A real outdoors type, loves being out in the elements and doing a lot of hard, physical work."

"Capricorns are known as the plow horses of the signs, the hardest-working and most responsible."

"Oh," he said, opening his palms, showing his array of calluses, "I'm all of that."

She turned her palms over. "I acquired these when I was a lot younger, working on Gertie's ranch, as well as Nell's. She sells grass leases every year to cattlemen from out of state who want to fatten up their beef on our lush, green grass in the summer. I was always fence mending at Nell's ranch,

69

or digging postholes."

"I was wondering where you got your calluses. I thought you might be working out in the gym or something. But you're a wrangler yourself." It made him feel good to know that, but he didn't understand why it counted so much to him. Sarah's face was free of the darkness of her past and she was smiling fully, laughter dancing in her eyes. Dawson liked the woman who hid behind the sheriff's uniform. He understood why she had a game face and why it was necessary. But it was also nice to know she trusted him enough to let down and be herself around him. It was a huge, wonderful discovery, and his heart swelled with so much emotion, it took him by surprise. No woman had ever caught his attention like Sarah Carter did. And he had no idea where the hell these feelings would take him.

Surely Sarah was engaged or married. There was no way she couldn't be one or the other. It wasn't something he could just ask her either. But damn, he sure wanted to know. Dawson would never entertain a relationship with a married woman; it simply wasn't morally right to him. His silly heart yearned to hear that Sarah was footloose and fancy-free, but he couldn't go there, as much as he wanted to.

The more he discovered about Sarah, the more he wanted to know about the woman beneath the uniform. Worse? He liked what he saw way too much. Still, Dawson dreamed, very sure his fantasies would never come true.

# CHAPTER FOUR

*June 8*

Sarah was looking forward to her grandmother meeting Dawson. From her perspective, he would be the perfect assistant. Best
of all, she liked his alertness, awareness of
others and his ability to read between the
lines. His mother training him in psychology as he grew up didn't hurt either. He
obviously used all those skills as a combat
medic. Now, if only Gertie thought as highly
of him as Sarah did. She would find out
shortly.

It was Friday, and she was going to meet
Dawson at Gertie's ranch. She'd given him
the address and he'd said he'd find it on his
map app. The sun was high in a semi-cloudy
sky. It had rained this morning, the front
passing through the area rapidly, leaving
patches of blue sky in its wake. Gertie had
listened without interruption the other night
when she'd called her about interviewing

Dawson. And typical of her grandmother, she hadn't had much to say. Instead, she'd said she'd eyeball him at her office when she saw him face-to-face. Sarah had smiled at that comment.

The only thing Gertie asked when she was done giving a readout on him was, "Can he take the heat in the kitchen?"

Sarah assured her that Dawson could. Both her grandmothers had found out through her father what had happened with the trap set by Gonzalez's soldiers on Route 89. Just because her father was no longer sheriff didn't mean he didn't have a police scanner. After talking with Sarah, and finding out she was all right, he'd told Gram Gertie and Gram Nell, so they wouldn't be blindsided. Gossip would flare up like a wildfire in the valley, so it was better it came directly from him. Her whole family was upset at the entrapment and her brush with death. Sarah was glad the tiny wounds along her chin and neck were pretty much healed. She didn't want Gertie getting more upset about the incident than she already was. Let her focus be on Dawson, instead.

Gertie had more than once lamented about Sarah being sheriff. She wished Sarah wasn't, for many reasons. But it was the perfect spot for her to try to rectify the family's dark, grief-stricken past, and maybe utilize the position to find out information she had always been looking for but had yet to discover. She'd give anything to change the past, and she frowned as she drove down the two-lane asphalt road that led to the Loosey Goosey Ranch.

The road gently sloped into a bowl-like valley below her. There were long white aluminum buildings with steeply built green roofs to shake off heavy winter snow accumulation. Around one side of each of these buildings were ten-foot-high wire fences, encompassing up to five acres of land. There were thousands of hens loose, happily being outdoors and scratching and pecking in the dirt and grass. That was Gertie's idea, to give her free-range hens a happy place to live. When the hen was ready to lay her egg, she went inside to one of the hundreds of wooden egg boxes filled with fresh straw, to lay her egg for the day. And then employees would come through once an hour, collecting them, sending them through a washer for cleaning, a stamp on each one indicating the farm name and then, packing.

On the other side of the valley were the fryer buildings. They, too, had huge areas where the older hens who were no longer laying eggs as often, were let out each day the weather cooperated. Two other buildings housed white geese. She saw the red, two-story barn near the three-story Victorian home where Gertie had lived with her husband most of her life. Sarah had fond memories of playing on the sunporch, which encompassed three sides of the 1900s' home. There was a large, bright green swing at one end of the front porch, and she loved sitting in it. Often, she and Gertie would be out there on a warm summer day, drinking iced tea and talking. Sarah loved those times with her grandmother.

To her surprise, she saw Dawson's pickup already sitting in the asphalt parking lot on the southern side of Gertie's home. He'd arrived early and was standing nearby, dressed in his jeans, boots, black Stetson and a blue-and-white long-sleeved shirt, the cuffs rolled up to just below his elbows. He was tall and strong-looking but not musclebound. Her heart thudded upon seeing him. Yesterday had been a busy day at the office and she hadn't seen him at all. Talking to Dawson, she found it easy to let down and be herself, not to have to be official and aloof as the sheriff of Lincoln County.

As she drove up and parked next to his truck and climbed out, Dawson ambled around the front of his truck to greet her. She was in uniform and went to meet him.

"Hey, stranger," he called. He touched the edge of his Stetson.

*Old-fashioned* and *courtly* were the words Sarah wanted to use for Callahan. "Hi, yourself. When did you arrive?"

"Oh, about ten minutes ago." He gestured toward the buildings in the distance. "I wanted to get a feel for Gertie's place. It's a huge, superbusy operation," and he placed his hands on his hips, his gaze focused on the trucking terminal at the other end of the valley. "I didn't realize just how big an empire it really is."

Standing next to him, Sarah said, "She and Isaac built this from scratch. One chicken at a time. One building at a time. One dream at a time, and then investing a lot of work and elbow grease in expansion. It took them fifteen years to get all the buildings constructed, have the truck terminal built and make it all work together."

He cocked his head, his eyes meeting hers. "And you grew up with them here?"

"Oh, yes," Sarah said, smiling fondly. "My mother worked and, of course, my dad was the sheriff, so we were brought over here to Gertie's after school or over to Nell's place, depending upon who had time to take care of us. Then, my mom would pick us up after work and we'd go home for dinner and to do our homework."

Nodding, Dawson said, "Well, it's a pretty big spread."

"You ready to go in? Gertie had Cece make some peanut butter cookies for you."

"For me?"

"Sure. You do like peanut butter cookies, don't you? They're Gertie's favorite dessert."

He fell into step with her, cutting his stride a bit as they left the parking lot, heading for a red-brick sidewalk and a white picket fence gate. "I like any kind of cookies. I'm not picky," he said, opening the latch on the gate, allowing her through first.

"Thanks." Sarah halted, looking at the early flowers studding the inside of the fence. Gertie's colorful tulips, which had been planted last fall, were blooming.

Dawson turned and gazed up at the three-story structure. "The house is an architectural wonder," he said, gesturing to the third story and the green tin roof over it.

"It's on the National Heritage register," Sarah told him. "And Steve Whitcomb, the resident architect in the valley, just dotes on this particular design. He loves to come over here with his wife, Maud, to have tea with

Gertie on summer afternoons, when they can all get away from their work demands."

Taking the wooden steps, Dawson followed her up to the screen door. "I can see why. It's in top condition, painted and obviously well cared for."

"Steve has a master carpenter from Driggs, Idaho, come over every summer to replace rotting or old wood. He does wonderful work. And he has a painter from Jackson Hole come in to keep the wood protected because the winters are so long and harsh around here."

"At least I'm not expected to do that kind of work," he said in jest, standing by the screen door.

"Are you nervous about meeting our force of nature?" Sarah asked, opening the screen and pressing the doorbell.

"Curious? Yes. But nervous? No."

"Not much rattles you, does it, Dawson?"

"Not after my years overseas; you're right."

The door swung open.

Gertie Carter stood in the doorway, peering critically at Dawson through her watery blue eyes.

Sarah squelched a smile. "Hi, Grandma. I want you to meet Dawson Callahan. Dawson? My grandmother, Gertie Carter."

"Nice to meet you, ma'am," he said, taking off his Stetson and offering her his hand.

"At least you got manners, young man," and Gertie slid her parchmentlike hand into his. Then she tilted a look in Sarah's direction. "He's got calluses on his hand. That's a good sign."

Chuckling, Sarah said, "He's a hard worker, Gertie. May we come in?" Her grandmother was in her typical workaday garb: jeans, a pair of beat-up old brown Oxford shoes and bright red socks to go along with her starched, long-sleeved white blouse with a red knit sweater vest over it. Her hair was silver and gray, short and bobbed. Sarah hoped Dawson didn't assume that because she was only five feet tall and wiry that she was a pushover. Gertie was tough as nails. He towered over her, and Sarah noticed how gently he took her hand to shake it. But Gertie was surprisingly strong, and she saw her grandmother grip his much-larger hand with a returning firmness that placed a look of surprise on Dawson's face.

Releasing his hand, Gertie said, "Of course. Come on in. We'll go to the kitchen first, and then to the dining room to chat. Cece's just taken out some fresh peanut butter cookies from the oven. I've got iced tea waitin' for us." She turned, leading them down the hall.

Dawson gestured for Sarah to go inside first as he held the screen door open for her. In his other hand was his Stetson, which he kept off his head. She liked his manners a lot. And she could tell Gertie was pleased with them, too. Maybe Westerners expected good manners from their men even in this day and age, when such gallantry was considered dead and buried. But it wasn't dead in the West. Her black boots thunked lightly down the mahogany floor, which shined a reddish hue beneath the lights above.

Waiting, she turned, seeing Dawson shut both doors and then walk over to a clothes tree and hang his hat on it.

"Ready?" she asked, watching as he quickly took in his surroundings.

"Lead on."

Sarah brought him into the kitchen. Cece was at the counter and waved her hand in their direction, scooping the last of the cookies onto a plate with a spatula.

"Those smell good, Cece," Sarah said, going over to pick up the plate.

"I've had trouble keeping Gertie outta here." The forty-year-old woman chuckled.

Sarah turned toward him. "Dawson, this

is Cece. She's Gertie's housekeeper and cook."

Cece smiled up at him, shook his hand and said, "Right nice to meet you, Mr. Callahan."

"Call me Dawson, ma'am. Nice to meet you, too."

Gertie walked across the huge kitchen toward another door. "This way, young man. Let's have a seat at the dining room table, and Cece will bring us refreshments."

Dawson followed her.

Sarah smiled at Cece, who smiled back.

Leaning forward, Cece whispered in her ear, "He's awfully good-looking!"

"I know."

"And he's got manners!"

"He's from Texas."

"Ohhh, that explains it all. Well, skedaddle! I'll bring the tray of drinks."

Sarah gave Cece a quick hug, then went into the dining room. It was as large as the kitchen but separate from the kitchen itself, as all turn-of-the-century homes were. The polished mahogany rectangular table was ten feet long and had been in the Carter family for over a hundred years. The chairs surrounding it were original to the antique table, all with nicely padded seats.

Gertie was going to pull out the main

chair at the end of the table to sit down, but Dawson beat her to it, pulling it out for her.

"Why . . . thank you, Mr. Callahan," she murmured, sitting down. Poking a finger to her right, she said, "You sit there. Sarah? You sit on my left, please?"

Sarah had placed the plate of cookies between them and then sat down. Cece brought in a sterling-silver tray with three glasses of iced tea, a saucer of freshly cut lemons and a sugar bowl, plus spoons and napkins. In no time, she'd served them. There was a pocket door to the main dining room, and the housekeeper slid it shut, leaving them in privacy.

"Well!" Gertie said to Sarah. "It's nice to see you again, my dear."

"I've been missing in action," Sarah apologized. She picked up two cookies and set them on her porcelain plate.

"Are you doing all right?" and Gertie motioned to her left arm, knowing she'd had some stitches in it at the local hospital after the attack by Gonzalez.

"Yes, fine. Everything is back to normal again, so don't worry."

Gertie took three cookies off the plate. "Young man? Don't be late getting these goodies or we'll have them all eaten before you can grab yourself some of Cece's world-famous cookies."

Dawson nodded and took two. "Ladies first," he told the older woman.

"Right nice to see your folks taught you right." Gertie busied herself with taking a bite of the first cookie. "Sarah, here, tells me you're from Texas. That your father is a wrangler on a major ranch near Amarillo. Why aren't you back there working on *that* ranch instead of lookin' for work here in Wyoming?"

Dawson squeezed some lemon into his tall glass of iced tea. "Because I've always wanted to fulfill my dream of coming to Wyoming."

"Isn't Texas big enough for ya?"

Lips twisting, Dawson said, "It's not about size, ma'am. It's about my curiosity regarding this state. Even as a kid, I wanted to come up here and explore Wyoming. I don't know why. I left the Marine Corps and decided to make that dream come true before I got too old to do it."

"I see. Well? What do you think so far?"

"I like it a lot. Compared to Texas, where unless you're in the greener parts of the state, it's pretty much a desert. Wyoming is lush and green here on the western border."

"Well, believe me, we have parts of Wyoming that are a desert, just like Texas. You just ain't seen 'em yet, is all. Go to Casper, on the eastern side of the state, and you'll see what I mean."

"Maybe it's the mountains that drew you here?" Sarah ventured.

Dawson raised a brow and thought about it. "You might have something there. Good call."

"Amarillo is flatter than a pancake," Gertie pointed out. "And Texas has bumpy hills, certainly not mountains. We have *real* mountains here in western Wyoming. The real deal. Is that what drew you here, then?"

"A good point," Dawson agreed. "It probably was."

Gertie held both her slender wrists toward him. "You're a paramedic. What do you think of these?"

Seeing the slight swelling, he said, "Do you mind if I examine them?"

"Nope. I want to know what you think about them. I'm sure Sarah told you I have arthritis in 'em." She laid her right wrist into his opened hand.

Dawson was gentle. "Well, this isn't very medical, but you have what I call bird bones," and he smiled a little, moving his fingers lightly across the area where the wrist joint was located.

"Bird bones?" she snorted. "Sarah, tell

84

him I'm *not* some little itty-bitty bird."

Laughing, Sarah met his warm gaze. "Her enemies call her the vulture of Wind River Valley."

"Ouch," he muttered, giving Gertie a kind look. "You don't seem like that to me."

"Never mind me! What do you think of my wrist?"

Smiling to himself, he concentrated on her wrist. "There's swelling around it, which is usually an indicator of bone rubbing against bone. Is that what your doctor told you?"

"Yes," she muttered defiantly, her gray brows rising and falling with consternation. "He said the same dad-burned thing! What about my left wrist?"

"Well," Dawson said, gently palpating it here and there, "it's pretty much the same thing."

"I was so hoping for another, better diagnosis."

He released her wrist. "Has your doc talked to you about going to a chiropractor or to a doctor of osteopathy, a bone doc?"

"No." Her lower lip pooched out as she regarded him darkly. "Why? What would you do if you were in my shoes?"

"I'm a great believer in alternative medicine, ma'am. I'd have X-rays done first to see if the small bones across your wrist are out of alignment. Often, when your spine goes out, it can travel up your shoulder and down your arm to those small bones." He gestured to her right wrist, which was worse-appearing than her left. "I'd go get an adjustment from a chiro first to see if they can't pick up on why it went out of alignment in the first place. Then, if that doesn't fix it, I'd see the bone doctor. She or he might have some cards up their sleeve that could be helpful to you."

"My doc wants me on damned mind-altering drugs. Hydrocodone. I took one and it knocked me out for four hours! I was so pissed when I woke up. I don't have four hours to waste in a day. I called him and chewed his ear off. He told me to stop taking them. I don't trust him. I hate drugs. Do you know of anything besides drugs that might help me?"

"Maybe," he said. "But you have to jump through other hoops, so we can really understand if you have the osteoporosis kind of arthritis or not."

"My family *never* gets sick! No one has ever had arthritis." Her nostrils flared, and she tapped her short fingers, angry. "I think he misdiagnosed me."

"Maybe, if he's not a good fit, Gertie, we

86

can find you another doctor."

"Yes," she snapped, "that's a good idea."

"Would that be part of my job?" he asked.

"Absolutely. I don't trust medical doctors further than I can throw 'em. I wanted to go to Taylor Douglas. Before this other doc rolled into our little community, Taylor took care of all of us just fine."

"Is she a doctor?" Dawson asked.

"She's a physician's assistant," Sarah said. "And she really has taken care of everyone around here."

"Plus," Gertie said, waving her finger in Dawson's direction, "she hates medical drugs as much as I do."

"Did you go to her?" he wondered.

"No, because I was stupid and listened to the medical doctor in Jackson Hole instead. He didn't trust PAs, didn't think much of 'em."

"Well, you need a second opinion, ma'am. Why not set up an appointment with Dr. Douglas?"

"Would you come with me?"

"Of course."

Gertie turned to Sarah. "I like 'im." Then she turned to him. "You're hired, Dawson. I need an assistant to help me sort out lots of things, and you're a man with a big curiosity about life. I like people who are thinking, asking good questions and have common sense. You know? Common sense is something very few people have, I've found out. Rather disappointin', if you ask me. But you have it. So, you want to work for me?"

Dawson smiled a little. "I'd be honored to work for you, Mrs. Carter."

"Pooh! You call me Gertie or I'll thump you good, young man!"

Dawson held up his hands. "I surrender. I'll call you Gertie if you call me Dawson."

"Fine," she grumbled, scowling. "And lose that ma'am stuff, too. All right? Everyone who worked with Isaac and me were seen and treated like family. I like family. Family is a good thing. And if it's cared for properly, it makes everyone within the family stronger. And happy."

"I come from a similar type of home," Dawson said, trying to still his sudden joy at being hired.

"I read your résumé and your DD Form 214, young'un, and you're a real hero. I was wondering if any of those wounds you got those Purple Hearts for were gonna be an issue around here. You got any physical issues?"

"No, I can work with no problem at all, Gertie." He saw her suddenly smile, her entire face wreathed in that smile. She exuded warm sunlight, and he took her change in moods in stride.

"That's good to hear. I'm makin' you foreman of the horses and cattle we have here on the ranch. In the coming weeks, I'll get you introduced to the women and men who run our egg and chicken business. And I think Sarah told you that you'll have a suite up on the second floor of my house here?"

"Yes."

"Cece has the bedroom at one end. The suite is at the other end of the hall. It's real quiet up there and I think you'll like it."

"After sleeping out on rock slopes in Afghanistan," he told her, "I'm sure it will be like a five-star hotel in comparison." He saw pleasure come to her eyes at his compliment.

"Sarah, here, usually comes over every few days to check on me. I know she's really busy, but we usually have a family dinner on Sunday afternoon. Cece makes it, and our whole family gathers around the table. You're expected to be there, too."

"That's very nice of you. Thank you." Shocked, Dawson understood Gertie, in her own unique way, was trying to make him feel like part of her family. "I'd like that." He glanced over at Sarah, who looked relieved, happiness dancing in her green gaze. At least he'd see her once a week, and that made him feel good on a completely different level.

"You got someone special in your life right now, Dawson?"

"Er . . . no . . ." and Dawson was caught flat-footed by her unexpected question. For whatever reason, he saw satisfaction come into her eyes.

"Good! Sarah isn't hitched yet either," Gertie informed him. "So she'll be comin' alone. I intend to put you two young'uns together at the Sunday dinner table."

Instantly, Dawson saw Sarah's cheeks grow a bright red as she stared, aghast, at her bold grandmother. Gertie, on the other hand, looked like the fox that just got into a big, fat henhouse, her pleased smile saying it all. He had the smarts to keep his mouth shut and simply nod his head. He wasn't about to throw gasoline on this fire. No way . . .

# CHAPTER FIVE

*June 8*

Sarah was astounded at Gertie's obvious matchmaking efforts. Her cheeks stung like fire and she saw deviltry dancing in her grandmother's eyes as she asked him about his love life. So why did she feel relieved inside, huh? Oh, she didn't want to go there. Her life was far too intense and stressed as it was. Sarah was *not* looking for a relationship. It was the farthest thing from her mind. Gertie then inquired if Sarah might show Dawson his new quarters up on the second floor and see if he approved of them.

Good! Anything to get Gertie's focus off her for a while. Walking quickly out of the dining room, Dawson followed her at a reasonable speed behind her, hands behind his back, a thoughtful expression on his face. Damned if she could read his real feelings, though. The man had just as good a black ops game face as she did.

The huge oak staircase curved gracefully in a half circle up to the second floor. The stairs were covered with a dark blue paisley carpet, her footfalls muffled as she quickly moved up the steps. At the top, she turned and waited for Dawson.

"I'm sorry about my grandmother," she apologized in an undertone, not wanting their conversation to get to Gertie's ears, as he came to a halt at the top.

"It's okay. Just sort of caught me off guard, I guess." He gave her a wry look. "You seemed shocked by it, too."

Making an unhappy noise, Sarah gestured toward the left hall. "Gertie doesn't mince words."

"Really?"

She heard the amusement in his voice as he walked easily at her side. "You'll see. I warned you beforehand about her not being PC. Remember?"

"Indeed, you did. I just didn't expect that sort of a question."

Sarah didn't see any real disappointment in his face, however. Why did she sense that he was very pleased about the whole damned, uncomfortable situation? And why? Oh, she wasn't going there with Dawson. Not after Gertie's high jinks!

"My grandmother can really stir a pot if

she has a mind to do it," she murmured, halting and twisting a hundred-year-old brass doorknob, pushing open the mahogany door. Stepping aside, she said, "Go on in. This is your new home, Dawson." Somehow, to her, it had a nice, comforting ring to it. His expression remained neutral and he released his hands from behind his back and stepped into the carpeted suite. She followed and quietly shut the door behind her.

In front of them was the parlor, which had an antique couch, a mahogany coffee table in front of it, a red-brick fireplace off to one side, two other antique chairs, two lamp tables, plus windows that allowed in a lot of light. She saw Dawson halt and swore she could feel him absorbing the room like a sponge. It wasn't anything obvious. Nothing about him really was, but her own sensing mechanisms were highly honed, and she could feel him taking it all in.

"I don't know if you're into antique furniture?"

Dawson turned, holding her gaze. "My family has 1900s' furniture from my great-great-grandparents who settled in the Texas Panhandle. I grew up with furniture somewhat like this. But that couch? It's a beauty."

Sarah moved over to it, placing her hand

along the top of the polished mahogany. "This is a very rare Duncan Phyfe couch. The crest rail shape, the curved legs, which are called a curule foot, is hard to find anywhere these days. My grandmother had this refinished in cream-colored-striped satin about twenty years ago. Before that? It had the original horsehair weave on it."

"It looks very rich and very expensive. I'm not sure I should sit down on it."

She laughed. "Well, as kids, we played on the couch. Gertie isn't the type to put a no-trespassing sign on something just because it's old. Her grandparents were very well off and bought the best of everything, and all the furniture you see was bought to last through many, many generations." She fondly patted the wooden polished rail. "This couch brings back a lot of happy memories to me."

He moved to the other end of the couch, sliding his hand across the curved end of the sofa. "The fabric feels soft. Inviting. I know my parents would love to see this."

"Take a cell-phone photo and send it to them. I'm sure they'd like to know you've landed a very nice job up here in Wyoming."

"Good idea." He turned, leaning down. The curved wood holding up the sofa rested on a large ball of the same material beneath each curved form. "Wouldn't a certain amount of weight break those balls?" he wondered, studying them.

"We never did," she offered. "And we were bouncing off and on this couch when we played on it. I guess if you put three grown men your size on it, maybe," and she grinned.

He straightened. "Well, it's quite an artistic piece. I like it." Turning around, he studied the fireplace. "Does it work?"

"Better. It's all the heating you have up here on the second floor during the wintertime."

"Will I be chopping wood for — how many fireplaces in this house?"

"Yes, you will. There are three of them. On the main floor, with the largest of three fireplaces, Gertie had wallboard heating installed, too. She just loves to hear the wood popping and crackling in the fireplace, but it's for show only. Cece and you will be building a fire every morning."

"I was always charged with bringing in the wood for our potbellied stove from age nine until I left for the Marine Corps at eighteen. I'm pretty handy with an ax."

"Not a deal breaker, huh?"

"Nah, chopping wood always feels good. I sweat, I work hard, and I like that."

"You really are an outdoors type."

"That was the only thing that concerned me about this job, but I think after listening to Gertie, I'll have my fill of outdoor activities, too."

"Oh," Sarah deadpanned, "she's just as much an outdoor person as you are, Dawson. I think you'll find that out pretty quickly. She's got a Polaris ATV parked out back, a bright red one she named Rocket. She drives like a bat out of hell around the ranch; I should probably warn you about that. Rocket takes her all over the place, and she puts the pedal to the metal. I told her if she didn't slow down on the property I was going to give her a speeding ticket."

"I'll bet that went over real well."

She chuckled. "You could say that."

Grinning, he walked to the red-brick fireplace, smoothing his hand along the reddish mahogany mantel above it. "Yet she can't drive her truck off the property and into town?"

"No, she can't. You'll do that for her. I think my suggestion for her to get an ATV after my grandfather died really helped her out a lot. She's got macular eye issues, and while she can see okay up to a point, she doesn't want to risk hitting someone out on an open highway because of her condition."

"I see." He moved to the two Edwardian mahogany chairs in different parts of the room. They, too, were very old but were lovingly cared for, with creamy satin fabric on them as well. There was a huge nine-by-twelve floral carpet with roses woven into it within the central area of the parlor. The blond oak flooring provided a nice dash of color surrounding it. The pale gold background color of the velvet rug was a backdrop for the red roses in bloom, the greenery mixed with other wildflowers at each corner.

There were two sturdy oak rocking chairs in two of the corners. The windows were open, showing the beautiful, transparent stained glass, and then a protective window behind it to shield them from the harsh winter weather. "I like that stained glass," and he walked over to the window, pulling the transparent curtains aside. There were heavy brocade gold drapes that could be pulled closed over all of it, if he wanted. Dawson was sure those drapes would stop some of the cold leaking in from the windows during winter.

Sarah joined him. "Gertie loves stained glass. Colorful types, I should add." She gestured to the red roses arcing across the top of the window, and then blooms, stems and leaves down both sides, leaving most of the window open so people could easily see out of it. "She hired a very famous woman from back East to come out and update each window. My grandmother loves rainbows, too, but I think you already know that," and she lifted her chin, meeting his gaze. Her heart thudded in her chest. The expression in Dawson's eyes seemed as if he genuinely was enjoying their conversation. She hadn't expected him to be very interested in the Victorian-era suite, but to her surprise, he was.

"My parents' home has some stained-glass windows in it, too. Nothing as fancy and pretty as these, but as kids, me and my brother liked watching the sun rise to a certain position in the sky, and then the sunshine would hit the window and there'd be rainbows all over the back wall and then the wood floor."

Sarah frowned. "You have a brother? I didn't see anything about him on your résumé." She recalled that he'd put down the names of his parents and himself; that was all.

Dawson's mouth thinned for a moment and he remained by the fireplace. "Yeah," he admitted heavily, giving her a glance, "I did. Toby was my younger brother by two years. When he was ten years old, he drowned. I tried to save him, almost drowned myself trying to do it, but I lost him."

The heartache was clear in his lowered voice; the pain and grief were there, too. Shock bolted through her system as she stared at him. "You lost your brother? I'm so sorry, Dawson." She felt her throat closing. The past came rushing back up to her, vignettes, like web pages being slammed into her again, and she struggled to push it all away. Forcing herself, she focused on Dawson because she saw the lingering sadness, the guilt, in his lowered eyes. Sarah made an inarticulate sound as tears rushed to her eyes, stinging and hot. A sheriff wasn't supposed to show emotions, and instantly, she lifted her fingers, brushing them away, swallowing hard several times, fighting back a past that had never been lain to rest.

Dawson regarded her in the hush of silence. "On some days, it's like a bad dream." Giving a heavy shoulder shrug, he added, "And other days? It's as if it happened yesterday. I'm sorry; I didn't mean to upset you like that." He pulled a white handkerchief from his back pocket and walked over to her, pressing it into her hand. "Here . . ."

His ability to transcend his own pain to care for her almost made Sarah want to burst out into sobs, throw her arms around his neck and have him hold her. How much she longed for that! Forcing herself to remain where she was, she dabbed her eyes. "Sorry," she mumbled.

"Don't be." He shook his head, remaining nearby. "It's not something I tell many people, but I know you have a soft heart. I'd appreciate it if you don't let this become common knowledge; it's almost too hard to talk about to anyone."

"Of course, I understand," she whispered unsteadily, fighting to force her tears to stop. Taking a deep breath, she pressed the damp handkerchief into his hand. "Thanks . . ."

"Anytime." He took it and folded it back up, pushing it into a back pocket. "Are you okay?" and he peered down at her, as if sizing her up, confusion in his voice.

"Umm, yes . . . fine, fine," Sarah said, taking a step away from him. "It just caught me off guard, was all," she admitted huskily. The need to cry, to wail, was so powerful, she could still feel that energy, like a closed fist, pushing upward into her chest, making her struggle to contain it all. And it was so hard to do that with Dawson's gentle questions, the way he was looking at her, as if he sensed something more about her reaction. Making one more swipe with trembling fingers, she moved away from him and pointed to the door leading to the bedroom and bathroom area. "Come this way. See what you think."

She stood aside after pushing the door wider. Dawson gave her another concerned look, walked past her and entered the next room, which was as large as the parlor had been. Pressing her hand to her throat, his back to her, she shut her eyes, forcing herself to breathe slowly in and out. That was the only thing she could do to force all the other reactions, the grief, the anger and haunting possibilities, the nightmarish answers, from pummeling her. Usually? She could put them in a box and shut the lid, focus on the present. But something in Dawson's demeanor, maybe that medic side of him, had blown the lid off the box that contained her past as well as her present. As he'd admitted, the pain and grief were in the past for his brother, Toby. But hers wasn't. She lived with it every day, and on days like this, it was excruciating. Sarah wasn't sure she could force everything back into that box deep within her.

This was too close for comfort, and as she

stood there, Dawson walked around the antique brass bed with the shining gold head- and footboard, his hand touching the bright patchwork quilt that served as a bedspread, Sarah continued to wrestle with her own dark emotions. "Do you like it?" she asked, her voice sounding off-key even to her.

"Yes, really nice. Kind of reminds me of my bedroom back at our home outside Amarillo. My father has worked for the Double Circle Ranch since I was born, so the owner gave him a Victorian two-story house to live in on the property. He's the foreman, so it worked out for everyone concerned." He halted at the six-drawer mahogany dresser, appreciating its ancient qualities and beauty. "Toby and I each had a room up on the second floor," he said, his voice quiet and contemplative. "Our brass beds were full-size. The people she helped as a social worker sometimes gave my mother gifts. One elderly woman made a quilt for her, and she gave it to me for a bedspread. Another woman with six kids made one and gave it to her, and that became Toby's spread." He turned, looking at the bed. "Funny how life comes around to repeat itself," and he gave her a slightly crooked smile. "I would never have thought

I'd be stepping back into the past, another Victorian home, with 1900s' furniture just like the one I grew up in. That amazes me."

Sarah stood there, thinking it stunned her, too. But in a different way. "Does it make you feel more at home, then?" she asked.

His mouth puckered, and he chuckled a little. "You could say that."

"Do you have two sets of grandparents?" she wondered.

"I do, yes."

"Are they anything like Gertie?"

He laughed softly. "No, they're pretty tame in comparison. They live in Amarillo, have their own small homes, and my parents see them regularly. They're getting up there in age and need help here and there."

"Is your mom still a social worker?"

"Oh yeah," Dawson said. "She'll probably never retire unless they force her to. She loves helping others."

Just as Dawson did, but Sarah didn't say that. There was a strong humanitarian and service side to this wrangler, no question.

"What about your dad? Is he still foreman?"

"Yes." Dawson craned a look in to the bathroom. It had black-and-white octagonal tiles across the floor, a large, a freestanding claw-footed bathtub, a shower and white tile on the walls where it sat. There was a white shower curtain pulled aside, the porcelain sparkling clean.

Easing out of the bathroom, he turned and met her gaze. "They live in the same place where we were born. My mother had both of us at home, had midwives helping her. She detests hospitals."

"Good for her. She sounds pretty independent, like the women of my family."

"I think so, but she's a Texan. And Texas women are strong. But I haven't met your grandmother Nell yet, or your mom."

"I'm sure you will this coming Sunday." She managed a smile in his direction. "Gertie and Nell trade Sundays for family dinners. I'm sure it won't take you long to get to know the cast of characters I've grown up with."

"I like Gertie," he said, coming around the bed, following her out to the parlor. "You know where you stand with someone who's like that. My mother is pretty PC, my father isn't. I think I took more after my mother on that one."

She smiled as she walked to the door. "From the looks of it, we have some things in common," and she gestured to the parlor. "We both grew up in turn-of-the-century homes, the same types of 1900s' bed and furniture. That's pretty interesting to me."

"Texas and Wyoming have something in common after all?" he teased, holding the door open for her.

She halted and turned in the hall. "I think they do. I'm leaving now. Once you get your things moved in here, go down and let Gertie know you're settled in. Then ask her if she has anything for you to do. I'm sure she probably would like to show you the egg and chicken business down below the house. She'll take you for a ride on Rocket," and she chuckled. She liked that his gray eyes danced with humor at her teasing.

"Think I'll be alive to make that first Sunday dinner?"

Laughter bubbled up in Sarah, and she felt the past starting to slip away. Dawson's easygoing nature was exactly what she needed at this moment. "Put on a Kevlar vest, wear a helmet and I'm sure you will."

"Has she ever been given a speeding ticket for driving Rocket?"

Her laughter deepened. "Gertie will never take Rocket off the property, that I promise you. Besides, it doesn't have a license plate on it."

"Just wondering. Sounds like I'll need that vest and helmet."

Dawson had lifted her out of the terror

and grief that had assailed her earlier in the day. He was leaning nonchalantly against the doorjamb, thumbs in his belt, grinning.

She chuckled and started down the hall. "No, you'll be fine."

"Okay, if you say so, Sheriff."

"See you Sunday, Dawson," and she lifted her hand in his direction and headed for the staircase. She didn't want to leave him, but there was apprehension bubbling up within her. How badly she wanted to share her past with him. As she quickly took the stairs down to the first floor, she knew Dawson would be a good listener. Looking around, she saw Cece in the kitchen, and Gertie was most likely in her office. Moving down the hall, she knocked lightly on the half-open door to her grandmother's work area.

"Hey," Gertie called, "you leavin' us, Sarah?"

She opened the door and stood on the threshold. "Yep, gotta get going."

"Is Dawson okay with his digs?" she asked, setting her pen aside over the accounting books in front of her.

"Yes, he likes them," and Sarah told her about his family living in a Victorian 1900s' home in Texas. There was a gleam in Gertie's eyes when she finished.

"I'm not surprised," she said.

"Oh? I sure was. It's as if we're in parallel universes," Sarah said.

"Nah, I just think he's the perfect guy for you, and it proves me right because you share a past that's similar."

Sarah's brows rose as she considered her grandmother's words. "Well . . . I'm not ready for a relationship, Gertie. I'm just too busy, and there are too many demands on a sheriff."

"Coulda fooled me," Gertie intoned, giving her that one-eyebrow-raised look whenever she knew she was right, even though Sarah was bucking in the harness over her insight.

"He's *very* nice, I agree."

"Oh, he's the kind of man you need in your life, Sarah. All I'm doin' is giving words to what you already know. Hmmm?"

Moving restlessly, Sarah looked down the hall, hoping their voices weren't carrying too far. The hall was empty, which meant Dawson couldn't hear them. Thank goodness! "Gertie, you have to stop matchmaking. I'm not ready to settle down. I love my job. I'm devoted to it. I'm helping people, and that makes me feel good."

Waving her hand, Gertie said, "Oh, I know, I know, but don't you get lonely in the evenings at home, alone? I know I do. Now that Isaac is gone, I get so I hate evenings because it's so quiet and boring around here. It must be the same for you."

Her radio saved her. Gertie rolled her eyes as she pressed the receiver down on her shoulder to answer it. It happened to be a fender-bender accident at the south side of town. Getting off the radio, she said, "I'll see you here for Sunday dinner," and she came into the office, pressing a kiss to her grandmother's head. "Don't work too hard, okay?"

"Oh, I know how to pace myself, child. It's you I'm concerned about. Stay safe out there, okay?" and she patted Sarah's arm.

"I will," she said. "See you Sunday. Love you . . ."

"Love you too, dumplin'."

# CHAPTER SIX

*June 10*

Dawson was helping to set the long dining room table for Sunday dinner under Cece's direction. It was an hour before the entire Carter family descended upon the home: David, Emily, Sarah and Emily's grandmother, Nell, would arrive.

Gertie was helping as well, bustling to and from the kitchen, taking out a one-hundred-year-old platter and other dishes of equal age. She said her grandmother had bought them in the 1890s and they were called the Spode Stafford Flowers collection. They were pretty American wildflowers on a white background, with 22-karat gilding around the edge of each plate. Gertie had placed a lime-green woven cloth on the table, and Dawson had laid it out, putting purple place mats beneath each plate, adding the silverware later. He liked the crystal amethyst-colored goblets with clear, transparent stems, all hand blown, all from the 1900s, she'd told him proudly. The table swam in sparkling dishes, crystal wine- and water glasses and real silverware that was a hundred and twenty years old. Cece had polished it last night at the table after the dishes were cleared. The woman never stopped working.

The doorbell rang. Gertie had asked him to go answer the door, introduce himself to the family who had just arrived. He hoped it was Sarah. But as he hurried into the foyer, he saw a tall, but very thin woman with her gray hair tamed into a bun on the nape of her neck, standing there.

"Hi, I'm Dawson Callahan, Gertie's new assistant," he said after opening the door for her.

"Nell Franklin," and she held out her thin hand to him, giving him a warm, gracious smile.

Dawson shook her hand very gently. "May I carry that into the kitchen for you?" She was holding a large bowl of something beneath a plastic wrap.

"Why, of course. Thank you."

Dawson set the bowl carefully on the foyer cherrywood Queen Anne table and then helped her take off her light, ivory-colored coat. It was a bit chilly today, and he knew older people got cold far more easily than younger adults or children. Nell had a long, thin face and green eyes the same color as Sarah's. At seventy-six, she moved rather well, and he was impressed. She touched her steel-colored bun, making sure it was neat and still in place. She had a blue knit cap around her head to match her blue and white springlike outfit. Everything about Nell was neat and pressed. She wore gold metal square glasses and nudged them up on her nose.

"Gertie said you were very nice and she was right." Nell looked up at him. "But you're a mighty tall drink of water."

It was Dawson's turn to smile as he stepped aside and picked up the bowl while she retrieved her white leather purse from the desk. "Six-foot-two. My dad wanted me to play basketball, but I never liked the sport. Would you like to go into the living room? Gertie's serving some finger food in there. Can I get you something to drink?"

"Oh, I'd love a spot of hot tea. And Cece makes the best appetizers. Yes, I'm going to go visit them and maybe catch Gertie the Whirlwind and say hi to her, also."

Dawson liked Nell's genteel ways and manners. He swore she had stepped out of the pages of a 1900 Sears Catalog. His

111

mother had a collection of them, and as a child, he and Toby used to go through them by the hour, fully entertained by all the black-and-white illustrations. It brought back soothing and comforting memories of his brash, athletic little brother, who loved anything mechanical. His heart ached because Toby hadn't grown up to become a man, have adventures and share his life with him and their parents. They'd always been supportive of each other, never antagonistic. They were best friends, which made his loss doubly hard, his inability to rescue his drowning brother in time. Dawson had never cried so hard, for so long, in his entire life. Nothing in his life compared to his loss of Toby, except for his divorce from Lucia at age twenty-five. And he knew Toby was never far from his parents' thoughts and hearts either, although they never blamed him for not saving his brother. It had been a terrible childhood accident, but it left a hole the size of a tunnel through all their hearts to this day.

Trying to gently put his grief-stricken feelings off to one side, Dawson finished laying the silverware just as Cece had instructed him. He wasn't one for Miss Manners, but he already knew Gertie very much wanted the good ol' days environment in her home, as she referred to them, no matter how much the world was rapidly changing around them. Every piece of silverware was laid in a certain order to the next one. Cece warned him that Gertie would come steaming through the dining room later to double-check his work, so he'd better have them in the correct order.

Grinning, he straightened the green crocheted lace at one corner of the table. Gertie had said her grandmother had crocheted this beautiful lime-colored tablecloth. Everything around him was a hand-me-down from the family, and each was an heirloom and had a provenance to it. He liked that, because it was similar to his own ranching-family upbringing.

The doorbell rang.

"I'll get it," Dawson called out to no one in particular. As he walked down the hall toward the foyer, he glanced left and saw Nell in a rocker, holding her flowery Spode wildflower painted cup filled with tea, chatting amiably with Gertie. They seemed to truly like each other, and Dawson drew in a deep breath of relief. He knew no family was perfect. Far from it. What he was hoping for at this Sunday dinner was that all the family members got along well with one another. He'd soon find out.

Looking through the stained-glass window in the door, he saw it was Sarah. She was standing alone. His heart galloped. Her ginger-colored hair was a soft frame around her face. He could see a silvery sheen blouse with a burgundy-colored scarf across her shoulders. She wore pink lipstick, her cheeks slightly flushed, but he saw no other makeup on her.

Opening the door, he teased, "Wow, you clean up well, Sheriff."

She laughed and touched her silk burgundy skirt, which hung to just below her knees. "Yeah, I'm out of uniform, aren't I? I imagine that's quite a shock for you; you've only seen me in my law-enforcement duds."

"Nice change, though," Dawson said, stepping aside. "Come on in. I'm playing meeter-and-greeter today because Gertie wants me to get acquainted with everyone before dinner." As she walked past him, he inhaled the subtle scent of almonds. Deciding it was the shampoo she used on her shining reddish-brown hair, he closed the door. The wine-colored scarf highlighted her proud carriage, the ends falling between her breasts, covered with that shining silver-gray blouse. The difference was striking, making him feel desire, because she had such long legs and sweetly rounded hips that reminded him of a ballerina. All beauty, grace and harmony in motion, he decided. It was a helluva turn-on for him, and he instantly reined in his testosterone; it had no place at this family table.

"Thanks," Sarah murmured, pulling her white leather purse strap across her left shoulder. "Mmm, something smells good," she said, walking beside him, their hands almost brushing each other from time to time. "What's Cece fixing for us this afternoon?"

"Prime rib, baked potatoes, sliced carrots with almonds and a strawberry parfait for dessert."

"I can see Gertie is getting you up to speed on helping in the kitchen."

His mouth twisted a bit. "Yes, she is. I don't mind helping because both our parents worked, so Toby and I were responsible for getting the table set, and later on, I was taught how to cook."

"So you're not flustered with all that silverware?"

"Well, that's another story." They halted at the drawing room, where Nell and Gertie sat.

"I'll drop in to see them," Sarah told him.

"Would you like something to drink?"

"No . . . maybe a glass of wine with dinner. Thanks."

Gertie launched herself off the over-stuffed, flowery fabric Edwardian chair. Nell wasn't far behind her. Gertie opened her arms as she approached Sarah. It was warming to Dawson to see such love existing between the two grandmothers, who literally encircled Sarah. Smiling, he aimed himself toward the kitchen to ask if Cece needed some help. He briefly cataloged a look in Sarah's eyes when he'd mentioned Toby's name. It told him her compassion for others was a major component of her personality because he'd seen sadness in them for him. Dawson wondered how she traded off those emotions during a crisis, which law enforcement had to do all the time. How did she handle her emotions? Did she stuff them in a mental box like he did? Was she able to cry at some point later and get relief from what she saw or had to deal with earlier in some human crisis? He didn't know, and he wanted to find out. Blame it on his paramedic's curiosity.

As he rounded the corner into the kitchen, he wondered how Sarah was dealing with damn near being trapped by that drug lord's ambush. They hadn't talked much about it. Still, he wanted the time to discuss it with her and would somehow find it, one way or another. The fact that he knew for sure that Sarah wasn't going out with someone meant the door was open for a man to walk through. *If* she wanted him to walk through it at all. That was the real question, but Dawson sensed she liked him, and that was special. She didn't seem to be the type of woman who revealed her personal side too much to anyone. And of course, she'd been in the military, where emotions were encouraged to be shut down, not turned on. How had she survived in that environment being the way she really was? And what had given her the shield or internal strength to put them into a box so she could react to life-and-death situations? Did it come from childhood? From her father's molding of her? He'd been in law enforcement, so he would have been a role model for Sarah.

Dawson's mother's psychology had stuck with him ever since he was seven years old and those were questions she had asked her own clients. Now, as a mature adult, he was more than grateful for her training. And he'd backed it up by attaining a minor in psychology with his paramedic college degree.

Sarah tried to fight the comforting warmth of Dawson sitting next to her at the dinner table. They faced her mother and father, Emily and David, with the two grand-mothers at either end of the table. Cece had served small cups of butternut squash soup, sprinkled with bacon bits and a dollop of sour cream. Her father doted on Dawson, and that didn't surprise her. And her mother gave her a look that signaled hope that she was interested in Gertie's new assistant for a possible relationship. There was nothing hidden by her mother, who yearned for her to settle down and have a partner in her life who could support her dreams and career. They wanted grandchildren.

Sarah loved her mother so much because she had always told her to go after her dreams. Emily was a worrywart, and Sarah tried to downplay the unexpected ambush by Gonzalez's drug soldiers to her, as did her father, who remained pretty much closemouthed about it. But he would text her or they'd talk on the phone about the ongoing investigation to find the perps who had tried to kill them that morning.

There was a lot of laughter, telling of stories and some serious talk in between the courses. A lot of questions were aimed at Dawson, who took them in good-natured stride. Nothing seemed to upset this man, and Sarah liked that rock-solid core about him. She was sure it was in part due to the military training and experiences he'd had. Now she wanted time to explore the other parts of his personality, one-on-one. How she longed for that! Everyone seemed to like Dawson, and he had a wry sense of humor, just like her father. Those two got along together, and that tickled Sarah's heart.

After dinner, Cece served the strawberry parfait, and it was the perfect light dessert after such a heavy, delicious meal of prime rib. She'd had a glass of burgundy wine and, because she rarely drank much, there was a bit of a buzz afterward. In her job, she couldn't afford to be inebriated or have alcohol in her bloodstream. Emergencies came in twenty-four-hours a day, and Sarah had lost count of the times she'd been awakened in the middle of the night with a call from the deputy on duty about an escalating crisis. Sometimes, she had to climb out of bed and into her uniform, going to the scene to direct it. At other times, her very capable crew could handle it. And she got more sleep, which she always knew was so important.

"Tell you what," Gertie said, aiming her gaze to Dawson and Sarah, "why don't you two young'uns go out and enjoy your coffee on the porch swing?"

"Good idea!" Nell chimed in, giving them her permission, too, her eyes alight with mischief.

Sarah glanced over at Dawson. "Want to?" She saw a gleam in Dawson's gray eyes, that wry hook upward of one corner of his mouth as he smoothly pushed back from the table and stood up. He placed his hands on the back of her chair. Well, that answered that.

"Sure sounds like a good idea," he said, giving the grandmothers an amused look that told them he knew what they were up to.

Sarah heard the cackle from the grand-mothers as she rose. "Come on," she told him, "let's go to the kitchen. Cece will give us our coffee."

In no time, they were out on the front porch and sitting on the swing, coffee cups in hand. She noticed Dawson gave her plenty of room. There were soft yellow fabric pillows at each end, and he'd taken his to the corner, placed it behind his back and relaxed. It was nearly five p.m. and the June evening was coming upon them. She had borrowed one of Gertie's hand-knitted small afghans and thrown it around her shoulders before sitting down. It would get cool real fast when the sun set behind the

Wilson Range.

"You've really been thrown into a pot of stew," she told him, balancing the cup and saucer in her lap. "Hired yesterday and twelve hours later you're probably thinking you've been turned into a butler in a 1900s' Victorian house." She saw the corners of Dawson's eyes crinkle.

"Gertie said the job wouldn't let me get bored, that there were so many things, all the time, that had to be dealt with. I don't mind it. I'd rather be busy than bored out of my skull."

"She'll keep you on your toes."

Chuckling, he said, "She warned me that she would. I think I can handle it. I like jobs where I'm learning something. This afternoon, I learned to lay out a trail of silverware in a particular hierarchy."

"When I was a kid, I used to do that for her."

She saw him become serious. "What's the latest on that ambush that was set for you?"

"The Teton Black Hawk helicopter crew located the van that was used, about two miles up a dirt road that led toward the Salt River Range. From there, once my deputies and forensics' team got there, they could see a second vehicle had arrived, more than likely picked up the crew, turned around and took off. We found fingerprints and we're running them through several federal and state databases right now. I don't think we'll get a hit. I think Gonzalez has what I call roving packs of soldiers who are all over the state, doing his bidding."

"All Hispanic?"

"No, all colors, countries and races. Central and South American drug lords learned a long time ago to mix and match. That way, they can't be profiled."

"I guess if you're a drug lord, that's a wise move. Camouflage and disrupting the expected for the unexpected."

"Yes," she muttered, shaking her head. "How are you doing after that incident? Any PTSD symptoms flare up? I know they did in me."

"Yes," Dawson said. "I have PTSD, so going through that firefight on Highway 89 brought it all back. I didn't sleep hardly at all that night."

"We were lucky," she said, giving him a sympathetic look.

"Don't we both know it?"

"One thing for sure, being in military combat makes you less susceptible in some ways to stuff like this when it happens in the civilian world."

"That's one way of looking at it. You seem

like you caught up on your sleep."

She grimaced and touched below her eye. "Makeup. Subtle, but it's there if you look close enough."

"I didn't see it."

"I don't normally wear it. But my parents, Gertie and Nell, are all shocked by the close call. I didn't want them to worry, so I covered up any shadows beneath my eyes. If I hadn't? They'd have climbed all over me and given me twenty questions."

"Because they love you and want you safe."

"Yes, but my job description doesn't guarantee that."

"Did they worry about your father when he was sheriff?"

"My mom did, and so did I. But Gertie and Nell are from a time when men were seen as strong, impervious and could dodge bullets, unlike nowadays. They don't hold such with women, though. It's a generational challenge. I try to low-key anything that happens because they worry too much already."

"David Carter is a man, so they expected him to be able to take care of whatever came up and live to come home to dinner that night?"

"Precisely. They just can't seem to see me

in the same light."

"Are you in this job because of your father? Or because you, personally, wanted to make a difference?"

Sarah liked his insightful question. Not much was missed by this man. "Honestly? I grew up with my dad serving our county. Both he and my mom believe we owe back to the community that surrounds us. That everyone should contribute what they can, and in their own way. My mom works with Delos Charity in Wind River because she feels guilty that she has so much compared to so many who live in the county who are below the economic poverty line."

"Duty and community service, then?"

"Sure. We joined the military, and that was about duty, honor and country. I don't see them as being different, but from the same cut of cloth. Service is service."

"Do most folks in the county think having a woman as a sheriff is a good thing?"

"I won eighty-five percent of the vote, Dawson. I think that answers your question." She sipped her coffee. "I don't think people care what your gender is as long as you can handle the job. Don't you?"

"I think there's a male part of this country who would continue to want to keep women down."

Snorting, Sarah muttered, "I'll be so glad when that assumption dies a hard, final death. I'm sick and tired of men like that. We've got more than our fair share in Wyoming, in case you don't know it. They believe women should be barefoot and pregnant, stay home, raise the kids and let the man of the house earn the money. Such crap."

"I like it when you're more yourself than your game face lets on. I know you have to remain unemotional outwardly as a law-enforcement officer."

He was teasing her again, but gently, because she could see he meant it in his eyes and the tone of his voice. "Who *are* you, Dawson? Really?"

His lips twisted. "Was that an insult or a compliment?"

"A compliment."

"Why do you see me as anything other than the guy sitting here with you? Do you think I'm hiding something from you? Not being myself?"

Shaking her head, Sarah said, "I find you refreshing in a way I've never seen in a man before. I guess I'm trying to figure out how you got to be who you are."

"Whew," and he wiped his brow, "that was a close call."

Laughing, Sarah saw the playfulness in his expression. "Come on!"

"I am who I am. Nothing more or less. You know all about me. You did more deep-diving background investigation on me than you probably do on a perp because I would be working directly with Gertie, whom you love and dote on."

"I'm a lot like Gertie; I don't beat around the bush, Dawson. I'm interested in you. Who you are. What makes you tick. And I don't know if you have a similar need to know that about me or not. It could be a one-way street."

"Oh," he murmured, "you interest me. I like the woman in the swing with me. She's intriguing."

"So? How do we do this? Find some quality time away from our day jobs to find that out?"

"I'm open to whatever you suggest."

"I try, at least one day a week, to work over at the Bar C. It's a military vet–owned ranch. I ride fence, repair it and do what I can to help them out. I work sunup to sundown. I pack a lunch, bring my fence fixing gear, a good set of elkskin gloves, a hat and they loan me one of their horses for the day."

"Sounds good to me, Sarah. I'd like to

meet some more vets. They're our kind."

"Shaylene Lockhart is the owner. Her husband, Reese, was a captain in the Marine Corps. Right now, they have three other vets, Harper Sutton, Garret Fleming and Noah Mabry. The women vets are Dair Wilson, Kira Duval-Fleming and Tara Dalton. Shay's dream was to have a place where vets with PTSD could heal, and she'd done that and more. Her father, a drunk, Ray Crawford, let the ranch go when Shay was in the Marine Corps. He had a stroke and she had to leave the military to come home and run the broken-down place. He used to have grass leases available for out-of-state ranchers who wanted to truck their cattle in and feed all summer on the rich grass of Wyoming. But Ray let the place go, and in three hard winters, all the many pasture's fences were broken down and in serious need of replacement. Without grass leases, the ranch would have been in foreclosure if not for Shay's efforts and vision. When I could, I spent a day repairing fence for her. Every little bit helps."

"It's vets helping vets. I'll ride with you, if Shay and Reese want a second wrangler working on those fences. Gertie is giving me next Saturday off. What's your schedule look like?"

"I'm off for the weekend unless all hell breaks loose somewhere in the county."

"Good; then you choose the time and I'll meet you."

"I can pick you up here next Saturday at 0800."

"Do you want Gertie to know about this?"

She managed to squelch a laugh. "Oh, it's better to do it in front of her; Gertie has her ear to the ground and gossip would tell her faster than I could if we tried to sneak off without her knowing we were working together over at the Bar C."

"Busted."

She joined his laugher. "Yes. Totally."

"Call me with the details when you know them. I need to go buy a good pair of fence gloves, but that's going to be easy enough to do over at Charlie Becker's store."

Sarah felt her heart inflating with such joy that it startled her. What was it about Dawson that drew her so effortlessly to him?

# CHAPTER SEVEN

*June 16*

"You look preoccupied, Sarah," Dawson said as he rode a gray horse named Ghost beside her chestnut gelding, Socks. It was eight a.m., the morning chilly, the sky a crystalline blue and the sun's rays shooting across the valley toward the Wilson Range in the west. Dawson had met her at the Bar C Ranch an hour earlier. There, he'd been introduced to Shay and Reese Lockhart, shook hands and found them to be warm and welcoming. After that, Reese walked with them to one of the two barns, pulled out Ghost and Socks for them.

He was busy with another issue, so Sarah promised him that she'd show Dawson where the tack room and equipment was located. Dawson had sensed strain in Reese, but it was merely an observation. And that was what led him, once they were out along a lease fence area to repair rotted posts they discovered as they rode the line, to bring up the subject. Sarah was wearing her black baseball cap, and she pushed it up a bit on her brow over his question.

"Two things," she said. "First, Reese and Shay just got hit with a lawsuit from Ray Crawford to take the Bar C away from them."

"I thought you said the property was in Shay's hands, not her father's?"

"Yep." She sighed, leaning down, stroking Socks's neck and pulling a few flaxen strands of mane out of a snarl. "That's right. But that doesn't mean he won't cause them years of legal stress, thousands, maybe over a hundred thousand dollars, in legal bills, as well. They may win the case but be so financially devastated by it, they could lose the Bar C to foreclosure. It's not a pretty picture. You've not run into Ray yet, have you?" and she narrowed her gaze upon him.

"No." Pulling the heavy denim jacket closed after dropping the reins on Ghost's neck, he added, "And I don't think I want to. I met Garret Fleming, who lives here on the Bar C, up at Charlie Becker's last Wednesday. I was there putting in an order for Gertie on hen food when he came in. We introduced ourselves, and Garret had

130

already heard I was hired as Gertie's assistant. When he found out I was a vet like himself, afterward, we went over to Kassie's Café and sat down to chat over a cup of coffee."

"Military people are good like that," Sarah said. "Garret's a stand-up guy, too. He's a tall, big dude, and you know not to mess with him."

"Yeah, I got that," Dawson said wryly, smiling a little as the horse swayed beneath him. "He's black ops, so you'd never see him coming."

"Not until he wanted you to," Sarah added with a sour grin. "So? Did you have time to find out more about the Bar C?"

"Yeah, we talked for about an hour before we both had to get back to other business. Garret said nothing about a pending lawsuit against Shay and Reese, though."

"That's because it was delivered Friday by one of my deputies to their doorstep, so he didn't know about it when he met you," she said. "It's heartbreaking. Shay has struggled so hard to bring her family ranch back from the brink of foreclosure and her father does nothing but throw monkey wrenches into all her efforts. No love lost there, for sure."

"He's an alcoholic, from what Garret said,

131

an unreformed one, drinking as much now as he did in the past."

Sarah shook her head. "Last Tuesday, Ray was driving fifty miles per hour in a twenty-five zone, and one of my deputies pulled him over and gave him a speeding ticket. Crawford started cussing him out and the deputy told him he'd better zip it up or he was going to jail."

"What happened next?"

"Crawford put a sock in it. None of us like dealing with him. He's ornery, a blow-hard and a liar. I honestly don't know how Shay managed to survive the bastard for the first eighteen years of her life. Her mother's dead. Crawford abuses everyone around him. That's why he lost his cattle leases and the ranch fell into disrepair. He was always cussing out the wranglers he hired, and one by one, they all quit because they weren't going to take that kind of crap from him or anyone. And then he couldn't hire anyone because they all knew what he was like, and no wrangler worth their salt was going to step into that buzz saw and get verbally abused daily by him."

"Didn't Crawford get it?"

Shaking her head, she muttered, "Nope. He's an alcoholic. He's selfish, self-centered and doesn't care about anything else but his own immediate needs." She rested her hand on the thigh of her Levi's, looking ahead, assessing the fence posts and the barbed wire between each one.

"Doesn't seem fair," Dawson said. He liked that Sarah had braided her hair, and it hung down between her shoulder blades. This morning she looked like a wrangler, not a sheriff. Normally, when he'd see her, she was tense, her game face in place, her lips pursed, as if holding back a lot of emotion. He knew she carried a lot of loads herself. Some known. Many unknown. And he wanted to know all about her: why she was the way she was.

Giving an abrupt laugh, Sarah said, "What in life is ever fair, Callahan? You of all people, with your skills and insights, know that."

Rubbing his chin with his gloved hand, he said, "Yeah, but you hate to see bad things happen to good people. When you look at the Bar C, the new horse arena, the two barns recently painted and a number of the fenced pastures having cattle leases this year, you know Shay and Reese, plus the other vets, are hauling ass and doing a helluva lot of work to make it all happen."

"Oh, they work their butts off, Dawson. All of them."

"Why can't Crawford just walk away?"

"He's angry at his daughter, angry at his dead wife, who was the owner of the ranch through her family, angry that in her will, she left it to Shay, not him. He's vengeful, on top of all the rest of his fine attributes."

"I wouldn't have left it to Crawford for love or money," Dawson growled.

"You can't choose your family members."

He heard the heaviness in her husky voice. "Is everything okay with your parents?"

"Yes, they're fine." She waved her hand. "I was talking obliquely, about another family living in Wind River Valley."

"I'm all ears. I learn a lot from you about the people who live here," he teased, seeing her lips purse once more. There was darkness in her eyes, so Dawson sensed whatever was bothering Sarah, it might be an old problem, not a new one.

"Good thing you're trustworthy," she said, pulling Socks to a halt. Up ahead, there was a rotted post leaning and straining against the barbed wire that kept it from falling over. "I'll tell you about it as we dig out that post."

Dismounting, Dawson placed the reins into the rich grass around them. Both horses had been taught to ground tie. Once the reins were dropped, they didn't move.

"No, I'm not a gossip, that's for sure," he said, opening his saddlebags, taking out the tools they'd need. They'd have to cut the five strands of barbed wire, dig out around the rotted post enough to pull it out. Once it was out, Sarah would note it on the GPS of her phone and send the info via email to Shay at her office. Then, two vet wranglers would bring out a truck with a new post, dig a proper posthole and place the new one in it. After that, they'd restring the barbed wire, making that section of the fence sturdy once more.

They got to work, cutting the barbed wire, looping it and carefully walking it back to the other posts so it wouldn't tangle in their horse's feet. Dawson smiled to himself as he began to shovel out a hole around the leaning post. Sarah knew her business when it came to the sharp, cutting barbed wire. She had a pair of wire cutters, wore thick, protective elkskin gloves, a pair of half chaps that hung from her waist to just below her knees. The lower legs of her Levi's were getting soaked and darkened from the dew-laden, nearly calf-high grass. But so was his. "So?" he prodded, "tell me about this other family who's on your worry radar," and he looked up to see her grimace.

"Have you heard anyone mention the Elson family who live in the south valley?" she asked, looping and then bringing the five strands together and using the twine from a hay bale to tie it to the healthy fence post eight feet away from where he was digging.

"No."

"You haven't been here long enough, that's why," she answered grimly, making her way over to the strands of barbed wire on the other side, snipping them off the rotted post, quickly removing the U-shaped rusty nails, as well. "That family has lived here in the valley for two generations. The present one consists of the parents, Brian and Roberta. They had four sons: Hiram, Kaen, Cree and Elisha. They're nothing but trouble on the loose. Brian is an alcoholic, plus a child and wife abuser. Roberta is on recreational drugs most of the time, and she refuses to press charges against Brian even though he's blacked both her eyes, fractured her right cheekbone, nose and broken her right arm. So, he keeps beating her up. Cree Elson kidnapped Tara Dalton when she was sixteen. He was in 'love' with her, so he grabbed her and carried her off to a cabin up in the Salt River Mountain range. We got her back safe and sound. Cree went to prison for years. Tara left the valley after high school graduation and went into the military. She got back from her enlistment and came home. Cree was out of prison, found out she was back in the valley. Within months of her arrival home, Tara was once again kidnapped by him."

Dawson gave a low whistle. "That had to be really hard on Tara. I haven't met her yet, but I know she's engaged to Harper Sutton. What happened when he grabbed her the second time?"

"We managed to intercept Cree up on the side of a mountain in the Salt River range and rescue her. He hadn't hurt her except to tie her wrists together in front of her with a rope."

"I'm sure it wasn't luck that got you to Elson in time to save her." He halted his digging, wiping his sweaty brow with the back of his gloved hand.

"It was a lot of good people, law enforcement and a drone owned by a father and son, all coming together to help Tara. That enabled us to find him before he disappeared into the forest with her. And there was no luck involved. It was hard, quick planning by my people back at the courthouse, and I ran the rescue from the canyon parking lot where he took her."

"But you organized it. Right?" He watched her tie up the strands to the other post.

Sarah was thorough. She approached everything with critical, detailed observation, putting the pieces together, first so she understood before reacting or creating a plan. She wasn't the type to knee-jerk in a crisis either. He'd already seen that when they were bushwhacked out on Route 89.

"Yes. I have good relationships with all the organizations in and out of our county. We have a drone club in Wind River, and it was a man and his son who came when I asked them to try to locate Cree and Tara. Their help was enormous."

"Eyes in the sky," he agreed. "When you talk about the Elsons, I hear a lot more in your voice than just worry."

"Because they've been a thorn in the side of this county and law enforcement for two generations. This generation of men has all done serious federal prison or jail time."

"What are they? Drug runners?"

"Yes. That's their MO. But I'm more concerned this past year that they might hook up with Gonzalez and his crew; enlarge their skill set into sex trafficking and slavery. We're having girls as young as twelve years old snatched right off our roads and streets, Dawson. Girls coming home from school, dragged into a van or truck, and they disappear forever. It's sickening. And it's escalating all over the country. It isn't just in Wyoming."

He heard a lot of pain in her voice over the last. Digging more with the shovel, widening the hole, he frowned. "Are you working with the FBI regarding Gonzalez trying to take over your county?"

"Absolutely. Also with the sex trafficking unit. It's an added burden on the FBI, as well as us. We just don't have the money to hire more deputies. These poor girls get kidnapped, carried off to another state or country, forced into giving sex to any man who pays for it. I've got a team of deputies who give educational talks to schools, clubs and anyone who wants information on it in our county. It's crucial we make all parents aware of what their young daughters and sons need to do if an unknown man approaches them. I've lobbied the governor for more funds, but Wyoming is in a bust cycle with the oil business, so there's no money for any county." Her lips flattened as she straightened, placing the wire cutters in a side pocket on her leather chaps. "I'm afraid if Gonzalez continues his move to get into our state, sooner or later the Elsons are going to become known to him."

"What can he do? Force them to work with him?"

"Not force, but he'll give them a piece of the action, which means they have to swear allegiance to his organization. He needs people on the ground who know the area. And the Elsons are more than acquainted with every nook and cranny of this county. It will just make our job harder if another girl or boy is snatched." She turned away, heading back to Socks, who was happily munching on the thick, green grass near his hooves.

Straightening, Dawson heard raw anguish in her voice. Where had that come from? He almost stopped digging and went over to where she was standing at the saddlebags, opening one of them. If he wasn't seeing things, he thought her hands were slightly trembling. What the hell! His gut twisted in reaction and he sensed something emotionally overwhelming to Sarah, but he couldn't name it and had no idea what it might be. But he was seeing it.

Ordering himself to mind his own business, Dawson went back to digging. How long had they known each other? Less than two weeks? Right now, he wanted to explore common ground with Sarah, as well as to create trust. He'd lain awake most of last night wondering why he was so enamored with her. Dawson had no answers, just frustration. Sarah had a secret. And it was a secret so huge that it had made her hands tremble.

Sarah gulped several times, keeping her back to Dawson. Dammit! She couldn't even discuss sex trafficking without seizing up emotionally about it. The look in Dawson's face, the care burning in his gray eyes, damn near made her unravel like a ball of yarn. She couldn't cry! The lump in her throat grew to almost a painful level, so much so that she grabbed a bottle of water out of the saddlebag and gulped down several swallows to stop the reaction.

Wiping her mouth with the back of her gloved hand, she heard Dawson once more digging. Relief spread through her. This wasn't something she could talk about to him, but God knew she wanted to do exactly that. He was a strong, quiet man with a level of maturity she found missing in so many men. He listened intently when she spoke, and she could feel him absorbing every word she said. The only people who gave her that full, undivided attention on personal matters were her parents and grandmothers. Because they loved her and cared about her in every possible way. Yet, Dawson was giving her that same level of awareness.

Twisting on the cap, she shoved the water bottle down into the saddlebag and felt less wobbly in the stomach, the tears receding and the lump in her throat dissolving. Closing her eyes for a moment, she dragged in a ragged breath to try to steady her shaken nerves. Somehow, just being around Dawson triggered her emotionally and she couldn't explain why. It wasn't that he was manipulating her or being anything but honest and straightforward, as he'd always been with her. It was her reaction that shocked her. Dawson seemed to just naturally create a safe haven for her when they talked. All the buried feelings in her had wanted to be released over the nightmarish years that haunted her, and then, to give them voice. Nothing and no one had ever made her want to share what had happened to her like this.

Sarah wasn't sure what to do about it, waffling and questioning her attraction to Dawson. The man wasn't a flirt. He was attentive, playful at times, and he made her laugh. There was a nice, heated vibe between them, and it seemed stronger and hotter the more time they spent together. She wasn't going to lie to herself: he was a hunk. She was sure he had some eccentricities, but whatever they were, they hadn't become apparent — yet.

*Time.* She just needed time, and to rein in her desire to entrust her emotional well-being to him. Oh, she wasn't innocent; that was for sure. And she hadn't peeked out from beneath a cabbage leaf yesterday either. Her gut compass, her heart and sixth sense, told her that Dawson was as steady and constant as the sun rising in the east and setting in the west. Even Gertie was thrilled to pieces about the guy. He had shadowed her the first week and now, at the beginning of the second one, was almost amazing her grandmother with his intuitive ability to be there at the right time and place to help her. And not only that — he'd gotten her to go to an acupuncturist in Jackson Hole last Monday and since then, her wrists had no pain. That just about made Gertie faint, because her wrist pain had been constant for the last five years.

Was it Dawson? His knowledge of medicine? Sarah got ready to help him pull out the fence post. She decided patience was the best course of action as she released the lariat from the leather around it.

"We about ready to have Socks pull that fence post out?" she asked, opening the lariat.

143

"Yeah, we're there," Dawson said, placing the shovel on another post and walking up to her. As she handed him the lasso, he carried it to the leaning post and tightened the loop around it. "Go ahead and mount up," he said, holding the rope up off the wet grass.

Nodding, Sarah threw her leg over Socks, wrapped the rope around the horn several times and guided him in the direction Dawson wanted the post removed. The rope grew taut as she backed Socks, watching the post begin to slide grudgingly out of the wet, muddy earth. Socks lowered his rear, front hooves digging in, using his thirteen-hundred pounds of weight to make the difference. In moments, the post lay on the ground. Sarah pulled Socks to a halt, giving him a well-earned pat. The horse snorted, as if it were nothing.

"Garret told me the other day that Socks used to be one of the top quarter horses in the state when it came to calf roping," Dawson said as he slid the lasso off the post, bringing it over to Sarah, who had her hand out for it.

"Yes, he was. He's fifteen now, and Shay said they retired him to only do ranch work. No more calf roping competitions for this big guy," and she quickly put the lariat back into place, tightening the leather loop below the saddle horn.

Patting the chestnut, Dawson said, "He's a quiet, steady horse with a lot of experience and knowledge. He's the kind that will keep you safe in a tight situation."

"Sort of like you," she said teasingly, smiling down at him.

"Me?"

"You."

"I make you feel safe?"

She saw the surprise in his expression. "Yes, you do." She leaned down, splaying her hand against Socks's sleek neck. It was then that the surprise in his eyes turned to pleasure, and he gave her a cocky grin.

"Well, unlike Socks, I'm not past my prime."

"Oh, I'd never make the mistake of thinking that, Callahan." She enjoyed their sparring repartee because Dawson was never mean or pointed with his teasing. She saw him move Socks's forelock and smooth it down the center of the white blaze on his forehead.

"So? In your world, Ms. Carter? A man who's slow, steady and experienced is a good thing?" and he met and held her gaze.

Her lower body went hot because the look he gave her was one of a man who definitely was interested in the woman he was with. "I like a man I can count on," she agreed, appearing outwardly unruffled but feeling far from it.

"Kind of like your father?" he wondered. "David strikes me as a quiet, earnest man with the patience of Job."

"As usual, your perception is right on the money. I'm not the most patient person in the world and my dad taught me the virtue of becoming that way. And I've learned to appreciate that same skill in the people around me."

Dawson nodded. "You've got red strands in your hair, Sarah, so I always thought there was a side to you that was wild, spontaneous and not necessarily patient," and he added a grin.

"Ginger-colored hair is not red hair. There's a difference."

"But were you a wild child growing up?"

She became somber. "For a while, I was, yes. But things changed, and I tempered that part of me after that."

"Hmmm, I'd like to see that wild little girl side of you come and play sometime when appropriate. I know you can't show that part because of the law-enforcement side of things, but I sense you can be pretty spontaneous when you're in a different situation."

Sarah moved a little uncomfortably in the saddle, seeing the glimmer in Dawson's eyes, that male confidence of his so sure about her. "That little girl is gone. What you see now is what you get."

"Pity," he murmured. "I learned a long time ago to play when I could, work when I had to and then go back and play some more."

"Did you get that from your parents?"

"Yeah, and my baby brother, Toby. He was the wild child in our family." He stroked Socks's neck, becoming more serious. "Toby was always up for adventure, risk taking and doing something new or different. I was pretty much the stick in the mud, as he used to accuse me of being. I only had ten years with him, but he taught me a lot, and I swore after he died that I'd become more like him. Toby was serious when he had to be, and he was responsible, but he always knew when to blow it off and go play and break that serious, responsible energy around him. He taught me a lot."

"I'm so sorry you lost him, Dawson. He sounds like such a fun-loving brother."

Tapping his chest, he said, "Toby lives with me to this day, in my heart. I carry a photo of him in my wallet and part of my losing him, the grief, has been healed because he does live with me to this day."

"That's a beautiful way to look at life . . . at such awful loss. I admire that you can do it."

Shrugging, Dawson said, "Well, I don't like the other choice. There's nothing that's bringing him back, but that doesn't mean we throw away our memories of him either. My parents are great role models for me. They didn't push Toby's death under a rug, they didn't jam it down inside them and never speak of him again. Instead? Even shortly after his death, my mom and dad would talk about him, the foods he liked or hated, at the dinner table at night. We had some good laughs about Toby's eating habits, among other things." His voice softened. "Looking back on those years, my parents did a lot to help me deal with the guilt I carried about that day. By the time I was eighteen, and maybe a little bit more mature? I no longer carried as much guilt over the accident."

"That's a blessing in itself," Sarah said quietly. "Maybe hanging around you when we get time will help me in some way."

Dawson looked up at her, frowning, but he said nothing.

"Well," Sarah said, "let's get moseying on down the line. I'm sure we'll find another

148

rotted post sooner or later." She had to get moving; the look he gave her scared her. It was as if he was looking in to her like she was a crystal ball, clearly seeing her own guilt and loss. Her mind said it was impossible, but the unsettled feeling, and then that warmth that enveloped her, was real. Or maybe it was just her imagination, because she felt safe and trusted him far more than she should.

# CHAPTER EIGHT

*June 18*

Dawson tried to quell the tension gripping his gut as he sat down in the living room of Reese and Shay's home. They'd invited him for dinner and then dessert afterward, promising everyone they had an important announcement to share with all the vets. Sarah had been invited, because she was a strong part of the fabric of the Bar C, and one of Shay's good friends.

He had been disappointed, though, when Shay received a call before dinner that Sarah was working a car accident about three miles outside of town. She said she'd try to make it for dessert with them, if she got lucky.

He tried not to broadcast how badly he wanted to see her. It had been Saturday with her that had stoked the fire in him, making him realize how lonely he was without a woman in his life. Women completed men and vice versa in his world. He had happy parents who were not only best friends, but who also deeply loved each other. And now, as he sat on one end of an empty couch, his gaze swept the room. Garret Fleming sat with his wife, Kira. Noah Mabry was with Dair Wilson. Harper had his arm around Tara's shoulders on a love seat. They were all radiantly happy, all hopelessly in love with one another, just as Reese and Shay were. He was surrounded by true joy and love, but he also felt the ache of loneliness so cutting, reminding him that he hungered for a partner as well. His parents loved him, of course. Oh, and he had good friends, but that was a different kind of love. He wanted what all his military vet friends had discovered: a special, deep, fulfilling love with the right partner.

Shay looked radiant, her cheeks flushed a deep pink and her eyes dancing with a secret she wanted so badly to share with everyone. Reese, who was normally taciturn and gave little away in his expression, seemed buoyant, a gleam in his eyes as he studied his young wife with her naturally curly brown and gold hair. He sat with her on another sofa, Shay's hand resting on his thigh, his large hand over her much smaller one.

There was a sense of protection from each man toward the woman they loved, Dawson noted. And the look of love in the women's eyes for their men warmed him. For once, these vets, who had suffered so much, had found an island of peace and happiness in the everyday challenges that went on in their lives. It was a touching moment for him and he absorbed it fully, happy for all of them.

The doorbell rang.

"Oh, I bet that's Sarah!" Shay cried, popping up, hurrying out of the huge living room and heading down the hall to the foyer.

Dawson's heart pounded harder when he heard Sarah's low, husky voice and Shay answering her. His hands stilled on his thighs, his gaze riveted on the hallway, waiting for her to appear.

Sarah was still in uniform and she looked stressed to Dawson as she and Shay halted at the entrance. He stood up, and instantly, her gaze swung to his, clinging to him for just a moment. He felt so much in that glance. Looking at her uniform, he saw blood splatters across her left arm and shoulder. It had to be a bad accident, was all he could think.

"Hey, everyone," Sarah called, lifting her hand to all of them, "sorry I'm late."

The room gave Sarah a welcoming chorus of hellos in return.

"Shay has agreed to lend me some civilian clothes." Sarah pointed to the bloodstains on her blouse. "I wanted to be here tonight, but I don't want the smell to be a reminder of the accident investigation, so if you'll give us about ten or so minutes? We'll be back and then we can hear what Shay and Reese have to tell us."

Dawson stood uncertainly, wanting to go to Sarah, seeing the tightness of the skin across her cheekbones. But there was nothing he could do about it in that moment.

"Sure," Garret called, "get cleaned up." He looked toward the kitchen. "Me and Kira will get the dessert ready. By the time you get back, you can make yourself at home with Dawson on that couch and we'll have the chocolate cake and vanilla ice cream ready."

"Sounds good to me," Sarah said, relieved, giving Dawson a warm look that was more than a casual hello.

"Come on," Shay whispered, gripping her hand, pulling her down the hall. "Let's go find you some clean clothes."

After they had left, Garret and Kira went to the kitchen. So did Dawson. He wanted to do something . . . anything. His protective mechanisms were working overtime. As he came up to where Garret was cutting the three-layer cake he had made, Dawson asked, "What can I do to help?"

Garret slanted him a glance, ignoring his question. "She's okay, Dawson. Really."

"How do you know that?"

"Sarah's been a fixture around here for as long as I've been here. She's one of us. There's been a few other times when she's come to our Friday-night therapy sessions with Lilly Hilbert, and walked in off an accident investigation she had to take care of first. She's solid."

Kira pointed to the cabinet above where he stood. "Get us plates, Dawson? You're taller than I am," and she smiled, resting her hand comfortingly against his upper arm.

"You bet," he said.

"Oh, and get the bowls next to them? I'm going to grab the ice cream out of the freezer," Kira said.

Garret began to place the slices on the large dessert plates. His voice was low. "I saw how Sarah looked at you."

Dawson held out another plate so he could put another slice of cake on it. "What do you mean?"

"There's something building between the

154

two of you, isn't there?"

One thing Dawson had learned was that no one could fool Garret Fleming. The man was a mind reader at times, he grimly decided. "I'm not sure."

"Are you sure you want it to happen, if there is?" and he arched a sandy eyebrow in his direction, holding Dawson's gaze.

There was no way around Garret, so he leveled with him. "Yes, I'm hoping there is."

"Thought so. Sarah leads a hectic life. She doesn't have much time for herself. She comes out here every Saturday, if there isn't something going on that requires her attention as sheriff, and that's her me time, from what I can see."

"Good to know."

"Yeah," he muttered, a grin edging his mouth, "and if I were you? I'd sure as hell take advantage of that situation. She works too hard, doesn't get enough rest, is overresponsible, like all women, has to work twice as hard to prove to the men that she's just as capable as they are. You know the routine."

"We're on the same page with that one," Dawson said. He saw Kira coming back with the ice cream. "Thanks for your input."

Garret nodded, continuing to slice cake and place it on the plates. "Anytime."

Dawson busied himself helping Kira with doling out the ice cream. He was carrying the dessert into the living room when he saw Shay and Sarah reappear at the entrance to the living room. His heart soared. Sarah was tall and medium-boned, while Shay was much smaller and petite. Somehow, they had found a set of gray gym pants and a gray T-shirt top for Sarah that pretty much fit her.

"Thanks to Reese," Shay announced with a grin, "Sarah is wearing his gym stuff, but at least it fits her. All my clothes are way too small for her."

Everyone laughed, and Sarah did, too.

"Well, I'm not exactly ready for a fashion runway, but this will do." Sarah reached out, squeezing Reese's broad shoulder, "And thank you for the loan, big guy."

Reese nodded. "You give them a whole new meaning, Sarah."

The room filled with approving nods and chuckles.

"They'll probably never fit you the same, Reese," she teased drily, coming over to the couch where Dawson had been sitting. Taking a seat, she added, "and I'd much rather be here tonight than anywhere else."

Shay beamed and sat down next to Reese, who took her hand and squeezed it gently, giving her a loving look. "This wouldn't be right without you here with us, Sarah."

Between Garret, Kira and Dawson serving, they gave everyone their dessert. Dawson had been the last to sit down, and he liked how relaxed Sarah was now. He slid the bowl and plate in her direction on the coffee table that sat in front of their couch.

"Have you eaten dinner?" he wondered, sitting about two feet away from her.

"I grabbed a sandwich one of my deputies made earlier," she said.

He knew how he felt after a firefight and there had been blood spilled. "How's your appetite?"

Sarah picked up her fork after placing a paper napkin on her thigh. "I'm hungry."

It served to tell him that even after traumatic accidents, Sarah had the ability to wall off that experience and still maintain a good grip on reality. But in her job? She needed to project that kind of calm and quiet to those around her.

"Okay, everyone, dig in!" Shay urged excitedly.

For the next fifteen minutes there wasn't much chatter, just a lot of spoons clinking in the ice cream bowls and forks used to eat the cake Garret had baked earlier. Lots of pleasurable sounds and appreciation came

157

from everyone. Dawson covertly watched Sarah out of the corner of his eye from time to time. She had folded one long leg beneath her, and he saw that she was seriously relaxed, which made him feel inner relief.

Sarah ate everything, just as everyone else did. She didn't take any prisoners, and Dawson was somewhat mollified to see she had a genuine appetite. His admiration for her raised another notch.

Garret and Kira gathered up all the emptied plates and flatware afterward, taking them to the kitchen and then placing them in the dishwasher.

Dawson was going to help, but Garret had caught his glance and gave a subtle shake of his head, so he remained at Sarah's side. He noticed Shay was almost unable to sit still. She kept casting a bursting, happy smile up at Reese, and then would survey everyone with undisguised affection. Shay considered everyone in this room to be more than a friend to her: They were her family. Her cheeks deepened in color as Garret and Kira returned and sat down.

"Okay," Garret said to her, "spill the beans, Shay. What's going on that you're moving around like you have ants in your pants?"

"Yeah," Dair spoke up, laughing, "you're

killing us with all the suspense!"

There was a lot of laughter and a unanimous chorus of agreement among the group.

Shay stood up, her hands gripped nervously in front of her. "Well," she began, "for the longest time, since Reese and I married, we've wanted to start a family." She placed her hand protectively across her abdomen. "I'm three months pregnant."

Dawson heard the women gasp and then give whoops of joy. All of them, including Sarah, got up, rushed over to Shay, surrounded her, hugging her and congratulating her. Reese beamed.

Garret, Noah and Harper all nodded and gave each other and Reese a thumbs-up. The women were bubbling with celebration, surrounding Shay, who was so petite and shorter than any of the other women vets that she disappeared from view. There were lots of tears shared among the women. Dawson understood from Garret in another conversation they'd had, that Sarah loved children. That was evidenced by her working closely with the Delos Charity food bank in the town. Her focus was on children from lower economic means, making sure they got solid breakfasts to start off their schooldays. She was ceaseless in going around Wyoming giving talks to any group or organization who invited her, to donate money so that Delos could keep feeding the children in her county.

Finally, the women broke up their circle around Shay, kissed her cheek and all sat down with their partners once more. Dawson saw the tears in Sarah's eyes as she sat a little closer to him this time. She reached out, placing her hand over his.

"Isn't this wonderful?" she quavered.

Turning his hand over, shocked by her unexpected touch, he curved his fingers around hers, squeezing them lightly. "Yes, it's a good thing." He didn't want to release her fingers, but he did, giving her the option to stay or leave. She reluctantly untangled her fingers from his. Still, there was a look in her green eyes, glimmering with unshed tears, and it was new and welcome. Sarah had wanted to be close to him. More warmth wrapped around his heart. Hope took root.

"Why didn't you tell us sooner, Shay?" Dair asked.

Wiping her eyes, she sat next to Reese. "Because I was afraid."

"Afraid?" Kira asked gently. "Of what?"

Making a muffled sound, Shay raised her hands. "With my father, the legal things he's hitting the ranch with, I was afraid I might miscarry. You all know I don't take stress real well."

"You take it well enough," Noah growled, frowning. "You're stronger than anyone I've ever met, Shay."

Reese smoothed his hand across Shay's tense shoulders. "She wanted to wait a while, get past all the legal issues. That's a new stress and pretty hard on everyone." He gave his wife a kind look. "We talked it over and felt it was better to wait it out for a while. Shay's now moving into her second trimester, and her doctor said that chances of miscarriage go down because she's learning to handle the new stresses."

"Sorry, gang," Shay whispered off-key, "but I wanted this baby so badly that I just didn't have the courage to overcome my own fear about losing her or him if I told you too soon."

"It's okay," Tara soothed. "We all understand. Don't feel bad that you didn't tell us sooner. The more important question is: What can we do to help you destress while you're pregnant?"

Sarah added, "Too bad we can't do what the Native Americans used to do before white men came to their country. When a woman got pregnant, she was set into a teepee away from the others, surrounded by other women, kept out of any stress within the village so she could be calm and focus on her pregnancy. They believed that when a woman was given that kind of calming environment, she's happy, and so is the baby she carries."

"I've heard of that," Shay said. "And Reese and I have talked about that very thing. It's my father who's creating the stress on me right now; I've just got to continue to disconnect from what he's trying to do to the ranch."

Harper Sutton spoke up. "Funny thing, Shay. Right now in my college classes on becoming a paramedic, they're all about how to deliver a baby," and he grinned crookedly. "At least you have me around. I may not be an MD, but my combat corpsman background gave me plenty of opportunities when I worked with Afghan midwives who were caring for mothers giving birth. I'd stand outside the hut and they'd come out and tell me what was going on, and I could give them feedback to help the mom in labor." He straightened a bit more, pride in his tone. "I helped deliver ten babies via the midwives because men aren't allowed by Islamic law to be with a woman in labor or deliver her baby. Only other women, midwives, can help her."

"Reese and I thought about you, Harper. And we're both grateful you're here on the Bar C while I'm pregnant." Shay gave him a look of relief. "And you have no idea how much we rely on you because you're a medic."

Harper wriggled his eyebrows, holding up his hands. "I have every confidence I could assist you in anything that came up, Shay. I can let the firefighters at the station, who are already paramedics, know about your condition, too. That way, everyone is prepared. Are you going to the hospital or going to have a home birth?"

Shay sighed. "I want a home birth. My doctor, Kate Donnelly, has her office in Jackson Hole and she isn't so sure, but she said as long as there are no complications, she'd be willing to come out and assist. And if I have to have emergency help, we have our small hospital five miles away from the ranch."

"Best of all worlds," Harper agreed. "Do you have a midwife picked out?"

"Yes. Kate gave me a list of midwives from the area and I hired two of them."

"Good," Harper said. "When they come over if I'm around, could you introduce us? They'll be happy to know they'll have another medical person with some experience around, just in case."

"Oh, for sure I will," Shay said eagerly. "We're so grateful you're here, Harper, believe me."

"Well," he said, losing his smile, getting serious, "after all you've done for us? I consider this dharma, paying you back in some small way for the support you've given us. We wouldn't be here, Shay, without your vision and dream for a vet-healing ranch where we could glue ourselves back together again."

"I second that," Dair said, her voice wobbly with emotion. "It's the least we can do for you, Shay. We need to have a girl confab soon so we can all sit down at the kitchen table and see what duties we can take off your hands to lighten your load these next six months. And plan a baby shower, too!"

Dawson saw and heard the grit in Dair's low tone. She was part Comanche and had lost her foot and ankle when an IED had exploded in Afghanistan. It had killed her bomb-sniffing dog, Zeus.

When Dair had arrived on the Bar C, the vet wranglers had all gotten together, with Reese heading them up, to build Dair a wooden ramp from where their homes sat all the way down to the main barns and arena. This year, they were going to pour concrete for a wide sidewalk so Dair, and anyone else, who needed that kind of assistance, whether in a wheelchair or an amputee, could travel easily up and down the slope. Dawson knew from talking with Noah in the barn on Saturday after fence mending that they'd helped Dair because of her amputation. She'd come to the Bar C at Shay's insistence, and everyone had pitched in to help Dair feel part of the team. It spoke a lot about the vets, working to support her needs. And he was so glad to be a part of this group.

"Okay, that's a great idea about a baby shower," Reese told Dair, giving his wife a warm glance. "Let us guys know what you come up with. I think we men should get together to see if we can make Shay's next six months a little easier on her."

"Well, for one thing," Garret spoke up, "if she'll let me back into your kitchen, I can cook nightly meals. I know how stressful it is to work like Shay does all day and then juggle house duties in the evening. When I first came here, I did all the cooking for her and the vets three times a day, seven days a week. I can do that again."

Shay's expression softened with gratefulness. "Garret, you're getting so popular in

165

the valley because of your construction background, I would never ask you to do all that cooking. But you're right: Some nights it's hard on me to have to tend to house stuff. I could use your help."

"How about I cook five days out of the week and you cook the other two? And if you're tired on some night, call me soon enough and if I'm not out on a job site, I can come in and fix dinner for you."

"Well," Kira said, "if you're going to cook a meal, why not cook for them and us? That way, after you get it served, you can come home and we'll leave them to their privacy?"

"Great idea," Garret said. "That okay with you, Shay?"

"Sure is. We can decide on a weekly basis what five days you can be here to do the cooking at night. Okay?"

Rubbing his hands, Garret said, "Fair enough. It's only for six months. And it's not a prison sentence to me because you know I love to cook."

Everyone tittered. They knew Garret was chef quality and no one ever left anything on their plate when he cooked for the crew.

"Now," Garret said, waving a finger in Shay's direction, "I'm still doing Sunday supper for everyone here. That will never change. Okay?"

"That's wonderful," Shay bubbled, grinning. "I was so hoping you would keep doing that for us, Garret."

Kira gave her husband a wink. "Garret might be a warrior, but beneath that is a soft heart, and he loves to cook for everyone, Shay. So no worries. All right?"

"All right," she breathed. "It just feels so good when everything works out, but I know it's because of our military training that we come together like a squad or company when something needs to be done."

Dawson relaxed. Maybe because Shay looked utterly relieved, knowing she had a safety net of vets who would watch over the baby growing inside her belly. And the women vets were tight with one another, no question, and they would make sure Shay didn't overdo and stress out. More than anything, he felt Shay needed this kind of nurturing. She'd worked so hard for so long to make this dream come true for all of them that no one deserved a rest more than her. He also knew that Shay's daily work in the barns would be curtailed a lot by Noah and Harper, who had a look in their eyes that told him just that. Shay was a hard, physical worker. Reese would probably talk her out of riding horses from now on, instead appealing to her to try walking, and maybe assign her to picking up eggs at the chicken coop every morning but not do any heavy lifting. She was young, and in great physical shape, but a pregnant woman should be given some easier assignments if it was possible. And looking at everyone, Dawson could see the commitment to give Shay the time off she needed in their expressions. That would destress her even more.

Sarah's phone rang. She gave everyone a look of apology, unwound and walked out into the foyer to answer it. Being sheriff of a county, Dawson decided, was 24/7/365. He told himself he should be grateful she'd sat with him, touched his hand and remained close to him. All those subtle signs were a green light as far as he was concerned.

After a five-minute conversation out in the hall, Sarah halted at the entrance. "Hey, gang, I've got to go. I'm needed out in the field." She gave Shay a look of apology. "I'm going to wear Reese's clothes and I'll change at home and then go on duty. I promise I'll bring them back to you soon, washed and folded."

Reese laughed. "Keep them for as long as you want, Sarah. I have three others."

Instantly, Dawson was on his feet, walking toward her. "I'll walk you to your cruiser," he said. He wasn't going to take no for an answer, but the expression on Sarah's face told him she appreciated his company.

"Thanks, Dawson," she said, moving into the room and going over and gently hugging Shay good-bye. She released her and then hugged Reese, too. Lifting her hand as she straightened, Sarah added, "See you guys and girls this Saturday. Pray that nothing major happens in the county that morning."

Dair laughed and said, "I've got my fingers crossed, Sarah."

Turning, smiling, she walked over to Dawson. "Ready?"

"As I'll ever be," he said, cupping her elbow, guiding her down the hall toward the wooden hooks holding everyone's lightweight jackets. There was a fine tension in Sarah. He dropped his hand and reached out, taking a plastic bag that held her bloodied blouse in it. Shay had used a black felt-tip pen to write SARAH on it. "I'll carry this for you," he said, going to the door.

"Keep this up, Callahan, and I won't have a thing to do except stand here and watch you do all the work," she teased.

Chuckling, he opened the screen door for her. "I wish I could do more for you, Sarah. This is small stuff."

169

She passed him, turned and stood out on the porch, waiting for him.

"What's going on?" Dawson asked, cupping her elbow again. He was going to claim her for his own, that was all there was to it. Yes, Sarah was a self-sufficient woman and yes, she could take care of herself, but he wanted her to know he was there to be her support, too. She could have wrested her elbow from his hand as they took the wooden steps down to the sidewalk, but she didn't.

"It's the Elsons. Again," she muttered, frowning. Lifting the key fob, she pressed it and opened the cruiser.

"You going home first to grab a clean uniform blouse, then?" he asked, setting the plastic bag in on the passenger side of the cruiser.

"Have to." She looked around. "It was such a nice night, Dawson. I don't get to see many happy endings in my line of work, and I was hoping tonight would remain upbeat."

He heard the discouragement in her tone as she slid into the cruiser. Standing and holding the door open, he asked, "Will you be okay?"

"Yes. I've got two deputies out at the Elson home right now. Everyone is waiting for me to arrive."

Nodding, he said, "I'm around if you need someone to talk to."

There was a glimmer in Sarah's shadowed eyes as she turned on the engine. "Has anyone ever told you that you're a big, bad grizzly bear in disguise?"

He shut the door and she lowered the window. "No. I'm generally pretty even tempered and try not to show that side of myself to anyone."

"You don't fool me," and she tossed him a slight smile. "But I like that side of you, too."

"That's a relief."

She laughed. "I'll see you Saturday, Dawson. It was a nice evening and I'm glad we could share it." Reaching out, she touched his shoulder momentarily. "You're a good person."

Her praise fell over him like warm sunlight in the darkness of the night. "Thanks. You take care out there. Okay? And yes, I'll see you Saturday. . . ."

Already, Dawson could see and feel the shift in Sarah as she prepared to back the cruiser out of the parking space. Taking a few steps away from the vehicle, he lifted his hand good-bye to her, wishing he could go with her. But he couldn't, and it left his gut tightening once more. The woman had a dangerous job. She'd left a war in Afghanistan and traded it in for a county war with a lot of dark players who lived here. The Elson clan, especially. Turning, he scowled and put his hands in his pockets, slowly walking toward the gate to the white picket fence.

He heard the screen door open and close. It was Garret. There was a porch light, and he could see the concern in the soldier's face as he came quickly down the steps and met him on the sidewalk.

"It's the Elsons again, isn't it?"

"Are you a mind reader? Yes, it is." Dawson could see Garret's face, the dark shadows across it, his eyes glittering, reminding him of a wolf on the prowl.

"Sarah rarely gets pulled out like this at night," he said, hands on his hips, looking around the quiet ranch, scowling. "And the one she always rolls on is when one of the Elson boys are involved in something illegal. Did she say what it was about?"

"No," Dawson admitted. "She did say two deputies were already at the Elson residence, though."

Snorting, Garret said, "Probably the old man beating up on Roberta again. The sick, crazy bastard."

"Is he dangerous?"

"About once a month, Brian gets drunker than a skunk, goes home and beats the shit out of his wife just because." Garret flexed his fist. "And Roberta won't press charges against him to save her own hide."

"What can Sarah do, then?"

"She seems to have a mollifying effect on Brian; no matter how drunk he is, she can get him to back off and leave his wife alone. There's an unspoken connection between them, and it's always been there. Brian was holed up in his house one time, with a SWAT team surrounding it. Sarah was able to pick up the bullhorn and ask Brian if she could come in and talk to him. He said yes." Garret shook his head. "Sarah just has a special thing about being able to bring madmen down and calming them. On that call, Brian came out of the house, handed over his weapon and the SWAT team went home."

"Damn," Dawson muttered, shaking his head.

"Hey, you're falling for a woman warrior," Garret said grimly. "And she's always going to be in the line of fire, so you'd better get used to it or it'll eat acid through your stomach lining and you'll get ulcers. That or step away from her now, before it's too late and you're too deeply involved with her. Sarah isn't for a man who can't stand the heat of the fire she lives in daily."

"I'm stepping," Dawson told him grimly, holding his dark stare, "toward Sarah. Not away from her. I'm not used to a woman being a sheriff; it's a learning curve for me."

Garret shrugged. "I didn't think you'd shy away from her." He clapped Dawson on the shoulder. "Come back in. Kira and Dair are serving coffee. Sarah will be okay."

# CHAPTER NINE

*June 18*

It was nine p.m. when Sarah rolled onto the Elson homestead, her emotions held in tight check. Brian's father, Jethro Elson, was in federal prison in Montana, never to see freedom again. Her mouth thinned as she pulled up outside the shantylike, two-story house that was surrounded on two sides by the Salt River Mountains. It was a broken-down hovel where Brian and Roberta had raised their four sons to be criminals, like their father and grandfather. The Elsons were still upset over Cree having been shot and killed when he kidnapped Tara Dalton for the second time. Reese had shot him in self-defense.

Her gut tightened as she saw Deputy Jeff Robson, once on the law-enforcement side of the Marine Corps, head in her direction. The place was muddy and unkempt. Sliding out of the Tahoe seat, she saw the twenty-seven-year-old's grim face.

He came around her opened door. "Brian is unstable. We think he's taken cocaine by his symptoms of constantly sniffing, and the way he's acting. We've asked him if he took the drug, but he's denied it. He's sniffing every twenty seconds, he's restless and complaining we won't let him pace the house, so we don't believe him."

She shut the door and settled the belt around her waist. "What else? Have you been able to talk him down?"

"Not really," Jeff hedged with a grimace. "He's spooked. Roberta is in her bedroom, the door locked, hiding from him. She doesn't want either of us to try to help her or to call an ambulance. We haven't seen her, so we don't know if she's injured or not."

"I see," Sarah muttered. "Have either you or Craig James tried to communicate with her?"

"Yes, but she screams at us and tells us to leave. That she won't unlock the door. We've tried to coax her out of there so we can assess her condition, but she won't do it."

"It isn't like this little pattern hasn't played out before," she agreed glumly. "Where's Craig at?"

"He's in the kitchen watching over Brian,

who's saying he's going to kill Roberta."

"That's nothing new either. He's always saying he's going to do it," Sarah said, moving quickly down the muddy path toward the house. How she wished Roberta would press charges, but she was too beaten down by so many years of abuse. Her life was her four sons and she was deeply devoted to them, never mind they were lowlifes just like Brian.

"No," Jeff agreed, "it isn't. But Brian's edgy, not like the usual behavior when he drinks too much or after he's beaten her."

This wasn't the first time they'd been called to this place. "And if I throw his ass in jail, he gets out in forty-eight hours, he comes back here and beats the hell out of Roberta some more, saying it was her fault we arrested him. Dammit!"

Lifting his black baseball cap off his short brown hair, Jeff growled, "Yeah. These two have their dance steps down perfectly, don't they? Really sick and sad."

Making an unhappy sound, Sarah took the stairs to the partly open door. "You stay with Craig and watch Elson. If he's on coke, he's not only unstable, he can lose it and become a danger to all of us."

"Copy that," Jeff said, pushing the door open for her. "You going to try to get to

Roberta to open her door and let you in?"

"Yes. Are any of their sons on the premises or somewhere on the property?"

"No, just the two of them, but we'll keep an eye out."

"Do, because any of those boys could turn violent in a heartbeat. I know they carry illegal firearms. I don't trust any of them."

"Yeah, well, their old man, I'm sure, has a firearm or two hidden around the house. We don't have a search warrant to go look for them."

"As long as Brian sits at the kitchen table and behaves, we have to let things remain status quo. Just keep your voice low and easy-sounding. You know the drill on dealing with someone who's high on drugs."

"Sure do."

Sarah made sure her radio was on a special frequency to her two deputies. They all wore earpieces, and on that channel, they could keep in constant touch with one another. "All I want to do is calm this situation."

"Good luck."

Sarah walked down the hall after trying to make sure the mud sticking thickly to her black leather boots was mostly cleaned off. The place reeked. Food, three or four days old, lay on paper plates here and there, dirty clothing was piled on a sofa or chair, or dropped carelessly on the dusty wooden floor. She knew from her two years of experience that the Elsons didn't take a shower for days at a time. Or brush their teeth, which grated on her sensitive nose, when smelling their cadaverlike breath.

Roberta never put food away, so it lay out in different rooms, rotting, tainting the air. Nor did she or any other member of her family keep the place clean or picked up. The place looked like a third-world-country hovel that had been bombed. Sarah knew this sordid house well. But she kept her emotions under lock and key.

Right now, she had to talk to Roberta, coax her to open the door and let her in. Someone needed to check her for injuries. She'd had her nose broken several times, both cheekbones, her left arm and, this year, four out of five of the fingers on her right hand. Roberta had allowed her in before, and Sarah hoped she would this time. They had established a tenuous connection with each other.

Moving through the living room, the carpet frayed and probably thirty years old, the overstuffed couch looking tired, pieces of cotton oozing out of the thin, torn fabric here and there. The place smelled musty, cloyed heavily with cigarette and marijuana smoke, making her wrinkle her nose against the assailing odors. Moving to the right and down the hall where the bedrooms were located, she halted and knocked softly on a door to her right.

"Roberta? It's Sarah Carter."

"Go away!" she screeched.

The corners of Sarah's mouth tucked inward for a moment. She knocked again. "Roberta, you know I won't do that. The sooner you let me in, the sooner we'll leave. How about it? I need to see that you're all right. Please let me in?" She knew the forty-five-year-old woman hated the police with a rabid passion. And because of that, she'd probably do anything to get rid of them sooner rather than later.

The lock clicked and the door grudgingly opened. Roberta glared up at her. "Okay, come in, but you're not staying long and I'm not pressing charges."

"Okay," Sarah said, stepping into the small room.

Roberta was five-foot-six-inches tall, skinny as a proverbial rail, her straight brown hair lying across her hunched shoulder, uncombed and framing her pale face. Sarah knew she was a chronic heroin user. She'd seen twenty or thirty track scars on each of her lower arms last year, when they'd been called out once again to this place for Brian beating her.

Tonight, Roberta was wearing a black cardigan sweater over a pink T-shirt, and jeans. Sarah saw the stress in her brown eyes as she sat on the edge of the full-size brass bed, her arms crossed, a defiant expression on her face. Her nose was dripping blood and Sarah could see her left cheek was badly swollen, the first purpling colors beginning to appear from Brian's fist striking her. Roberta kept swiping at her nose with her hand and then wiping it across her jeans, refusing to look up at Sarah.

Shutting the door quietly behind her, Sarah gazed around the place. It was a habit to ensure no one else was lurking in the room. She returned her attention to Roberta, who was sitting hunched, her shoulders up and tight, her gaze focused on the floor in front of her. Pulling her white linen handkerchief from her back pocket, Sarah shook it open and walked over to her. She gently pressed the cloth into Roberta's hand. The woman wouldn't look at her but quickly took it and pressed the handkerchief against her bleeding nose.

"Can you tell me what happened?" Sarah asked quietly, taking a chair from the corner, sitting down about six feet away from Roberta.

"The usual," Roberta said in a low tone. "Brian drinks. That's it."

Sarah stood, went to the bathroom, poured water into a glass and brought it back to her. "Here," she said, slipping it into Roberta's other hand, "take some water."

"Thanks . . ." Roberta drank thirstily. She put the nearly empty glass on the bed stand, her hand none too steady.

Sarah sat down. "Did Brian punch you in the stomach?" That's what he usually did because that way no one would see the bruises. Sarah could feel nothing but compassion for this woman. She was Brian's whipping post when drunk or high on meth or cocaine, just as his sons were targets of opportunity for him as well. He was a violent, angry, mentally unstable man.

"No . . . he just pushed me around, was all." Lifting her head, Roberta's eyes narrowed. "Now? Are you satisfied? You've seen me. I'm okay. Leave us alone, Sarah. There's nothing I can do. And I'm not pressing charges against Brian, so don't even ask."

"Were you two taking drugs before he started hitting you?"

Hitching one thin shoulder, Roberta said, "Like I'd admit anything to you."

"Brian has taken cocaine. That makes him dangerous and unpredictable, Roberta. Usually he drinks, but that's not what happened this time around."

Roberta sat there, her mouth moving into a hard line, staring straight ahead, hanky pressed firmly to her nose.

"Look, I need your help here," Sarah urged quietly. "I've got two of my deputies out there and there's only four of them on duty to cover the entire county. We all know Brian took coke. I don't feel good about leaving you here alone with him, Roberta. Depending upon how much of the drug he took and when, he could come after you again. People on coke kill other people." She reached out, gently smoothing the fabric of the cardigan along her shoulder. "I don't want you hurt any more than you already are, Roberta. Let me help you this one time?" She saw the woman's face thaw momentarily and cut her a quick glance.

Sarah saw terror in her eyes. Roberta didn't scare easily. She made her hand firmer on her shoulder, feeling a sliver of an opening. "Please? Let us help you. If nothing else, I can take you to the county Red Cross shelter. Just for the night, until Brian comes down off that cliff he's on. I'll have one of my deputy's drive you home whenever you want. By then, Brian will be off the effects of the coke. He'll be more stable."

Roberta hung her head, her hands gripped in her lap. Her voice was rough with fear. "You know what he'd do, Sarah. He'd come after me. He'd kill anyone who stood in the way of gettin' to me."

"We wouldn't tell him where you were being taken. I promise. But I can't continue to protect you here, Roberta. There are other people in this county who might have life-and-death emergencies, too. I can't park Craig and Jeff out there to watch him all night." What Sarah wanted to do was handcuff the sick bastard and haul his ass to jail. With forty-eight hours of incarceration, he would no longer be on coke, and then he wouldn't try killing Roberta. Probably beat her up again, though.

"In order to do that?" Roberta rasped, putting her hand against her eyes, "I'd have to press charges. I'd have to tell you that yes, I saw him take cocaine." Her hand dropping away, she stared up at Sarah. "Wouldn't I?"

With a slow nod of her head, Sarah said, "Yes, you would. I can't haul him out of here otherwise. You know the law pretty well. My hands are tied if you don't tell me Brian took cocaine. I can arrest him for forty-eight hours, but legally, by the end of that time, I have to release him, and he'll walk free unless I can charge him with a crime." She held her breath, wanting so badly to help Roberta, to protect her. One day, Sarah knew Brian would kill this woman. She didn't want that to happen. Roberta was a victim of continuous, nonstop violence, too afraid to protect herself by turning over evidence of Brian's abusiveness to her or her sons.

"I-I'm so tired, Sarah. . . ."

Wincing at the sudden, raw emotion in Roberta's voice, Sarah came around and crouched in front of her, holding her weary gaze. "Then let me help you."

"Why would you?" she whispered, tears beginning to dribble down her taut face. "Jethro kidnapped your sister. He sold her . . . how could I trust you? I'm sure you hate us for what happened."

It felt as if a nest of angry bees had gotten loose inside her gut. Sarah quelled them, focusing on Roberta. "I don't hate you or your sons, Roberta. Jethro was the one who kidnapped my sister." She halted, scrambling inwardly to halt the rise of her rage and grief over Lane's eventual death at the hands of a kidnapper.

Putting a tight grip on her feelings, she

added, "I care what happens to you, Roberta. I don't blame you for what happened to my sister. I never did and never will." Reaching out, Sarah laid her hand lightly on Roberta's. Her skin was so cold, so paper thin, obviously from malnutrition. The woman didn't eat right, just junk food. "I'm here. I'll help you, but you have to say those words, Roberta. Let me cuff Brian and take him in." Her voice turned rough with emotion. "You and I both know what will happen when we leave. Brian's going to come in here and beat you. Only this time, he may kill you. Is that really what you want? Is it?"

Giving her a sad look, Roberta whispered brokenly, "You know, at this age, I'm so tired, so worn out that death looks pretty good to me on some days. At least I would be out of pain and suffering, wondering when Brian was going to stalk me and jump me again. But then, I pull myself out of it because my sons would miss me, and I love them."

Wincing, Sarah's hand tightened on hers. "Please, Roberta, let me help. . . . I'm begging you . . ."

There was a sudden commotion outside the door. Sarah jerked her head up toward the sound. She could hear a scuffle going on out in the dining room. Straightening, she whispered as she drew her pistol, "Roberta, stay here. Don't leave this room . . ." and she ran to the door.

Shots were fired.

Grabbing the doorknob, Sarah was suddenly thrown off her feet.

Brian leaped inside, gun in hand, breathing like an angry bull.

Sarah landed on her back with a crash into the chair, stunning her for a moment.

Roberta shrieked.

"You bitch!" Elson roared.

Muscle memory took over for Sarah. She rolled over on her back once she hit the floor, both hands on the pistol, taking aim at Brian.

The deafening roar of the pistol echoed, hurting her ears. Sarah saw Elson halt, change his mind, whip his pistol in her direction, to where she lay on the floor.

He fired at the same time she did.

Sarah let out a gasp, slammed back into the floor. Her whole chest ballooned with burning fire. She saw Brian staggering backward, a surprised look on his face. She had shot him in the left shoulder, spinning him around. He windmilled backward, slammed into the wall, but still held on to the gun.

Roberta was screaming, scrambling off the bed, trying to hide from him.

It was milliseconds for Sarah. Gasping for air, stunned by the bullet striking her Kevlar vest, she tried to focus. Brian scrambled upward, once more on his feet, teeth bared, eyes wild as he lifted the gun in her direction.

Sarah fired.

Her whole left leg suddenly went numb.

She watched her bullet strike Brian in the center of his chest. It flung him backward as he fell out of the doorway to the hall, his gun listlessly tumbling out of his fingers.

*Hit! I'm hit!*

Where were Jeff and Craig? Gasping for air, feeling a tsunami of pain spreading across her chest, Sarah jerkily rolled to her side, trying to reach the radio on her shoulder to call for help.

Jeff Robson, his left arm covered with blood, staggered to the bedroom and leaned heavily on the doorjamb. "I," he gasped, "called for backup and an ambulance."

Sarah's gaze never left the unmoving Brian Elson. "Check Elson. Where's Craig?"

"Got hit in the head with Elson's bullet. He's unconscious," he rasped, holding his hand against his shoulder, leaning down, making sure Brian was down for good. His hand shook badly. Looking up, he said, "No pulse. What about you? Your leg is bleeding, Sarah."

Stunned, her mind feeling as if it were stuck in neutral, Sarah pushed herself into a sitting position. Roberta had leaped off the bed, crouched and hidden on the other side of it. Her head popped up, her eyes wide with terror, gripping the edge of the covers.

"Okay," Sarah whispered, feeling as if her voice were hundreds of miles away in an echo chamber, "okay . . ." Help was on the way. The other two deputies would arrive at some point. So would the paramedics and ambulance. Glancing down at her numb left leg, Sarah saw the entire thigh of her trousers was blood-soaked. There was no feeling in that leg. She put her gun aside, reaching out, seeing a pool of blood gathering beneath it.

"You're bleeding bad," Jeff muttered, stepping inside. He lifted his right hand away from his own wound, grabbing the tourniquet that was in his belt. "Lay down, Sarah. Let me get this around your leg. You're bleeding out."

Feeling woozy, Sarah nodded and flopped down on the floor. The room spun. She felt weak and helpless, two things she never did. Jeff had been trained in emergency medicine, an EMT in his own right. She saw the pain and tightness in his square face as he came to her side, kneeling down, floundering to put the tourniquet around her thigh above the bullet wound. He was injured himself, his left arm barely working at his commands.

"This is going to hurt," he warned her, and he tightened the loop around her thigh, yanking it tight, trying to stop the loss of blood.

Pain ran up her leg. Sarah grunted, a small cry tearing out of her. Black dots danced in front of her eyes. She felt Jeff tightening the tourniquet even more, the agony racing upward into the trunk of her body. A black veil descended over her eyes. She could hear Jeff's heavy, sporadic breathing, hear Roberta sobbing loudly. And then she fell into an abyss.

The phone rang at Reese and Shay's home. Dawson was helping to clean up the kitchen, putting dishes into the dishwasher. He shut the door and punched the Start button, hearing the water begin to fill inside it.

"Hello," Shay answered.

Dawson heard her gasp, her hand flying to her mouth. Her eyes were huge with terror. A terrible sensation ripped through him.

Reese saw and heard his wife's gasp, going instantly to her side, standing next to the wall phone, close to her, worried looking.

"Oh . . . no! No! Are they all right? Please, tell me they're all right," Shay cried.

A feeling of dread came over Dawson. Shay's voice was shattered with disbelief. She stared at Reese, and then over at him. Her hand was pressed against her throat, as if to stop another cry.

"Y-yes, tell me where they're taking them? Oh, okay. Have Sarah's parents been called? Good . . . good. We're on our way . . . thank you. . . ." And she hung up.

"Oh, God, Reese, Sarah, Jeff and Craig were all shot at the Elson compound!" and she burst into tears.

Dawson felt an icy coldness coat the inside of him. He moved over to Shay, who was being comforted by Reese. "Are they alive?" he demanded hoarsely.

"Y-yes. . . . Craig has a head wound and is unconscious, Jeff has a left shoulder wound. Sarah . . . she got hit in the chest with a bullet fired by Elson and her vest saved her, but he shot her a second time, in her left thigh. She nearly bled out. She's still alive, but in critical condition. The ambulance is on its way to Wind River Hospital. It's the nearest place they can get to stabilize them."

Reese turned to him. "Can you get our truck ready? Go down to the barn and bring it around front? The three of us will leave immediately."

"Yes, I'll get it," Dawson said, quickly moving to the door after pulling down the keys from a hook in the kitchen. His mind spun. Sarah was critical. His mouth grew dry, he wanted to scream, but he funneled all those emotions into focusing on the job at hand. Running down the hall for the front door, his heart beat in time with each footfall.

*Get the truck. Get to the Wind River Hospital. Sarah was there.*

Could they save her? Or not?

It hurt to even think those words as he jerked open the door, ran out, slamming it behind him and heading swiftly for the barn below which the vehicles were kept. It was dark, but the huge floodlights from the houses and the arena lit his way so he could race down the wooden walk toward the second red barn, where all the vehicles were kept. The air was coolish. Above him, he could see stars winking back at him. Everything seemed so quiet and peaceful as the wind tore past him, his stride long and cadenced.

*Hurry! Hurry!*

Sliding into the ramp of the barn, he quickly pushed open the tall, heavy sliding doors. His emotions were going to swamp him any second. He had to focus! Running for the silver Ford three-quarter-ton, extended cab pickup, Dawson leaped inside, jamming the key into the slot. Instantly, the engine turned over, a deep growl.

*Turn on the headlights.*

He was forcing himself to slow down, to think moment by moment, to concentrate on what had to be done. Jerking the truck into gear, the vehicle roared out of the barn, up the road, kicking up thick plumes of dust behind him. By the time he'd swung into the gravel parking lot in front of Reese and Shay's home, they were standing there, waiting for him. Shay was distraught-looking. Reese was grim.

Throwing it into park, he waited impatiently for them to climb in.

"We just got a second phone call from Dispatch," Reese told Dawson. "Sarah is AB Positive. The hospital has none of that blood type on hand."

He stared at Reese's shadowed face as he helped Shay into the cab and then hopped into the passenger-side seat. "AB Positive? Are you sure?"

"Yeah," he grunted. "They're gonna give her Type O. It's the only thing they can do. She's lost too much blood —"

"Get on the phone," Dawson instructed, jerking the truck into gear, slamming his boot down on the accelerator. "Call Emergency and tell them that I have AB Positive blood. Tell them to get ready to take whatever they need once we get there. And then let's get hold of the Teton sheriff's department, speak to whoever is on duty. Ask the sheriff's department to fly any AB blood that's at their hospital in Jackson Hole."

"Good idea," Reese said, some relief in his tone.

Gasping, Shay cried, "You have the same blood type?"

"Yeah," Dawson ground out, swinging the truck out from the dirt road and onto the highway, heading for Wind River.

"Oh, thank God!" Shay whispered. "How many units can you give? Do you know?"

"An adult has anywhere between eight to twelve pints of blood in them," Dawson told her. "The larger and taller you are, the more blood you have. Normally, when you give blood, they only take a pint. But in my case, they can easily take two or three pints."

But would it be too late?

# CHAPTER TEN

*June 19*

A nurse was waiting for Dawson at the entrance to the Wind River Hospital ER. He told her his name and she quickly escorted him into a room to begin the life-saving transfusion.

"I'm Nurse Karen Siebold, Mr. Callahan," she said, gesturing for him to sit in a comfortable chair and roll up the sleeve on his left arm.

"Call me, Dawson. Have you heard how Sarah Carter is doing?"

"She's in surgery," she said, quickly swabbing the inside of his arm. "We're really lucky. We have the best ortho surgeon from Jackson Hole, John Martin, who was giving a talk to a group of our doctors this evening. I heard she took a bullet to her Kevlar vest high on her chest. That's going to cause a lot of bruising, but that's all. The X-rays didn't show any broken ribs or sternum."

195

"What about her leg? They say she was shot in the leg."

"The left midthigh," the nurse said. "The bullet cut her femoral artery and she almost bled to death. It also nicked the femur itself and, according to what I heard, she's got a Greenstick fracture to it."

"Greenstick," Dawson said, his brows moving upward. "You're talking a lateral fracture of the femur, then?"

"That's right. But it's a closed fracture, not an open one. Greensticks never are."

A closed fracture meant the bones had not broken in two and torn the skin open, a much more serious break. Dawson's mind clicked through his medical training. "That means the fracture is going to weaken her femur, but the bone isn't broken. Right?"

"Right you are," she said. "Sarah got lucky. Really lucky. It will take her six to eight weeks to heal from that kind of fracture. I know her pretty well because we see her in here from time to time, when an accident victim is brought in to us, and I know she hates being bed bound. She's a restless tumbleweed," and Karen smiled fondly. "She won't like being trussed up and then being tied up in a wheelchair, bed or crutches that long."

A sliver of relief threaded through him as

the nurse set up the blood transfusion. "That's good to hear. How about the deputy with the head wound? How is he doing?"

Karen grimaced. "Craig Jacobs is in surgery as well. We called in our neurologist, Dr. Susan Costa, and she's operating on him." She straightened. "Both Craig and Sarah are critical."

An icy knife plunged into his heart and he tried to shield himself from the emotions erupting within him. "How much of my blood are you going to take?"

"Two pints."

"No, take three."

"I can't do it because of hospital regulations —"

"Good news," Reese Lockhart called, walking swiftly into the room. "I just got word from the second-in-command deputy for Lincoln County that the Teton sheriff has already picked up four pints of AB Positive blood from the Jackson Hole Hospital and they're taking off right now, flying them here. They should be here in thirty minutes."

Relief melted some of that icy knife within him. "That's good news. What about Sarah's family? Are they here?"

Reese nodded. "Yes. They're all up on the second floor, surgery. Her parents, as well as the two grannies. They were already up there when Shay and I arrived. Everyone is deeply shaken."

"Who isn't?" Dawson agreed quietly. He looked at the red blood flowing below the chair into a bag. "How's Shay doing?"

"Better," Reese said. "You may not know this, but Shay and Sarah went from first grade through twelfth together. They're close friends."

"No, I didn't know that." It explained Shay's extreme response to that life-changing phone call. Looking over at Karen, he asked, "Do you know how much blood Sarah lost?"

"No, but the operation team will. I'm to get your blood up to them as soon as possible. It's going to help save her life. The other AB Positive blood coming in from Jackson Hole will be used by the surgical team instead of O positive blood. Your blood is going to stabilize her."

Urgency thrummed through Dawson. He knew if Sarah didn't have enough blood in her body, her heart would stop working and she'd die on the table. Sure the surgical team was on top of that possibility, he wanted to hurry the transfusion process along, get up on the surgery floor and ask the nurse there for an update on her progress. He couldn't lose her! He was just getting her trust, slowly but surely, and now this. Dawson didn't know if she would live, and that shattered him in a way that left him feeling helpless.

Dawson entered the surgery lobby, looking for the Carter family. Nurse Siebold had taken the two pints of his blood directly to surgery. He spotted Sarah's family standing huddled together, along with Reese and Shay. They all looked in his direction when he entered.

Emily, Sarah's mother, gave him a wobbly smile and threw her arms around him. "Thank you," she said against his chest. "Karen told us earlier that you were coming in and volunteering your blood for her. I don't know how to thank you."

He squeezed her gently and released her. Emily's tears touched him deeply. Wrestling to keep his own personal feelings for Sarah aside, he rasped, "It's the least I could do."

David, Sarah's father, clapped him on the shoulder. "I just got word the Teton sheriff's helo is landing on the pad just outside here. Thank you. I know you've given our daughter a fighting chance by giving your blood first."

"You're our hero," Emily whispered, pushing the tears away.

Dawson saw Gertie aimed, fired and coming for him. He managed a slight grin. "Sorry I couldn't be the one to drive you over here."

"Pshaw!" Gertie growled, throwing her arms around his middle, squeezing the daylights out of him.

Warmth flooded his chest as he squeezed his short, thin boss. Releasing her, he saw Nell coming at a slower pace in his direction, gratefulness in her expression. "Who brought you here, Gertie?"

"One of the men from the chicken side of the ranch. Don't worry about it," she told him gruffly, releasing him, standing aside so Nell could hug him, too.

Dawson was overwhelmed with the family's thanks. Nell said nothing more than "thank you," but it was more than enough. When he released the grandmother, he looked to Emily and David. "Have you heard anything?"

"Just before you arrived," Emily said, "a surgery nurse came out to tell us they had given Sarah your blood and that it stabilized her numbers."

Relief swept through him. "Good," he managed, his voice sounding strangled. So many emotions were going through him in that moment. He saw so much of Sarah's face in Emily's. Dawson felt as if his heart were being torn in two. The expressions on the faces of her family as they surrounded him nearly drove him to tears. Gulping several times, he rasped, "Why don't we sit down? We just have to wait to hear from the surgeon."

They had no more than sat down when a nurse came out of the operating room. She was dressed in green scrubs and gown, her mask pulled aside. Going directly to David and Emily, she said, "We've given Sarah two more AB Positive pints. She required four pints. She's stable, no longer critical. The operation is going well. Dr. Martin says he's about finished. He should be coming out to speak to all you in about half an hour."

"Thank you," David said, a catch in his voice. "For everything . . ."

Sitting across the room on a red plastic couch, Dawson felt as if someone had suddenly breathed life back into him. Sarah was stable. *Stable!* He wanted to get up and yell it to the heavens. Because he was a paramedic, he knew Martin had sewn the torn femoral artery back together again. All that remained was for him to see if any other muscles were involved in the trajectory of the bullet, so he could repair them as well.

There was nothing they could do about a Greenstick fracture except keep Sarah off her feet, give her a brace; she would be stuck in a wheelchair for a while as her leg healed.

Looking around, he saw the utter relief on the faces of her gathered family. Emily was clutching her husband's hand, her other hand across her mouth for a moment, as if to stop a sob or cry of elation at the good news. Dawson could feel the raw emotion of the Carters. He was no less affected, but none of them knew of his growing affection . . . maybe love . . . for Sarah. It was far too early to say anything to them about it. First, he and Sarah needed those deep discussions between themselves, and time.

But now? Dawson wondered how being shot would affect Sarah's head and her career. He knew from too much experience what a bullet wound did to Marines. It changed their lives. How was it going to change Sarah's? And how would it affect their growing, tenuous relationship? He knew Sarah liked him. Hell, they hadn't even kissed yet. His whole life felt upended, as if he were in free fall. How desperately he wanted to be at Sarah's side, holding her hand, supporting her, giving her purchase after this terrible, life-changing event. But he wasn't going to try to wedge himself into her family to do it. They loved her as much as he did.

That sudden thought made him sit up. Shock rolled through him again, only this time it was over something intensely personal and known to no one. He knew what love was. *Maybe.* He'd fallen for Lucia Steward and married her. That went to hell in a handbag real quick, thanks to his PTSD. Whatever he felt for Sarah was so much more than what he'd felt for Lucia. The first time he met Sarah, it was like meeting an old, dear friend, but it was more than just a friendly response from deep within him. His heart had tugged violently in his chest and he couldn't explain the powerful reaction he'd had to her. That feeling had never gone away, only grown intensity and joy within him. Being with Sarah was like breathing fresh air for the first time in his adult life. Was that love? A part of love? Confused, Dawson wasn't clear or sure about it. Yes, he was drawn to Sarah; yes, he wanted to kiss her and take her into heated oblivion with him. Yes, he wanted her in his bed, at his side, sharing, giving and taking from each other. That had to be love? Or was it just lust?

With his PTSD staining his whole reality from a mental and emotional perspective,

Dawson couldn't easily separate love from lust. Both started with an *L,* but the two were not friends. Lust was about sex without much emotion involved, just satiating one's sexual desire. Love was so much more; he'd seen it in his parents' relationship as he grew up.

Sitting back on the plastic couch, lost in his internal reverie, Dawson tentatively decided what he felt for Sarah, what he dreamed about with her, followed a pattern of love more than simple lust. He liked being with her, liked her laughter, was curious about how she saw the world and how she regarded him. Dawson knew there was something good and healthy growing between them. Would he have a chance to act on it? Would being shot and wounded change Sarah's life not only in small ways, but large ones as well? He was from her past. This bullet wound was her present. And as much as he wished he could foresee a future with her, he couldn't, no matter how much he wanted to.

Dr. Martin, dressed in scrubs, his hands free of gloves but his cap still on, with his mask hanging down his chest, entered the surgery lounge.

Everyone's head snapped up and the low

sounds of talking stopped instantly.

"Mr. and Mrs. Carter? I'm John Martin, Sarah's surgeon. The good news is that your daughter is going to live."

A collective sigh filled the room.

"Right now, we have her in recovery. As soon as she's conscious, we'll take her to her room. And once the nurses have gotten her comfortable, one of them will come down to get you so you can see her."

David stood up, gripping the surgeon's hand. "Thank you, Doctor. Thank you so much."

"You're welcome," Martin said, smiling a little. "I'm glad I was down here to give the hospital doctors a talk on ortho. Sarah has a guardian angel or two."

Emily stood. "We're so grateful to you and your team, Doctor. Can you tell us more about Sarah's condition? Is she still critical?"

"No, she's in guarded condition, but that's a good upgrade," Martin told everyone. "She has adequate blood in her now, and all her stats are in the normal range. We're giving her an antibiotic IV drip, which, after a bullet wound, is standard procedure. The bone in her left thigh, the femur, has a six-inch lateral crack in it. We call that a Greenstick fracture."

"What does that mean?" Gertie demanded, coming up to him. "Speak English, Doc."

Martin grinned. "Yes, ma'am. If you have to break in a bone in your body? This is the best break to have. It's a vertical fracture, which means it has fewer complications and can usually heal up one to two weeks faster than a horizontal fracture. Sarah will have to be in a wheelchair for at least a week, maybe two, depending. I'll be seeing her seven days from now, and I can tell you more at that time."

"Oh," Nell said, "Sarah hates being bedridden, Dr. Martin."

"That's what one of my surgery nurses told me. The wheelchair is just a way to keep the weight off the leg so it can knit back together properly. As soon as we can, we'll get her on crutches, plus a leg brace that will help the bone continue to knit and heal."

"Well," Gertie muttered, "what kind of time are we talkin', Doc?"

"Bones in a woman of her age will heal in four to six weeks. I'm sure that by week four, she'll be walking on her own, still in the leg brace. By week six, if all goes well, the leg brace will be gone, too and she can begin physical therapy to get her muscles back."

"What about the injury to her muscle tissue?" Dawson asked, joining the family, standing in the back of the semi-circle.

"She'll need some physical therapy after her bone knits fully, as I said. but I anticipate in the next six months she'll be as good as new and won't have to rely on anything but her own two feet."

Murmurs moved around the group, and another layer of worry dissolved from Dawson's shoulders. "That's good news. What about her femoral artery tear?"

Martin nodded. "That was major and why she needs to be in a wheelchair for at least one week so it can fully heal. I'll be dropping in to see how Sarah is doing before I leave tonight. My advice is to see her two at a time. She's going to be very groggy coming out from under the anesthesia, plus the shock of the surgery, not to mention getting shot. She might not have much mental clarity, so don't expect it. Anesthesia normally wears off in twenty-four to forty-eight hours, so she should be back to her normal mental state at that time."

"David and Emily should go first," Gertie said.

"Absolutely," Nell said.

"Then you two," Dawson told the grand-mothers. "And if Sarah is too tired and wiped out after your visits, I'll come back to see her tomorrow during visiting hours."

"Good enough," Gertie said, and then slyly added, "but I think my granddaughter is gonna get in a snit if you don't show up after Nell and I visit her."

Feeling a flush move up his neck and into his cheeks, Dawson avoided the sharpened stares coming from David and Emily. Wishing Gertie hadn't said anything, he moved uncomfortably. "Well," he told her, "let's see where she's at after you two visit. Okay?"

Gertie gave him a merry look. "Okay, Dawson. But I know she's gonna want to see you."

Wanting to deflect, Dawson asked the doctor, "What about Deputy James? Do you know anything about his surgery?"

"Yes. They're closing him up right now. The bullet struck the bone of his skull, cracking it. They're going to watch him for swelling of the brain. They won't know much about his mental state until he gets out of recovery and becomes fully con-scious."

"Does he have any family here?" Dawson hadn't seen anyone else in the surgery lounge.

"His folks are in Virginia. The hospital has been on the phone with them, updating them. They're catching a red-eye flight to be out here with him, but they won't arrive until tomorrow, late morning."

"What's his condition?"

"Critical. We'll know more after he awakens. He'll be placed in ICU."

"And Deputy Robson?" David asked. "How is he?"

"Already in recovery and conscious. Shoulder injury. He's in good condition. His parents are flying in from Caspar right now. Should arrive shortly. The hospital called them on their cell phone to update them so they wouldn't worry about their son."

"Great," Dawson said. "Good news all around." Brian Elson was dead, so there was no sense in asking about him. He felt sorry for his wife, but in the back of his mind, he realized she was free from being his punching bag for the rest of her life. Her hell on earth had ended.

"Sure is, folks," Martin said. "If you'll excuse me . . ." The surgeon gave them a nod, turned and walked out of the room.

David Carter heaved a sigh, giving his wife a long look. "This could have been so much worse."

"Got that right," Gertie agreed. "Anyone up for some coffee down at the restaurant on the first floor? I need to drink something. A good teaspoon of whiskey is what I had in mind, but they don't sell liquor here."

Nell tittered and shook her head. "Oh, Gertie, there you go again."

"Hey," she said, waggling a finger in Nell's direction, "I'm the comic relief for all of you. Now, come on, follow me and Dawson to the restaurant." She hooked her arm around his, dragging him forward.

Brief chuckles and smiles broke out as the group followed Gertie's hard-charging lead toward the elevator down the hall.

Dawson cut his stride, giving Gertie an amused look. "Everyone dodged a bullet."

Gertie punched the button on the elevator, the doors whooshed open. "We said a lot of prayers, young man." She strutted into the elevator, still holding on to his arm. "And the two pints of blood you gave Sarah gave her a lifeline. If you hadn't done that, she might not be with us right now." She punched his arm with her index finger. "And none of us are going to ever forget what you did for our Sarah. You're her angel in disguise."

"Well," Dawson said drily as they moved to the rear to let the others get on, "you two grannies have a lot more pull than the rest of us."

More chuckles as the doors closed.

Gertie poked him in the upper arm again. "You're too modest, Dawson. We all owe you so much and none of us are gonna forget it. I've got the devil on one shoulder and an angel on another. Luckily, I deferred to my angel today, and she brought it home. And that angel was you."

Dawson heard the others agree, nodding their heads in unison, giving him a grateful look for his part in saving Sarah's life. Each of them reached out and touched his arm, his shoulder or squeezed his hand in thanks.

Dawson grinned, and he was fine with Gertie holding on to his arm. He knew sometimes she got dizzy and refused to use a cane; it hurt her pride too much to use it. And he recognized one of those times as now. "Let's pick out a table in the restaurant," he told her, "then I'll go get everyone coffee."

"Sounds good to me!" Gertie crowed.

Nell said, "They might have small bottles of wine available, Gert. Maybe get one?"

Giving a loud snort, Gertie muttered, "That piss? Whiskey is a real liquor, not that grape stuff mixed with water. No, thank you!"

The group broke into laughter as the doors opened.

Dawson knew the family needed some relief from knowing they'd nearly lost Sarah. Gertie was the perfect foil. As the family trailed out of the elevator, they waited for the others to step off. Leaning down, he whispered into Gertie's ear: "You know exactly what you're doing. Don't you?"

Gertie's thin lips curved upward. She cackled loudly. "Every minute of every day, Mr. Callahan. And don't you ever forget it!"

Chuckling, he led Gertie out of the elevator to the restaurant across the hallway. "No, ma'am, I'll never forget it," he solemnly promised her. "I'm just glad you're a warrior for the light and not the dark, or we'd all be in a helluva lot of trouble."

Gertie's laughter floated up and down the hall.

# CHAPTER ELEVEN

*June 21*

Dawson felt exhaustion creeping upon him. It was 4:00 a.m. by the time he was allowed to see Sarah. The two groups of family members stayed for ten minutes each, not wanting to tax her. They would come back during regular visiting hours, from ten a.m. to eight p.m., from here on out. Everyone agreed Sarah needed her rest. As he took the elevator up to the third floor, where her room was, he tried to rein in his emotions. What he wanted to do to comfort her, and what he should do, which was keep his hands off, were in a tug-of-war within him.

At the nurses' station, he was given Sarah's room number. Everything was pretty much dark on the floor because the other patients were sleeping. He wiped his smarting eyes as he moved soundlessly down the highly polished hall toward her private room. The door was partly open. As

213

he pushed it wider, he saw a nurse fiddling with the IV stand near Sarah's bed. The room was semilit, the shadows deep, and he was sure she was probably asleep. Removing his hat, Dawson stood just inside the door, making sure the nurse saw him. She looked up, smiled briefly and finished her work on the IV, then turned toward him.

"She's very tired, Mr. Callahan. Make it brief, please?"

"I will," he promised, stepping aside so she could leave.

Moving quietly into the room, he saw how Sarah's leg was supported beneath the light blue blankets across the lower half of her body. Her eyes were shut, her skin frighteningly pale. If Dawson hadn't seen this same kind of pallor in combat, when one of the Marines was shot, he'd have been even more worried. Her skin was tight, and he wondered as he approached her bed if she was in pain. Just getting to be with Sarah fed his heart, his soul, in unexpected but wonderful ways. She was going to live.

He pulled up a chair, not making any noise, and sat down, facing her. Her ginger-colored hair was mussed, and he wanted to gently smooth some of those strands away from her face, knowing how most women hated when their hair wasn't in place. He saw the light sprinkling of freckles across her cheeks and nose now. Her lips were chapped, parted, and he watched the slow rise and fall of her chest beneath her blue hospital gown. Looking up, he could read the monitors, seeing that her functions were all within normal ranges. Another layer of angst peeled off him. He was damned glad he'd had medical training, as well as combat experience with wounded comrades. It served to tell him much more than the untrained civilian, who wouldn't know how to read those numbers, much less interpret them. Sarah was stable. That was the best sign of all.

There was no such thing as quiet in a hospital; the beeps of the machines, the low noise floating into the room from the nurses' station was constant. Noise pollution. It was a wonder anyone slept at all in them, or got well. The smell of bleach was prevalent. Sitting there, hands resting on his thighs, Dawson absorbed Sarah as she slept. She was beautiful in his eyes, strong, confident and just the kind of woman he'd always wanted to meet but never had. *Until now.*

Glancing down at his watch, he saw his time was almost up. Dawson wasn't about to wake her up to ask how she was doing. Sarah had almost died. She would go through a helluva evolution about her dance on the blade of death. Dawson had seen it in his friends who had walked a similar combat path and nearly died. He'd been there when they finally opened up days afterward, and he'd watched the realization sink into them. Some of them cried, some struggled to come to grips with why they'd lived and their buddy hadn't. Survivor's guilt was very, very real. And it had sharp, savage teeth. He hoped Sarah wouldn't go through that.

At least he'd found out earlier that the two wounded deputies had survived. One was in ICU, still in critical condition, but the nurses had told him he was improving. There was great hope he'd recover fully or near enough. Sarah would feel responsible for her deputies being wounded; Dawson knew it. She would take on the guilt of not being able to protect her people. Never mind that she was far removed from the kitchen, where Brian Elson had pulled a gun and shot them.

He slowly stood up, taking the chair back to the corner where he'd found it. Walking to her bedside, he leaned over, barely touching an errant strand of hair, carefully pulling it away from her temple. The powerful desire to hold her, make her feel safe in her highly unsafe world, ripped through him. Just holding her, Dawson knew, would be good for Sarah's state of jumbled, torn-up emotions.

It would have to wait until another day. Straightening, he turned and left as quietly as he'd come.

Sarah's heart thudded when she saw Dawson come moseying into her room. It was shortly after lunch. He had his hands at his sides, looking so strong and confident in that quiet way of his. Wearing jeans, a red-and-white-plaid shirt, sleeves rolled up to his elbows, revealing the dark hair on his lower arms, a black Stetson in one hand and a bouquet of pink roses in the other, buoyed her ragged emotions. She looked up, meeting his dark, unfathomable gaze, his expression unreadable. Oh, she knew that military game face, for sure. She watched his gray eyes thaw, and warmth flooded her. That very male mouth of his, the sculpted lips she wanted to touch and outline with her fingertips and mouth, lifted a little, greeting her silently.

"Shucks," Dawson teased, "here I thought you'd be asleep again and I could put these roses by your bedside so that when you woke up, you'd see something pretty."

"Hi," she managed, her throat sore, her voice scratchy. Picking nervously at the blanket, Sarah tried to harness the violent churn of emotions. Her family had come with flowers earlier that morning, and that had lifted her spirits, too. But his bouquet meant something else to her that made her feel less edgy, calmer.

Dawson smiled and halted at her bedside after placing his hat aside. "You're looking better, Sarah."

"As opposed to what?" she asked, lifting her hand weakly as he placed the roses near enough for her to inhale their wonderful fragrance.

"I visited you around four a.m. this morning and you looked exhausted even while you slept." He eased the bouquet away and spotted a vase sitting on the window ledge. "You've got some color in your cheeks now. How are you doing?"

There was no one she'd wanted to see more than Dawson. Swallowing, pain coming on its heels, she said, "Better, I guess . . . I'm still woozy, I can't think hardly at all. It's awful," and she followed him with her gaze, watching him set the bouquet on the window frame and take the glass vase to the bathroom.

"You're still getting rid of the anesthesia

that's swimming around in your system. It usually takes forty-eight hours before it leaves completely, and your thoughts actually work. Drink a lot of water. That will help you get rid of it quicker. It's a long process you've got to go through," he warned, coming back with the vase filled with water.

Didn't she know that? She had IVs in both arms. So many lines going here and there to take her pulse, her oxygen level, her heartbeat. She watched Dawson put the flowers into the vase.

"Where would you like your roses, Sarah?"

"There on the window ledge is fine. Thank you . . ." and she saw his face thaw some more, that unreadable look beginning to dissolve, replaced with an expression she thought might be compassion.

"I stopped at the nurses' desk before coming in here," Dawson told her, walking over to the chair and bringing it to her bedside. "I don't know if you got the latest medical update on your deputies?"

Touched deeply that he'd think of her, of what was bothering her most, the people she worked with and were her close friends being wounded, she said, "My dad visited me at ten a.m. and said that Jeff had been released this morning. His shoulder injury is a lot better than the wounds Craig and I got. We're stuck here."

"Yes, Jeff is back home, from what Gertie told me earlier. The nurse said Craig James is still in ICU, but he's slowly improving. They have him in a medically induced coma until the swelling in his brain recedes."

Grimacing, she whispered, "This is so devastating, Dawson," and her voice trailed off. She avoided his gaze. Her stomach churned and she tasted bitterness in the back of her mouth. She'd killed a man. Brian Elson was dead. She'd heard Roberta was hysterical over his death. Their sons were threatening to kill the deputies, come after her. Which explained why there was a deputy on guard outside her door and would be there 24/7 until she left the hospital.

Unnerved by so many unexpected events, she absorbed Dawson's nearness. If only she could crawl into his arms, have them wrap around her, hold her for just a moment because she didn't feel safe at all. Worse, she worried about those three grown Elson sons coming into the hospital, which was now on high alert, another deputy down on the first floor in the ER, watching for anything suspicious. The hospital wasn't on lockdown, but she could feel the tension in the nurses who cared for her. They didn't want a crazed Elson coming into the hospital with an AR-15 or AK-47, murdering doctors, nurses and patients to find and kill her.

"You did what you had to do, Sarah," Dawson said gently. He looked out the door, to where the deputy was standing. There was a chair nearby, so he could sit when he wanted to. "We've both been in combat. We've had friends who were killed or wounded and we've seen it happen." He reached out to where her hand rested against her belly, caressed it briefly. "As I understand it, you were in the bedroom with Roberta when Brian pulled a gun and shot the deputies in the kitchen."

Her brows dipped. "Y-yes." How warm and consoling Dawson's hand felt on hers. Sarah almost blurted that she wanted him to keep holding her as he drew it away. He gave her a respite from raw feelings ravaging her.

"I imagine you're feeling pretty rugged right now," he ventured.

The kind understanding in his eyes spilled over her, making her feel less guilty. "Rocky," she muttered, clasping her hands, avoiding his gaze. "If I'm honest? Really, really rocky."

"Are you in pain?" and Dawson turned, looking at the leg beneath the lightweight covers.

She lifted her hand, touching her gown over her chest. "No pain in the leg, but where that first bullet of Elson's hit me in the vest? It's throbbing like a banshee."

"Would you consider a chemical ice pack over the area? I think it could give you some relief. Bruises can hurt worse than a wound."

"That's right, I keep forgetting you're a paramedic."

"One of my specialties," he agreed. "Are you game?"

"Did you bring your medic pack?" she asked, slight amusement in her hoarse tone.

Shaking his head, he smiled a little, then stood. "No. But I'll tell the nurse you could use a couple of those chem packs. I'll be right back."

Watching him move silently out of her room brought back to Sarah once more that Dawson had been recon Marine and had survived in deep black ops. The man had lived six months at a time in Indian Country or the Sandbox, as they called it, in enemy territory in Afghanistan. And like many of the operators she had known, he was self-effacing and humble. A civilian meeting

Dawson would never realize who he was or what he had sacrificed for their country. Operators knew they were the best-trained people in the military world; there was no need to tell anyone about it. In fact, the operators she'd known never bragged, but always gave their team the praise, not themselves.

Her heart swelled with so many emotions for Dawson. Seeing him today was exactly what she'd needed. She'd loved seeing her parents again this morning, along with the grannies. They had surrounded her with a loving safety net. Dawson fed her on another level, but she was too worn and shocky to think more about it.

Dawson came back ten minutes later with two packs in his hands. "Success. Want me to get one ready for you?" and he held up one of the plastic bags.

"Yeah. I'm not exactly keen about slapping it against my knee to start the chemical reaction, though."

"I'll do the heavy lifting for you," he said, and slapped it hard against his knee, which released the chemicals to mix and then turn icy cold.

Sarah smoothed down the top of her gown and said, "Put it over this area?"

Dawson did, making sure he didn't touch

her. She gave him a look of thanks, settling it exactly where she wanted it on her upper chest. He could see signs of deep bruising where the collar revealed the damaged skin beneath it. The color was a deep, vivid red mixed with purple.

"Thanks."

"Is there anything else I can get you?" he asked, sitting down once more.

"Out of here, maybe?"

Grinning, he said, "Spoken like a type A that's been hobbled and can't be on the move like they prefer."

Giving him a sour look, Sarah said, "Got that right. I've already ordered my second-in-command to bring me up to date on what's going on at our office." She stared at her left leg. "I hate hospitals . . ."

"Yeah, they're not big on my list either. You look worried about something. Want to share?"

"My mom and dad want me to recuperate at their home. Did they tell you that?" Because they were the ones who had told her this morning that he'd been there from the beginning, and that he'd given two pints of his blood to her. They'd become somber when they'd admitted that if Dawson hadn't done that, she could have died or, at the very best, not recovered as quickly as she had. Her heart stirred; she wanted so badly to let down and blither to him about being shot, about what had happened, but her law-enforcement side won out and she suppressed it. She would thank him, however. The man was a true hero in her eyes. He'd helped save her life.

"Gertie was saying your parents had made their offer, but she was adamant about having you recover at her house."

She settled back against the pillows, closing her eyes for a moment, suddenly feeling very weary. "There are two things to consider. Only my family knows that my dad is battling prostate cancer right now. I just don't think it's a good idea to drop myself with all my needs and demands for the next four to six weeks, on top of his medical condition. And the Elsons want a shooting rampage. I don't want them attacking my home, my parents' home or even Gertie's."

He frowned. "I'm sorry to hear about your dad. What's his prognosis?"

"The doctors don't want to do surgery. They're using drugs right now, and they seem to be working."

"That's good news, but I think you're right about not placing yourself in their home. I know chemo really tires a person out, and I'm sure your parents are under a lot of stress. And I talked to Gertie about the Elsons this morning over breakfast. She didn't mince words about them."

"I don't want to put anyone at risk, Dawson." The words came out low and filled with anguish. "My family just didn't need me getting shot right now. I-I feel so damned bad about it . . . about becoming a burden . . . another worry for them. My mother has always been afraid for me, afraid of me getting shot or killed, and I've fulfilled that fear for her. And now she's scared out of her wits about the Elson boys coming to their house to kill me. And if they did, they'd shoot my parents, too. It would be a bloodbath. My poor grandmothers could have strokes or heart attacks if that happened. It's a mess."

"It's not an easy time for anyone," he agreed. "Gertie told me when she got back from seeing you this morning that she begged you to let her take care of you." He saw her open her eyes, saw the turmoil in them.

"I-I really think going to Gertie's would put her and a lot of her employees at risk."

"You're in for six weeks of healing with that leg wound. I think you need a place to hole up and get well. What do you want to do, Sarah? Really?"

Her eyes filled with tears. No one had asked her; her parents and Gertie had ignored the possible danger to themselves, wanting to care for her no matter what. Dawson had a way of getting to the heart of the issue without the emotional baggage that came along with it, interfering with the logic of what should be done. Swallowing several times, she managed, "Gertie isn't up to taking care of me; I know that. Yes, she has the room." She stared at him. "What I really want? I want to disappear after I get out of the hospital, find somewhere I can stay without the Elsons finding me. I want to confuse them so I can get well enough to get back to doing my job. I don't want to put anyone else at risk." Her voice became choked. "Enough good people have already been hurt. I refuse to have more."

"Do you know of a place to hide?"

"Yes. There's a US Forest Service cabin up on the slopes of the Salt River Range. I can make a call, talk to the supervisor, and I know they'll give me permission to hide out up there." She pushed strands of hair away from her face, eyeing him. Her heart began a beat of dread. What if he wouldn't go along with her request? What if he said no? Sarah knew she'd need someone to care for her. "I need your help, Dawson. You're the person I want to stay with me up at that cabin. You'll do double duty: helping me medically as well as being my bodyguard. Are you willing to do that? If not, I understand. I'll find someone else."

Nodding, he pushed his hands slowly up and down his thighs, considering her request. "I have the medical background. I would know enough to care for you, and if you needed further medical help, I could make the right call to get it."

Her heart leaped. "You'll do it, then? You'll take care of me for a while?"

"Yes." He saw her face crumple with so many emotions. "We're a good team. I'll do it."

"You understand it's going to be dangerous? That you'll have to go back into black ops mode? The Elson boys will probably be hunting me as soon as they bury their father."

"I know that." One corner of his mouth hitched upward. "I survived Afghanistan. I'm sure I can get us through the next six weeks. I want you alive and getting back on your feet."

Tears burned in her eyes, but she fought them away. "Okay . . . thank you . . . I couldn't ask for a better partner in this. We'll be stronger because of our shared background. Two is better than one."

"SEALs have a saying," he told her. " 'One is none, two is one.' And they, more than any other black ops group, understand teamwork. We'll get through this together, Sarah, so wipe that look of anxiety off your face. We'll outwit the Elsons. It won't be easy, but we'll work like the good team I know we'll be. Do you think your parents and grannies will be upset over your choice?"

"No. Probably, if Dad were to be honest, he'd be relieved because he's got enough on his plate right now. So does my mom. Gertie and Nell will understand. Gertie will squawk a lot, but underneath, she knows this is a better plan to keep our family safe."

"They won't be able to visit you; I'm sure the Elsons will stake out their and the grandmothers' homes, thinking you're at one of them," he pointed out. "You won't be that far away, but you'll have to rely on Skype, phone calls and emails to stay in contact. They won't like it, but they'll accept it."

"And they will want to stay in touch. According to Dr. Martin, I have a long way to go yet. You really want to do this, Dawson?" She saw his gray eyes lighten, felt a wonderful sensation enveloping her as he considered her question. Every cell in her body screamed at him to say yes.

"I gave you my word I'd be there, and I will, Sarah. I promise not to play jokes on you either."

She laughed a little. "What? Were you the joker on your team, Callahan?"

"Just a little. I never did mean teasing, though. When we were behind the wire we got bored as hell, so I used to liven the guys up with a joke here or there."

"I'll bet you did." She pointed to her leg. "Well, you can't scare me to death or anything like that or I'm liable to tear my bullet wound open."

"I wouldn't do that, Sarah. Not ever. I promise to be on my best behavior with you."

"Then you'll be my medic?"

"I'll be more than that. I'll protect you."

She tried not to allow his low voice, the look he gave her, affect her, but it did. "Gertie has you doing a lot of things around her home and business. Will you have time for me, Dawson? Really?" His eyes narrowed, and she saw a brief flit of emotion, unsure of what it was. The impression he was burning her into himself, as if this conversation mattered more than anything else in his life, flowed through Sarah.

"I wouldn't want it any other way, Sarah. When I leave here, I'll go talk to your parents and then speak to Gertie and Nell. I'm sure they'll be relieved for you and for themselves."

"When the Elsons figure out I'm not at any of their homes, they're going to come searching for me, Dawson. But at least they'll leave my family alone."

Shrugging, he said, "Let them. We need to get permission from the Forest Service to use that cabin. I'm assuming it has Wi-Fi?"

"Yes, it's a central station for them during the summer months, when people sometimes get lost up in the mountains. It has all the electronics you could want. There are solar panels on the roof to provide electricity. It's hidden up at the end of a little-used dirt road, high on a slope where you can see anyone coming your way from below. No hikers go there because it's not on any Forest Service maps. It's a well-hidden jump-off point for rangers searching for missing persons."

The burning look in his darkening eyes sent a shiver of light and hope through Sarah. He was so serious, it served to tell her how loyal he really was, that she could lean on him all she needed to. Ordinarily, she didn't look to any man for her safety.

Her parents had raised her to be completely self-reliant. Right now, however, she was feeling weak, unable to fully defend herself. She hated the feeling, but she was more than relieved Dawson would be with her.

"I'll talk to your family. Are you up to calling the forestry supervisor? Or is that something you want me to handle?" Her cell phone was on the bed stand.

"I'll handle the cabin. I know they'll approve our use of it. I'm going to push my surgeon to find out how soon I can leave the hospital. The longer I'm in here, the more this hospital remains a possible target."

Slowly standing, Dawson nodded. "You've got my cell number. Call me when you know something?"

"Yes, I will."

"You're looking whipped, Sarah. Want to sleep for a while? Sleep is the most important thing you can do to heal your body."

Her lips twisted as she leaned over, picking up her cell phone. "In a little while."

"What about groceries? Is there anything you don't like to eat? I'm pretty good around a stove."

She managed a soft smile. "I'll eat anything that doesn't move first."

Nodding, Dawson went to the door. Lifting his hand, he said, "Okay. I'll be in touch with you a little later."

The look in his eyes, that intense quality deep within them, that sense of protection swirled around her, immediately made her feel better. "See you soon," she said, her voice hoarse, but full of emotion.

Sarah watched him disappear after speaking briefly with the deputy at the door. Dawson seemed unperturbed by the turn of events. Maybe Marine recons were all of that same temperament: confident, unflappable and easygoing. Yet, she'd seen something else in his eyes, recognizing it as his warrior side. She had no doubt that if one or more of the Elsons did find them in that hideaway cabin, he'd turn into a highly dangerous opponent. Recons were known for their stealth, their ability to fade into their surroundings, make absolutely no noise, then use surprise as a way to win the battle against any enemy. They, like snipers, were known as force multipliers; one recon could wreak havoc on a company of enemy, 120 men. It served to assure her that Callahan really was best suited to take care of her under the circumstances. Once she explained that to her family, Sarah was sure they'd be enthusiastic about her disappearing to heal.

Dragging in a breath, Sarah admitted she was scared. Scared for her family, worried that the Elsons might go after them to get even for her killing Brian. This was such an ugly, dangerous mess. It felt as if the malignant situation might overwhelm her, a strange feeling for her because this wasn't the way she normally thought. Dawson was right, she acknowledged; the anesthesia was playing hell on her mind and emotions. Inwardly, though, she was breathing easier because he was going to help her get through these next weeks. The look on his face when she'd asked if he would consider doing it had shaken her. He'd leaped at the chance to care for her.

Sarah didn't know very many men other than her deputies who would have the same reaction. But she didn't want to use any of Lincoln County's deputies now, because there were fewer of them on duty because of budget constraints and the loss of Jeff and Craig to their injuries. The people of Lincoln paid their taxes and Sarah was damned if she was going to haul one of the few left to guard her. Dawson was the perfect choice in every possible way.

Her mind moved over the many things that had to be done and handled. Most important to her was being able to run the sheriff's department even though she was in hiding. It could and would be done.

# CHAPTER TWELVE

*June 20*

Dawson tried to minimize the feelings for Sarah rushing through him because they distracted him. Now was not the time for them. Issues revolved around his worry about the Elson boys coming after Sarah and her family. After visiting her parents and the grannies, he was glad she didn't have to go through the process. Her family was just as stressed over the possibility of having their home attacked and going after Sarah as she was.

David Carter was particularly relieved to hear that Dawson would be at Sarah's side, rendering medical support as well as being her badass guard. Nell understood and agreed with the plan. Gertie didn't, saying she'd hire armed security guards and Sarah would be safe at her homestead. It took a lot of diplomatic wrangling on Dawson's part to get the upset oldster to see the wisdom of keeping everyone safe. Just the same, Gertie was hiring three security guards. She had a lot of employees working on her ranch and she was going to make sure no one got through the front entrance without being fully vetted and checked and on the list of people who were allowed on her property.

He was driving to the courthouse, where the sheriff's office was located, when he got a call on his cell. Pulling off to the side of the road, he placed his truck in park and answered it. It had been three hours since he'd left the hospital.

"Callahan," he answered in a clipped tone.

"It's me, Sarah."

"Are you all right?" All the brusqueness dissolved from his tone. She sounded tired.

"I'm fine. Everything's quiet around here. Listen, Commander Tom Franks of the Teton Sheriff's Department is having his dog trainer, Deputy Sheriff Jasmine Delano, drop off one of their working dogs, King, to my office. Can you go there to meet her? She should be arriving any minute now. She's going to show you the commands King knows, and how to work with him. Then, you'll bring the dog back to Gertie's place until I can get moved into that cabin. King will be with us for the duration of my healing."

"Hey, that's great! I worked with a number of working military dogs in Afghanistan. We used WMDs on our recon missions with great success."

"Oh, good! Tom is a longtime friend of our family and he told me that they're sending their best combat-trained dog to help keep me safe. King has better hearing, better vision and can smell an intruder better than any human."

"For sure," Dawson said, grinning. "This is a great break for us. I'm about ten minutes outside of Wind River. How are you doing?" She was never far from his mind — or his heart.

"Exhausted, but feeling better. The supervisor for the Forest Service has okayed my request to use their missing person's cabin headquarters, so that's good news, too."

"I knew the people of the valley would rally around you, Sarah," he said, hearing the sudden emotion in her voice. Her speech was still hoarse; it would take days for it to return to normal.

"I hope you're including yourself, Dawson," she whispered, her voice cracking.

It felt good to hear that. As injured and still in shock as she was, she was able to move beyond her own pain to connect with those around her. "Well," he murmured, his own voice growing husky with feeling, "thanks, but from where I stand? You rock. You always did and always will." For a moment, she was silent. Dawson wasn't sure if she was insulted or complimented by his statement. He knew Sarah was trying to coordinate so many things from her bedside a day after getting shot and having major surgery. It was far too soon for her to be doing it.

"Let me help you," he urged. "I don't need you stressed out any more than you already are, Sarah. You need your rest. If there are other phone calls to make? Or people to see? Tell me. I can come back to the hospital and we can create a mission plan so that most of that is off your shoulders."

She sighed. "You're right. I'm feeling raw, Dawson. There's just so much I didn't anticipate from that domestic disturbance call. It was a FUBAR in every possible way."

Both of them had unconsciously slipped into military speak because that was still stronger than their civilian slang. He smiled a little. FUBAR meant fucked up beyond all recognition, and it was a favorite maxim in the military. "FUBAR is the right word for it. Domestic violence calls must be the most dangerous you folks in law enforcement have to answer. It's always a crapshoot, from what I can see. A FUBAR in the making."

She gave a short, bitter laugh, but Dawson heard relief in her voice, too. Sarah was a one-person army as sheriff of her county. She was used to juggling God knew how many issues and problems all at once with her super-capable staff. But she couldn't do it herself right now. She couldn't rise to that level of physical energy or mental focus while she was dealing with the violent ups and downs of emotion ripping through her. It was a major distraction for her, and he could hear the frustration in her voice because no one could completely control their emotions forever. He needed to situate himself in her life a lot more than he was doing presently to remove the demanding loads he knew were coming for her in the days and weeks ahead. He wanted Sarah to focus on healing, not try to run the sheriff's office from her bed. Add to that the threat of the Elsons' revenge against herself and her family, no small threat.

"Okay . . . you're right." She sounded defeated.

"I'll go see that deputy and her dog at your office," he said, trying to sound soothing and calm. "Once I get the lowdown, and take King to Gertie's, I'll call you from there. We'll keep him there until we get you moved to the cabin. If you're a glutton for punishment? I can eat supper with you, if you want," he teased.

"Cece's a great cook. I'd love to eat anything Gertie has in her refrigerator. I'm not on a restricted diet here at the hospital. Bring whatever it is to my hospital room, okay?"

"Consider it done. I'll call you when I'm coming your way. Get some sleep."

Dawson arrived at Sarah's room three hours later. He had a large brown bag in one hand that contained leftovers from Gertie's fridge. Sarah's entire bed was covered with files, papers and a notepad, a radio and a cell phone, plus her iPad tablet, where she was typing something, as he entered.

"Did you get any rest?" he asked with a grin. He knew from talking to Cade Jameson, the assistant commander at her office, that Sarah had had the work on her desk brought to her earlier.

She looked up and gave him a wry glance. "A little."

Laughing, he brought the huge sack that contained their dinner and set it on the nearby bed stand. He wasn't going to chide her for working. Dawson understood Sarah's drive. She took her responsibility as sheriff first, above her own suffering or personal issues. Silently, he applauded her stance, but it wasn't a good one right now. She needed good, quality rest, to be nurtured and cared for, to be made to feel safe once more. Few people knew what a bullet wound could do to a person, but he did. And he knew what steps could be taken to help Sarah through the horrendous emotional process that anyone who'd been shot had to go through. He could help her.

Dawson turned, shutting the door after letting the deputy on duty know they needed to talk privately. Coming back into the room, he saw her gathering up the files from around her bed. Every once in a while, if she stretched too much, he could tell by the thinning of her lips that she'd aggravated her wounded thigh. He brought the rolling bed stand closer to the right side of her bed. When he opened the sack, fragrant, mouthwatering odors wafted into the air.

"Mmm, that smells good," Sarah murmured, placing the closed files on the other bed stand, to the left of her bed. "What did Gertie give us?"

"She had leftover meat lasagna, French

bread slathered with butter and bits of garlic, and Cece made you a fresh salad with your favorite dressing: Thousand Island. Best of all?" He pulled out a large plastic container. "She had Cece make tiramisu the day before yesterday, and she wanted to put some in for us. Said you loved it." He saw her face mirror gratefulness.

"That's so sweet of Gertie," she said. "I love tiramisu."

"There's a thermos of coffee in here, too. If you want? I'll put it all together on your tray?"

"That's wonderful," she said, smoothing out the blanket and pushing a strand of ginger-colored hair away from her face. "You saw the dog, King. What did you think of him? Did you take him over to Gertie's? Did King get along with Gram?"

He placed several containers on her table, smiling to himself at her rapid-fire questions. "Yes." He pulled out his cell phone and clicked on the photos he'd taken. "Here, take a look. King is a Belgian Malinois male. Deputy Delano gave me instructions and the commands to use. He was a combat WMD from age three to seven. Then the Marine Corps retired him, and Commander Franks bought him when he was brought back to the States. Jasmine

Delano, who you'll see in one of these photos, worked with him for a year to bring him into the way law enforcement works versus what he was trained to do in combat circumstances. He's ten years old now. Pretty-looking dog, don't you think?" He slid the cell phone into her hand and went back to getting her dinner ready.

"They're a nice-looking pair," Sarah said. "I've never met Deputy Delano, but I'd heard of her good work with King. She looks to be in her late twenties?"

"Yes, twenty-seven. And she's typical of dog handlers: quiet, calm and doesn't get rattled easily."

"Sort of like you," she noted, lifting her lashes, meeting his amused gaze.

"Callin' me a dog, Sheriff?"

Sarah laughed a little. "No, but when I was in Afghanistan, all the dog handlers I met were like you in temperament."

"Hope that's an unqualified compliment." He opened all the containers, placed the plastic ware and several white napkins next to them.

"It was a compliment, so relax, huh?"

"Whew." He saw her shake her head, amusement dancing in her eyes. Their parrying was good. He wanted to lift her spirits because he knew how stressed out she still was. Typical of all military-trained people, she jammed down what wasn't essential for survival so she could place her attention on what she felt was vital. But that skill had a negative side to it, too, and he was determined to try to stop that from happening. It would take another military person to do it, too. And he was up for that challenge.

Sarah was getting her old self back little by little. At least for the moment. Dawson said nothing, continuing to unload the fragrant contents from the sack. He cleared off a space on the bed stand for his containers of food as well. Sarah was intently studying the four photos he'd taken of Jasmine and King. He could almost see her committing both to memory.

"How's your leg feeling?" he asked, opening his containers, inhaling the spicy, garlicky fragrance wafting from the lasagna.

"The pain medication keeps the worst of it away. I asked the nurse to reduce the opioid IV drip because I couldn't think straight. All I wanted to do was go to sleep." She dug into the square piece of lasagna with her fork. "I'm more clearheaded since she did."

Sitting down next to her bed, he pulled his containers to him. "You seem more alert. But do you still have some pain in your leg?"

"A little," Sarah hedged. "I'd rather deal with that, though, than feel like I have nothing but cotton balls rolling around in my brain so I can't string two sentences together."

"Give yourself another twenty-four hours, Sarah, and you'll probably feel like you have your brain fully back in line. Very few people realize how insidious anesthesia and its aftereffects are."

She swallowed. "Do you like King? Did he like you?"

He noticed she'd pivoted away from herself, but he let it go. "It went okay. He's a beautiful dog. I like that black mask on his face and his fawn-colored body."

"Is he all work and no play?"

"Pretty much. He's not an ordinary dog. His job is to be alert and protect."

"Kinda like you?"

He met her warm gaze. "I don't have a tail, Ms. Carter." His joy amped up as she laughed a little, some pink flushing her cheeks. He wanted to make Sarah happy. He wished for some time out for her sake, to let her be a carefree girl once more because he saw when he saw that sparkle in her eyes, that deviltry that made her winsome, she was so damned desirable.

"No, good thing you don't have a tail, Callahan," she deadpanned between bites.

Dawson chuckled. For the next minute or so, silence cloaked the room except for the usual hospital sounds.

"I can hardly wait to get out of here, Dawson."

"Are you looking to me to abscond with you to that cabin without them knowing you left?" he teased, hooking a thumb toward the door and the nurses' station. He saw her lips flex with frustration. Getting serious, he said, "Have you talked to your doc yet about a release date?"

"Yes. He said tomorrow. I wanted to leave today, but he said no."

Brows raised, he said, "Has anyone made plans on how to get you to the cabin without being seen leaving here?"

"Yes. There are going to be two ambulances at the ER entrance at around 4 a.m., when it's dark. I'll be put into one of them, and the other will turn and go south on the highway, in the opposite direction. I'd like you to tail my ambulance in your truck. Keep some distance, looking for any suspicious vehicles." She pointed to the stack of files on her bed stand. "I've got color photos of all three Elson boys. And the vehicles they drive. You need to commit all of this to memory."

"Easy enough to do. So? What kind of stuff do we need besides groceries for that cabin?"

"The supervisor is sending two of his rangers up there today to make sure we have linens, towels and other supplies. We just need to bring food."

"And your favorite pillow? Gertie said you had a special pillow you liked to sleep with."

"Yes, but it's back at my house," she muttered, shaking her head.

"Is anyone watching your house, Sarah?"

"No. I don't have the person power to do that kind of thing."

"I can go over there after we eat and check it out, pick up your pillow and any clothes or other stuff you want."

"That would be great. I'll make a list. Thank you for doing this. I'm so glad you're helping me, Dawson."

"I try to put myself in the other person's shoes if I can," he said between savory bites.

"Just before you came in? I got cleaned up by a nurse, who came in and gave me a bed bath. The doctor wanted one more day with no weight on my leg so the artery will heal fully."

"Not exactly like a real shower or bath, though."

"No, but it sure feels good to be somewhat clean."

He gave her a wry look. "Is the doc going to let you take a shower at the cabin?"

"Yes. He's got watertight dressings packed in a bag that I'll take with me in the ambulance. The head nurse is putting all other medical items, prescriptions and anything else you'll need to take care of me and this wound."

"Good to know. But who's going to clean your backside?"

He saw her ponder the dilemma. "Just getting to stand up under a warm shower with water running down my back will be good enough for now."

"I understand. Water's always been healing and calming for me, too." Dawson wasn't about to tell her about the torrid dream he'd had about her last night. He hadn't gotten much sleep. As confident and able to take care of herself as Sarah was, he still wanted to protect her. Chalk it up to him still being a Neanderthal in an age when women didn't need men rescuing or protecting them anymore. That was passé. What was really needed, in his view of the changes in relationships between men and women, was an equal partnership, and that was what he dreamed of with Sarah. He'd stopped avoiding a deep truth about his growing feelings for her last night. The woman turned him on, turned him inside out; simply thinking of her made his day go better. She had that kind of positive effect on him. Never mind the more intimate sexual component he kept trying to tamp down, ignore and push into the background.

After eating, Sarah murmured, "I'll be glad when we can get to the cabin, Dawson. I'm so worried about my family . . ."

"One good thing? Your family isn't helpless. They know what's going on and they're very capable of defending themselves."

She fretted with a thread from the blanket, brows drooping as she focused on it. "I know, but the Elsons are known for taking their revenge on anyone who crosses them." Lifting her chin, she looked at him. "Their father's funeral is tomorrow. That's why I thought it would be strategic to get out of here unseen and to the cabin. I don't think any of them are going to miss it."

"We'll take precautions anyway. One thing I learned a long time ago about the enemy: you never underestimate them."

He saw her mood turn somber. "You're right. Still, I'll be glad to leave here for so many reasons. I have a county to run."

He rose and came close, moving her table

aside, beginning to put all the leftovers and containers back into the large paper sack. "The cabin will be a good place for you to heal."

Sarah would never be able to thank the small army of men and women who transported her from the hospital to the log cabin on the slopes of the Salt River Mountain range enough. The cabin was hidden from view by the Douglas fir that surrounded it. Exhausted, she lay in one of the four bedrooms. Most of the people had left by eight a.m., only one ranger remaining behind with them. He would go over all the radios and electronics utilized when searching for a missing person with Dawson. It didn't take much time — he was a quick learner — and she was once more glad he was there with her. King, the Belgian Malinois, lay on a brown-and-white-braided rug near her full-size bed. He was alert, ears up, listening and watching through the partially open door that led into the hall.

The orthopedic nurse had fitted her with a removable brace for her thigh, to give it stability when she got up to walk every few hours. It was on the oak dresser opposite her bed, ready to be used shortly. Right now, she was relegated to taking a few painful, careful steps with it on, using a pair of lightweight aluminum crutches. She had a wheelchair, which she would have to tolerate being pushed around in. She insisted on the crutches, too. She didn't want to be seen to rely on the wheelchair. Her pride just wouldn't allow her to go there.

Sarah hadn't felt so helpless in a long, long time, not since she was seven years old. Dr. Martin had a daily regime for her to follow to get her up and moving, to strengthen her healing bone and wound, to minimize the possibility of a blood clot forming. At the hospital, they'd taken her out of bed every hour with the wrap around her thigh, walking in mincing baby steps around the room on her crutches. Exercise brought blood to the wound and would help it heal faster, they explained. It was painful, but Sarah wasn't going to whine. Anything to get her leg back under her and working was her goal. Anything to get out of that damned, confining bed.

All the clothes Dawson had gathered from her home had been put into the dresser or hung in the closet on the other side of the door. She had her pillow, which was great. It looked as if Dawson had combed through her small house, picking up any items he felt she might need that weren't on the list.

As worn out as she was? Her heart blossomed with warm feelings for the man. Everything he did, it seemed, was on her behalf. She'd never met a man quite like him before. And on top of that? He was a warrior. She felt a new sense of safety because King and Dawson worked like a well-oiled team. The dog obviously respected the man, and Sarah could understand why. She did, too. She just wasn't going to admit it to him yet.

Hearing the main door to the cabin open and close, and then Dawson's footsteps echoing down the pine hall and coming her way, she looked expectantly at the half open door of her room. King was already up, focused on the sounds coming their way.

"Hey," Dawson called, pushing the door open all the way, "how do you like your new digs?"

King lay down once again.

"Much better," she admitted. "How'd things go with all the electronic gadgets the ranger showed you?"

He leaned down, patting King's head. "No problem." Straightening, he held her gaze. "You look happier," he said, and he grinned.

Warmth flowed through her, sweet and filled with promise. "I am. I'm relieved that if the Elsons try to find me, they'll realize pretty quickly I've disappeared. It would be like them to stake out my family and grannies' homes. There are three of them, and they'll lay in wait in the weeds, trying to figure out where I am. I've already had my deputies let out word that I'm in Denver. That's far enough away that they may be too lazy to try to follow me. And it leaves my family no longer suspected of harboring me."

"Will there be extra swings by the houses for a while?"

"Yes. I worked out a schedule where we'll use our unmarked cars for that. We all know the Elson vehicles and can spot them in a heartbeat. If they do find them nearby? They'll haul them into jail for forty-eight hours. I'm hoping when one of my men sit down with them, one of the Elsons might slip and let the cat out of the bag about what they're doing to find me. I've talked to another of my men, Jesse Hernandez, about going to see Roberta. Jesse's going to let her know we have an eye on her sons. And he'll advise her to tell her sons to leave my family alone. That I'm not with any of them."

"Good plan."

"I hope so."

"You didn't get to see how nice this cabin is. The ranger helping me with the electronics said it has four rooms, one of them the radio room. There are so many bedrooms so the trackers looking for lost people have a place to sleep and get some food in them to start another day of search and rescue."

"This area of the Salt River Mountains has a lot of beautiful trails, and we get called in to assist them from time to time, looking for lost hikers." She looked around the large room. "I've known about this cabin but never been here before. A number of my deputies have, especially in the summer, when the tourists arrive."

"Well, on to you," he said. "We need to get that brace on your thigh and then get you out of bed and walking to at least the bathroom on this first trip. What do you say?"

"Sounds good. I'd love to noodle around to see what the place looks like."

With a chuckle, he said, "Let's get that brace on, then."

Sarah was glad to be in a pair of loose-fitting gray gym pants instead of her hospital gown. She wore a red T-shirt that hung on her. Right now, loose-fitting clothes that were easy to take on and off were her new uniform. She was sitting on top of the bed and inhaled Dawson's scent as he leaned over, gently affixing the stabilizing device around her thigh. His touch was incredibly gentle. She instinctively knew he'd be a good lover. Trying to erase that unexpected thought, she touched the black brace as he straightened. "Feels okay. Next time? Let me put it on. I need to get friendly with the contraption."

Stepping aside, he said, "Sounds good. Now, try to move your legs over to the side of the bed. Or do you want some help?"

"No, I need to do this, Dawson. Let me try first." The device would minimize the pain of the movement, but Sarah knew there would be some, regardless, until her bullet wound healed. She moved slowly, relishing the act of moving at all. She no longer wore a catheter and both IVs were gone from her arms. That felt so freeing to her, as if she owned her own body once more. She struggled, but finally made it to the edge of the bed, proud of herself.

"In much pain?" Dawson asked.

"Like a toothache. I'll live."

He took the set of crutches leaning against the wall next to her bed, handing them to her. She'd been shown how to use them at the hospital. "I'll shadow you," he said, and stood back to give her room, but not so far away that he couldn't help her if she needed it. Sarah was bound and determined to do it on her own. She *had* to get well.

Sarah suddenly felt strange as she stood up on the crutches. Opening her mouth, she felt as if someone were tearing her consciousness away from her.

"Easy," Dawson said, moving in, placing his hand on her upper right arm, positioning himself to her side, his other arm slipping around her waist. "You got up too fast," he said. "The blood is leaving your head and you might faint. Lean on me for a moment until your head clears."

There was no choice. Not that she wanted one. Dawson had placed his tall, powerful body against her right side, one arm around her waist in case her legs decided not to support her. Sarah leaned against him, fighting not to faint. He stood without moving, silently coaxing her to lean against him. She inhaled his scent, part woodsy and part male. Resting her head against the span where his shoulder met his chest, Sarah closed her eyes, feeling dizzy. If she shut them, the dizziness went away.

"Good," he praised, his lips against her hair. "Anchor yourself. Let your heart pump blood back into your head."

Giving out a tremulous sigh, Sarah reveled in the hard warmth of his body, his arm embracing her, keeping her upright.

"What happened?"

"In medicalese, it's called hypervolemia. In common terms, it means you stood up too fast and your heart didn't have time to pump enough blood volume back into your head to compensate for your quick action. It usually happens to the elderly or people who have been sick in bed and off their feet a lot of the time. It should go away in another minute; just lean against me until that happens."

Snorting softly, she opened her eyes. It felt incredibly wonderful to be in his embrace, as awkward as it was with a crutch standing between them. Sarah could feel care radiating from him, felt the taut strength of his body against her weaker one. He smelled so good! The dark green cowboy shirt he wore, the fabric rough beneath her cheek and the scent of him combined, called to her in a very intimate way. She wanted much more of this. Of Dawson holding her. Sarah tried to tell herself that she had to remain strong, not become entangled in him as a man who set her heart and body to yearning for more of his touch.

Dawson didn't move. He kept his arm light around her waist, not trying to haul her against him or do anything that suggested intimacy. She felt tiredness overwhelm her as they stood there in the silence. Killing a man had upset her more than she dared connect with until now. Almost getting killed herself was piled onto it. Coupled with her own drive, and her responsibility to continue to protect her county was a third weight pushing down on her shoulders. Tears burned at the backs of her eyes and she gulped once, forcing them away. So much of her, the human being, wanted to turn fully toward Dawson, allow herself to be weak, allow herself to be cared for.

# CHAPTER THIRTEEN

*June 20*

Dawson closed his eyes for a moment, absorbing Sarah leaning against him, trusting him. The warmth of her cheek against his chest, the silky quality of her hair against his jaw told him just how much he wanted to love her. His heart soared with unparalleled joy as she finally trusted him completely, allowed him the honor of caring for her, if only for a minute. He ached to take her into his arms, carry her to bed and love her. All dreams, he told himself. But he'd never dreamed she would lean on him like this either. For a moment, he felt her quiver. It wasn't anything obvious, and maybe it was his imagination. But he sensed something was going on within her, felt her inner turmoil.

"I — uh," she whispered unsteadily, "feel so broken, Dawson."

"Anyone would under the circumstances

you just survived," he rasped, pressing a kiss to her hair, slightly tightening his arm around her waist and then relaxing it. Sensing she was on the verge of crying, he remained unmoving. This was the first time they'd embraced, albeit a highly awkward one. Dawson didn't want to try to remove the crutch between them, to break the spell that was warm and caring swirling between them.

"Only you would understand," she admitted, nuzzling her cheek against his chest, seeking safety.

"The military connects us," he agreed. "It always will. You can never get rid of it, even if you wanted to." He wanted to ask why she was feeling that way right then, but he clamped down on the question. Sarah was a strong, proud woman. She wouldn't be browbeaten, herded or pushed into a corner to reveal her inner workings to anyone. No, her coming to him had to be earned, her letting down her shield and being brutally honest with him. Dawson tried to temper the joy thrumming through him over this simple act. "What else?"

He felt her sigh more than heard it. She pressed her face into his chest, as if to hide from what she was feeling.

"I-I'm afraid to start talking about it,

Dawson. If I do? I feel like I'll let out a dammed-up bunch of emotions and I'll break down. I can't do that right now. Too many people are counting on me . . ."

Tackling his frustration, he closed his eyes, savoring her body against his. "There are times in everyone's life, Sarah, when they need to put themselves first, not last." He could feel the curve of her breast against his chest despite the crutch. When she had leaned into him, silently asking for his support, he'd dropped his left hand from her arm and curved it, instead, around her sagging shoulders. Loosening his right arm around her waist, he lifted his hand, smoothing some of those ginger strands away from her face. Dawson wasn't sure how she would receive that caress laced with care, not lust. Oh, he wanted her, but his smoothing those strands away from her pale cheek was about care. He felt her quiver. This time, he knew it wasn't his imagination. He sensed she wanted to cry but did nothing but wait, being a witness to whatever she wanted, trying to read her need correctly. That was the trick: reading her accurately, not projecting his own selfish desires.

The silence cloaked them. He could feel her need for him, feel her wanting to be closer to him. It washed across him like a lover's caress. The sensation he absorbed from her was sweet, filled with promise and so much more. Sarah awkwardly pulled away, lifting her chin, looking up into his eyes. He saw so much anguish in their green depths. Drowning in her warm gaze, he saw her lips part.

"I feel like my heart is going to explode with so many dark, scary emotions. I keep fighting them back, keeping them at bay. I feel if I let go, if I cry? It will destroy me. . . ."

The last words were tremulous. But there was nothing weak about her. "You've just been shot, Sarah. You had to shoot a man who wanted to kill you. You could have died. That's two strikes against you that you've still got to move through, to deal with, to cry about. I can't tell you how many times, after a battle when we lost someone, that we all cried about it. Maybe it wasn't in front of one another, but sometimes it was. Tears, I found out a long time ago, are healing." He caressed her cheek. "I've never seen a man or woman cry that it didn't help them, and it didn't make them lose control. It will be the same with you when you're ready to release it." He removed his hand. If he was reading her right, Sarah was asking for simple human care. To feel safe enough to unload how she was really feeling, no longer willing to hide from him. A sliver of him felt triumph coupled with an ecstasy he'd never experienced before. She wasn't a weak woman in any way.

"D-did you feel like you'd tear apart if you cried, Dawson?"

He lifted his chin and looked above her head for a moment, then settled his gaze back on hers. "I didn't really have a choice. I felt if I didn't let go, my chest was going to explode and I'd die."

"It was that intense?"

Seeing her confusion, Dawson wondered how often Sarah had cried in her life. He assumed because she was a woman, she'd cried often, as he'd seen others do. And that was probably a huge miscalculation on his part. Instantly, he wondered what trauma or experience in her life had shut her down. It was human to cry, but he also knew from the traumatized Afghan children and adults in their war-torn country, they didn't cry either. They were beyond tears, beyond feeling anything. What had pushed Sarah into that corner of emotional numbness? He wanted to ask but knew it wasn't the right time. Instead, he said, "Very intense. I didn't have a choice. I started crying until my throat hurt, my heart ached and I ran out of tears. There wasn't a choice for me."

"I just feel . . . God . . . so over-whelmed. . . ."

"Yeah," he murmured sympathetically, "anyone would. You're strong, Sarah, but sometimes, like now? I want you to lean on me. I'll hold you if you want. Do you feel a little bit better with some comfort?" He saw her lips twist a little and her gaze skitter away from his for a moment; then she met his gaze once more.

"It's . . . wonderful. . . ."

"For me, too," he admitted thickly, reining in his emotions. Sarah was deluged, suffocating beneath the need to cry and get so much dark hurt out of her system. Her eyes flared with some emotion, but he couldn't translate it. He felt her response but was afraid to misinterpret it. To him, it felt like a dizzying joy, a sense of camaraderie, of coming together on equal footing. With mutual trust. And, most of all, he felt her need for him at that very moment. Too much was going on for him to sort it all out, though. That meant a lot of caution on his part, and not jumping to conclusions. "I know at some point, Sarah, this whole experience will grab you and not let you go. And when that happens? I hope you'll come to me. I'll hold you and let you cry. I'll understand,

and that's as good as it gets. All right?"

She shifted away from him, leaning on her crutches, her weight on her right leg. "I'm hoping I can avoid it, Dawson."

Shaking his head, he said, "You won't."

"I saw men I worked with in Afghanistan wounded."

"But did you lose anyone you had a friendship with? Did you see them shot and die in front of you?"

"N-no. I never wanted to either."

"Neither did I, but it happens." He touched her right elbow. "How's that left leg feeling? You've been standing for quite a while." Dawson knew he had to get to safer ground for her sake.

"It's okay, a little achy, but I'm putting a little weight on it."

"Still want to tour the palace?" he teased. Instantly, he saw her respond in a positive way. The darkness haunting her eyes, the grimness of her expression, began to dissolve.

"Will you shadow me? The nurse always had a strap she put around my waist as I moved around on my crutches, in case I fell or got dizzy."

"I'll shadow you. I'll put my hand near your waist and be on your left and slightly behind you. Okay?" Dawson wasn't assuming anything with Sarah. She would let him know what she needed from him as she hobbled around.

"Thank you," she said, her voice soft.

He smiled a little, opening the door for her and then coming to her side. "Come on, you need to give that leg of yours some exercise. The more you put weight on it, use it even a little, the more blood and circulation will come to that area. That means faster healing."

"Oh, to have it heal overnight," she said, moving her crutches forward.

"It won't happen that fast, but your doctor wanted you up every waking hour. How about we check out the bathroom across the hall first? If you still feel frisky after that, we'll wander down the hall to the living room and kitchen."

"That's a plan, Callahan. Let's go."

He smiled down at her, watching the way her hair glinted with reddish highlights, the thick strands swinging back and forth as she confidently took to her crutches and left the bedroom. She had such courage and fortitude. It was as if their moments of intimacy had been healing for her, opening her up, too, and giving her permission to be human. Sooner or later, Dawson knew it would happen. And when it did? It would

267

be a thunderstorm of tears, but he was the right man to be there to help her work through it.

Sarah didn't want to leave Dawson's arm around her, wanted to continue leaning against his stalwart body, which comforted her. If she hadn't been in such a highly agitated state, she would have deferred to being a woman, and he was an incredibly desirable man. If only things were different. She felt like a layer cake, and those layers were toxic, him being the only positive one among the angst she carried within her.

The bathroom was large, with pale green tiles on the floor, a shower on one side and a large white tub on the other. They were functional, not designer quality, which was fine with her. She found the light blue towels nubby, more male than female oriented, when she ran her hand down one side of one. Reminding herself that this was more a work cabin than a touristy type, the towels should reflect that.

"What do you think?" Dawson asked, poking his head in the open doorway as she looked slowly around the huge room.

"That tub looks so inviting," she said.

"Are you a tub gal, not a shower type?" he teased.

She smiled faintly. "Getting in a hot tub of water up to my neck is one of the things I look forward to on some days."

"I noticed at your home you had an enclosed hot tub in the back. You probably use it often."

"Very often," she agreed, swinging out toward the door where he stood. "I feel okay. I'd like to explore the rest of this place."

Standing out of her way, he saw a bit of a flush to her cheeks. It was as if those moments when they had stood together had somehow given her a healing. Her green eyes no longer looked dark and filled with worry. Dawson knew from his broken marriage, the love he'd felt for Lucia always made him feel better. It was no different now with Sarah, only far more intense. Whether Sarah felt like he did toward her didn't matter. He had witnessed their intimacy, as chaste as it was, and had, in some good way, helped her. He saw it in her eyes, in her relaxed expression and the energy she seemed to have derived from the comfort he'd given her.

Following her down the highly polished pine hall, he saw her stop at the end and absorb the tall ceiling, the huge logs that held everything in place above them. She studied it for a long minute, missing nothing. Just as they would never completely leave being Marines, or their military ways, that moment out of time they'd just shared wouldn't be forgotten by her either. Nothing he could prove, but he knew it as if it were written on his soul.

"This is a beautiful cabin," she said, turning, looking up at him as he joined her.

"If you like wood and lots of logs, this is the place for you," he said.

"It's huge. A lot larger than I realized." She looked at the two comfortable sofas, separated by a long, pine coffee table. There were plenty of wood chairs around a long, oval pine kitchen table, enough to seat at least a dozen people if need be. She liked the overstuffed chairs, the Victorian flowers in the fabric. "I think a woman chose the furniture," she said, sliding him a glance. "What do you think?"

He placed his hands on his hips, surveying the room. "I think so. Men are more into steel, glass and concrete. The living room looks like a nice nest you'd want to sit down in and get comfy."

"I'll be glad when I can sit in one of those chairs."

"Well, you keep up this exercising, Sarah, and you'll be doing it real soon."

"I'm looking at the L-shaped bank of windows over the kitchen area," she said, nodding toward it. "My law-enforcement gaze."

"There aren't any curtains you can pull closed at night. Someone, the Elsons maybe, could look in and see where we're sitting."

"We need to do something about that."

"We're on the same wavelength. I was thinking that tomorrow I'll go visit Patty Davidson's Sewing and Quilt Center in Wind River. I made a call to her earlier about making us some opaque curtains. I gave her the measurements and she said she'd take care of it. She got her quilting club together and they're going to not only make curtains for each window but go over to the hardware store to get the rods and everything else so I can put them up."

"Good thinking," she praised. "You work fast," and she smiled a little. And then added, "You're really amazing, Dawson."

"Nah," he rumbled. "It's just my recon assessment of this cabin that told me those curtains needed to be made and mounted so we'd have privacy here."

"Still," she insisted, "that was a great call." She looked around. "There are two entrance/exit points?"

"Yes," and he gestured to the large wooden

271

front door, "there, and down the end of the hall is a door that leads to a small back porch."

"I couldn't see much coming in on the ambulance. How hidden is this cabin?"

"Very well hidden. You'd have to come up the dirt curve in our driveway to see it. Otherwise, we're surrounded by thick forest on all sides. Now, there's a clearing cut around the cabin because of wildfire issues, but even then, you'd either have to walk through a pretty thick stand of forest or walk up around that curve to see it."

"That's good." She noticed King had come out when she left the bedroom, sat outside the bathroom door and now joined them, watching them, always alert. "Where's King going to be at night?"

"Jasmine said to let him roam the cabin at night. That way he can see both entrance/ exit points, hear anyone coming from any direction and give us a bark of warning." He pointed down the hall to his bedroom, which was at the other end, near the second exit. "I'm leaving my door open in case he barks. I'm a light sleeper anyway; one bark out of King will shoot me out of bed."

"And our weapons?"

"Your pistol is in the bed-stand drawer nearest to where you're sleeping. I've loaded it, placed a bullet in the chamber and the safety is on. I've done the same with my pistol. I've also got an AR-15 semiautomatic rifle in my room. You don't. If King barks, I'll be the one doing the hunting with him at my side. I'll want you to stay in your bedroom."

"I hate that," Sarah muttered. "I'd much rather be mobile and able to scout the area with the two of you."

He reached over, patting her shoulder lightly. "That day's about five weeks away."

Making an unhappy sound, she continued toward the L-shaped kitchen. Outside, the sun was shining, the green of the Douglas fir reminding her of lace against the pale blue sky. How she wished she could go outside.

"What's the chance of me going out to get some fresh air?"

"Not today," Dawson said. He reached down, patting King's black head and ears. "As soon as you're done with your exercise and have gone back to your room to lay down, he and I are going to fully recon the area."

Pouting, Sarah said, "I hate this. I yearn for fresh air, and to go hiking, Callahan. I've never been good at staying indoors for very long."

He smiled and touched a strand of hair dipping over her left eye. "You have the notorious tumbleweed gene."

His touch, while fleeting, was exactly what she needed to quell her frustration over her situation. How did he know that? Her scalp tingled where he'd moved that ginger hair aside. Was he that in tune with her? Sarah thought so, appreciating him on a whole new level. "Tumbleweed gene," she said defiantly, smiling because he entertained her in a gentle, creative way. Who would have thought of that?

Shrugging, Dawson managed to grin as he followed her into the large, roomy kitchen. "I have the same one, so don't feel so bad."

She looked at the concrete counter, a light gray. The backsplash had a feminine touch once again, with blue, green, yellow and clear glass, taking away from the ugly concrete. The cabin, she was sure, had been built on a tight budget. Laying concrete as a counter was a lot cheaper than anything else.

"Did you tell Patty about the fabric you wanted for the curtains?" she wondered.

Grimacing, Dawson pointed to the backsplash. "I tried to give her a visual on the place. I told her there were eighteenth-century flowers in the fabric of the living room furniture. She asked me what colors in the kitchen. I don't know if she can match it exactly, but she'll try. I thought flowers might be a nice touch in here if she can find a similar fabric to make the curtains from. Do you think I gave her bum steer?"

"I think your description was perfect. Flowers should follow through a large room like this into the living room. If you have it in one section? It should be the same in the other one." She smiled up at him. "You're pretty good at this. Maybe you got the hausfrau gene."

He laughed deeply. "You catch on fast. Good move. My recon side is coming out. You don't miss any details where I come from. It can someday save your life."

"When were you over in the Sandbox?" She moved to the stove, glad to see it was gas. Everything in the kitchen was sparkling clean. The cabinets were made of pine, but someone, she guessed a woman, had had a say in them. There was green, yellow and blue opaque stained glass in each door, the same colors as the backsplash, making it beautiful to look at. When she got out of this mess, she was going to talk to the forest supervisor to find out who'd designed things. It had to be a woman.

"I joined the Corps at eighteen. Because of my tracking and hunting skills, I went from boot camp directly into recons, where I stayed for the next four years."

"Were you ever at Bagram?"

"Just to fly in and out on deployments. We were shipped around to different firebases in northern and eastern Afghanistan, with a lot of action on the Pakistan border. What about you?"

"I was deployed to Bagram on all my tours. Part of law enforcement. When you have twenty-thousand-plus people on one base, there's plenty to do law-wise. I never got out to any firebases."

He leaned against the counter, watching her touch the stove and then reach up, running her fingertips along the emerald-green stained glass in one cabinet. "We would never have met," he said.

"Might have been interesting if we had," Sarah admitted, turning, studying him. She saw interest in his eyes, felt him sensitive to her plight. Was he as drawn to her as she was to him? She could still remember the scent of him, and it stirred her physically, reminding her it had been a long time since she'd desired a man.

"Think so?" he teased.

"We seem to have a lot of things in common." Moving on her crutches, she went past him and carefully began to tackle the two wooden stairs down to the living room. She was slow on purpose and felt Dawson standing nearby in case she fell or slipped a crutch. He meant safety for her, and she hungrily absorbed his nearness, knowing he would catch her should she not make it down the two steps under her own power. At one point she felt the heat of his hand hovering near the small of her back in case he had to save her.

"You can tell I'm an amateur when it comes to crutches," she grumbled, her full focus on the second step.

"Actually? You're doing real good," Dawson said. She could sense his hand still hovering near her lower back.

"There," and she let out a breath of air as she made it to the solidity of the floor. Turning partly, she saw his face, his eyes narrowed and fully focused — on her. It was a good feeling, not an unsettling one. "I'm sure you'll be glad to get me on two working feet sooner rather than later." It came out as an apology, acknowledging this was taking a lot of Dawson's time. She saw the corners of his mouth hook upward as he took the steps and stood nearby. Again, she drew in a deep, quiet breath, purposely inhaling his scent. He was like perfume.

"How's that thigh feeling now? You've been up on it for a good fifteen minutes."

"It's a toothache pain coming on," she admitted. "But it feels so good to be able to move around, Dawson. I hate being bed bound."

He chuckled a little, following her as she crossed the room to one of the huge sofas with the bright flower fabric. "Did your mom ever get exasperated over your constant wanting to move around? I wonder," and his smile grew as he tossed her an amused look.

"No, she's real patient, though for sure, I was a restless kid. The schoolteacher said I should be tested for ADD or ADHD. My parents refused, saying kids in the first six grades should get at least three or four recesses outside to play in the sun, run and have fun."

"Good for them."

"I want to push myself, Dawson. I'm going to try to sit down on that couch."

He nodded. "Okay, type A, go for it."

She laughed a little and moved toward the couch. "It just looks so inviting. Heck, I'd rather sit out here with my leg propped up than stay in a bed. At least out here? I can see the world and life go by."

"Not a bad idea. I think we could get that to happen."

She could feel Dawson nearby as she maneuvered herself around. At one point, she handed him one of the crutches, using the other to balance herself as she stood close to the sofa. "I'm going to try to let myself down slowly," she told him, leaning over, placing her left hand on the arm. She saw him nod again, focused on her. King came around the coffee table, sat near it, watching her intently. It wasn't exactly balletlike as she grunted and groaned as she allowed herself to sit slowly on the thick, fluffy cushion. Sarah didn't want to fall, and she didn't know the strength of the cushion. At one point, Dawson stepped in and slipped his arm around her left upper arm to give her more strength if she needed it. Eventually, she made the landing.

"There," she huffed, "I made it with your help. Thanks." Easing her back against the cushion, she began to relax.

"How's the leg feeling?"

"Stressed. I can feel the wound pulling."

"Let's try this, then." He released her arm and brought the coffee table closer. Grabbing a throw pillow, he placed it on the table. "I'm going to slowly lift your leg so you can place your heel on that pillow. If I can get your heel on the pillow, you shouldn't be in pain, just comfortable."

"I'm willing to try it," she said. In no time, he'd done as he'd said. By sliding the table even closer, the stress was markedly reduced on her knee. "That feels so nice," she said, giving him a grateful look.

"Want to sit here for a while?"

"I'd like that."

"Is there anything I can get you?"

"My laptop?"

"Okay," he said, a grin coming to his mouth as he left her and headed down the hall to her bedroom.

He came back with the laptop, handing it to her.

"You still comfy?"

"Yes." She glanced over at King, who had settled on the floor near her right foot. "Do you have things to do?"

He glanced toward the kitchen. "Well, it's about 1300. Do you feel like some lunch? You need to eat to keep up your strength."

"Whatever you want to fix, Dawson. I'm really hungry for the first time since before I was shot."

"I think coming here was a good healing decision."

She gave him a warm look. "I have you and King. I'm going to Skype my parents and my grandmothers. I know they worry about me and I don't want them to."

"They'll be more than happy to hear you're okay up here. I'm going to make us some grilled cheese sandwiches."

She watched him saunter away from her, his stride balanced, fluid and once more telling her that he was in top athletic condition. There wasn't anything she didn't like about his body *and* his personality. He was ruggedly good-looking. His hands, although callused, were always gentle when he touched her. And did she ever look forward to any time she could connect with him. His mouth had been so close to hers earlier, when he held her in the bedroom. How much she'd wanted to kiss him! Sarah told herself that he probably would have gone into shock with her spontaneous need of him. Besides, she was in no position, literally, to do much more than kiss him.

Really? Sarah had constantly entertained loving Dawson and having him return those needs and feelings. She saw the look in his eyes sometimes and was experienced enough to know when a man desired her. Lust was a part of it, but there had to be more. As she lingered over starting up her laptop, she watched him from beneath her lashes as he moved quietly around the kitchen. It was like watching a wonderful, sweet dessert. Only right now? She couldn't have the dessert.

There was danger around them, and she shouldn't be thinking about things like that. Feeling a little guilty, Sarah logged on to the laptop and began to answer emails from her office on a number of open cases. Just listening to Dawson puttering around filled her not only with peace, a sense of safety, but something else so beautiful she didn't dare name it. Not yet. Maybe never. They were living in a chaotic time, and Sarah had no idea what might happen. None.

# CHAPTER FOURTEEN

*June 22*

"King and I took in the area earlier this morning while you were sleeping," Dawson told Sarah. She had worked hard to get herself to the kitchen table to eat breakfast with him. The crutches were unwieldy, and he could tell she hated using them. Glad that she wasn't trying to keep on a game face, he understood that yesterday something good — something wonderful — had magically happened between them when he'd held her. He'd lain awake half the night, replaying the unexpected intimacy between them, the trust she'd given him. He stopped fooling himself about Sarah. The truth was, he wanted a deep, ongoing relationship with her. What would she think if he confided his deepest wish?

Sarah sipped her coffee. "It's nine o'clock. What time did you two leave? I sure didn't hear you or wake up when you left."

"Got up at dawn. I wanted to scout a mile around the cabin from the entrance road, memorize the layout and let King get a sense and scent of the area."

"How did he do?" She looked over to see him lying next to her chair. Always the protector.

"Fine. I had him on a sixteen-foot leash and he obeyed all my commands without a problem."

She smiled down at the dog. "I'll bet he loved getting out and getting some exercise."

Dawson nodded. "And I'm sure you're feeling the same way."

"Got that right. But I can't, not yet. I'm just no good at being sick or injured."

"You're young and your body is going to heal fast." He saw she was unhappy. "What would you like for breakfast?"

"I already ate some oatmeal. You go ahead, though. I'll sit and drink coffee with you."

"How are you and the crutches getting along?" he teased, moving to the kitchen.

"It sucks. I'm a very impatient person."

Chuckling, he leaned over and opened a cabinet beneath the kitchen counter, drawing out a big black iron skillet. "Coulda fooled me. At least you know you can feed yourself. What's on your agenda for today?"

She smiled over his teasing comment. "I want you to teach me about the electronics in that room, the radios and stuff. I need to Skype Cade, who's running the sheriff's office in my absence. I need a morning report from him on what happened overnight."

Pulling eggs from the fridge, Dawson asked, "Did you have someone from your office at the funeral for Brian yesterday?"

"I had a deputy, out of sight and in civilian clothes, watching. All three boys were there."

"So now," Dawson murmured, cracking the eggs into a bowl, "those three are at large."

"We have tails on them."

Brows rising, he asked, "I thought you said you didn't have the manpower to do something like that."

"Tom Franks loaned me three of his deputies."

"Can you afford that?"

"He's paying for it out of his county budget, not mine." She shook her head. "I never saw that coming. Tom's always been a good friend, great to coordinate law-enforcement issues with, but his offer took me by surprise."

"You always find out who your real friends are when you're sick or injured," he said, stirring the eggs briskly in the bowl. Sliding her a glance, he saw how grateful she was. There was fragility about Sarah this morning. He didn't know what else to call it. Sooner or later, she was going to crash and split open from the trauma she was still holding inside.

"I just worry what the Elsons are going to do now. I worry about my family . . ."

He poured the eggs into the hot skillet. "Having tails on them will be a huge help."

"Yes. I'm more worried about my family than me."

"Well," he said, giving her a look as he stirred the eggs, "you can worry about them, but I'll take care of you. Me and King, that is."

Hiram Elson studied a map of the Salt River Range. It paralleled the entire valley that created the western boundary for Wyoming. Sitting at the truck stop just outside Wind River, in the café section, he had the map spread out before him. He'd gone over to Sarah's parents' home and watched from a grove of trees across the street for five hours. Although he'd seen David and Emily Carter coming and going, he never saw any sign that Sarah was staying with them. Leaving there, he went to get lunch. Where had they hidden Sarah? In his gut, he knew that was what they'd done. He wasn't stupid. He knew Sarah would realize that by killing their father, she'd guaranteed they'd kill her to settle the score.

He pushed his long fingers through his short red hair, wanting a cigarette, but even the truck stops forbade smoking these days. He growled in frustration. Studying the map, his mind leapfrogged over possibilities. It would stand to reason, Kaen, the middle brother, twenty-nine years old, had argued yesterday, after the funeral, that Sarah would disappear. She would know they were coming for her. She wouldn't want her family involved in it, so she wouldn't stay with them.

At first, Hiram blew off Kaen's reasoning. But after this morning, nearly to noon, he'd seen absolutely no evidence Sarah was at her parents'. They'd check out the two grannies, too. Kaen was going to watch Gertie Carter's place and Elisha, twenty-four, would watch Nell Franklin's home. It would take a couple of days to determine whether she was with one of them. Kaen, who was the geek in the family and always bragged he was the most intelligent of the four brothers, argued that Sarah Carter was keeping her family out of this revenge hunt and hidden somewhere else.

But where? Scowling, his thick red brows lay straight over his narrowed green eyes, ruthlessly studying the map. The four boys had all grown up in this valley. And they'd done a lot of rooting around in the Salt River Range, creating what were known as ratlines, new trails to offload drugs coming into the county that their father had bought to distribute. These trails led to meeting points, where dealers could pay them and then drive off with the purchased drugs. They had several meth labs up in the mountainous region, well hidden, so the smell of cooking wouldn't be inhaled by anyone or give them away. The trails were well hidden, used only by them. They never wanted the Forest Service to find them.

He wished Cree, the third brother, was there. Hiram had always admired his brother's ability to think outside the box. Unfortunately, Cree was dead, the dumb shit. He was obsessed with that Tara Dalton, and look where it got him: six feet under. So, there was no way to talk to him about this.

His mind clicked over the fact that the sheriff was wounded. An ambulance would have taken her out of the hospital. Moving his thick finger along the slope of the Salt River Range, he began to circle, in pencil, known trails that might allow an ambulance to drive on it. All the roads leading into the range were dirt. Some were better, even graded, and cared for by the county. Hiram was sure they would choose a cabin that had a well-graded road. They couldn't bring a buslike ambulance on a bad road; the vehicle simply couldn't handle the potholes, the dips or rough surface conditions. Ambulances weren't ATVs.

Rubbing his square jaw, he considered his epiphany. Knowing he was making a decision to start looking for roads, he designed a plan. He'd start with the nearest roads into the range from the hospital. After Elisha and Kaen ended their observation of the grannies, he'd make a call on a burner phone to tell them to meet him at the family homestead. There, they could plan in privacy. Sarah Carter was a dead woman. She just didn't know it yet.

Dawson couldn't sleep. He'd quietly gotten up, padded barefoot down the hall, peered into the gloom of Sarah's room and seen King's head come up, looking at him. The dog knew not to growl or bark because he recognized him. Sarah was sleeping.

It was three a.m. He hated being jolted awake, but it was part of his PTSD. One therapist had told him, while he was still in the military, that when he woke up at the same time every night, it had to do with a traumatic event that had taken place at that time. That his mind, and maybe his dreams, were revolving around it, trying to dissolve another fragment of the terror he'd felt at the time. Moving out to the kitchen, a small stove light on, he opened the cabinet and found some tea. Not about to drink coffee — then he'd never get back to sleep — he filled the copper kettle with some water from the faucet.

The clack of King's paws striking the pine floor caught his attention. Looking up, he saw the dog come around the corner and into the kitchen.

King whined, then looked toward the hall.

Frowning, Dawson put the cup and tea bag aside. "What's going on?" he asked the dog.

Another whine. And then he wagged his long, whiplike tail, turned and trotted down the hall, disappearing into Sarah's room.

Concerned, he rubbed the T-shirt across his chest and set the kettle aside, then moved toward the hall. Was something wrong with Sarah? He wasn't familiar with this command or training in a dog, but he knew from growing up with dogs that they sensed things humans didn't. And it wasn't unusual for a dog to run to get help for a human in trouble either.

Halting at the door to Sarah's room, he saw King sitting tensely near the head of the bed. His gaze flicked to Sarah. She was muttering and mumbling, restless and pushing the covers off her body to her waist. Silently, he moved inside, trying to hear what she was saying but not wanting to startle her awake. King was like a statue, his ears up, his sole focus on the woman he was to protect.

". . . Lane . . . no . . . hold on . . . hold on . . ."

Frowning, Dawson moved closer to her bedside. Sarah couldn't toss and turn because of her leg injury, but he saw her gripping the covers at her waist. *Lane.* He'd heard mention of that name at different times. He'd wanted to ask Sarah about this person, but things had been moving so fast in their complicated lives, he hadn't had the opportunity. With the light from the hall falling silently into the room, he could see her face, which looked pained. Surmising the medication to stop the leg pain had run out; that could be the reason for a bad dream.

Sarah suddenly screamed.

Flinching, Dawson saw her snap into an upright position, eyes wide open and staring, unseeing at him, but seeing something beyond him that he didn't. She was breathing hard, her face taut, perspiration across her brow. Her hair had fallen forward, framing her face, showing how pale she was. She was having a flashback.

He didn't wait any longer.

Moving to the side of her bed, he called her name softly but firmly. She was breathing roughly, moaning, closing her eyes and then opening them. How badly he wanted to sweep her into his arms and hold her. Sensing that was what she needed but not daring to do it, Dawson kept calling her name. He knew that people with PTSD or having nightmares shouldn't be touched. Instead, a calm, quiet voice calling their name would eventually break through the terror and awaken them.

The fourth time he called her name, the glassy look in her eyes changed. They moved to where he was standing beside her bed, as if hearing him for the first time. Her breathing was harsh and labored, her chest heaving beneath the nightgown she wore. She stared up at him, looked around the room, her gaze swinging back to him once more.

"W-what are you doing here?" she managed, her hand against the column of her neck. "Is something wrong?"

"You were screaming, Sarah. I was in the kitchen making myself some tea." He pointed to King. "He came to get me. When I walked in, you were screaming out a name."

Her brows fell and she stared at him. "A name? What are you talking about?"

"Did you have a nightmare, Sarah? You were calling out for someone named Lane." Instantly, he saw what little color was in her shadowy face drain away. Her eyes filled with anguish and the corners of her mouth tucked inward, as if to stop from crying or screaming. Opening his hands, he said, "Who's Lane? Were you having a dream?"

"Oh . . ." she whispered brokenly, "oh, God, no. . . ." and covered her face with her hands.

Dawson felt as if an invisible bomb had gone off in the room. He didn't know who Lane was. Sarah's shoulders had tensed. He could feel and see her trying to control her reaction to his words. Her breathing was less harsh, but he could see her lips moving, tightening and then parting, as if fighting back something. He wasn't sure what it was, but it appeared to be either a scream or a cry. The room felt as if it were shrinking around them, as if it were closing in on Sarah. The pain and terror he saw in her eyes snapped him to attention.

*To hell with it.* He was going to sit down on the edge of the bed and face her.

Sitting gently so as not to disturb her healing leg, he grazed her upper arm with his fingers, trying to calm her. He rasped, "Can you talk about it, Sarah? Who's Lane?"

A little cry tore from her and her hands fell away.

Dawson felt as if he were looking at a Marine with a thousand-yard stare in his eyes. Sarah's gaze was empty, as if she was physically there with him, but in every other way somewhere else. Another time and place. He slid his callused hand down her bare lower arm, encasing her fingers, which were icy cold and damp. "It's all right," he told her in a low, quiet tone. The blankness in Sarah's eyes scared him. He'd never seen that look on her before. Who was Lane? Obviously someone important to Sarah. Squeezing her hand gently, he felt her fingers curve tightly around his. She was struggling with something so huge that he couldn't even begin to guess what it might be.

"It's all right, Sarah. You're safe here with King and me. You're safe . . ." because he thought Lane might have been someone in her military life, a good friend who had been killed in front of her perhaps. He guessed perhaps Lane was so important to Sarah that she was still grieving her. And the way she was reacting? It reminded him of too many of his Marine friends who had PTSD and would wake in the middle of the night with a similar look and reaction. And every time it had happened in their barracks at the firebase? After they had awakened from the claws of the nightmare that captured them, it was about a buddy lost in combat. Dawson remembered that terrified look, the horror plainly written upon taut, sweaty faces.

He watched her closely, saying nothing. Because other than comforting her, he didn't know what to do. Maybe later, when she got over the rocky awakening, when the grip of the flashback eased, she might fill him in. At least now he'd made contact with her, and her breathing wasn't as strident.

"Keep slowing your breathing, Sarah. Take in a deep breath and let it out slowly. Count to ten, breathe in, then slowly let it out. . . ." He felt her fingers tighten a little around his. It felt as if she were clinging to him, afraid he'd let her go. But he wouldn't. He would be there for her. "That's it . . .

good . . . you're doing fine . . ."

Sarah lifted her other hand, hiding her eyes from him.

He felt a shift within her, but it was nothing outwardly obvious. Her mouth opened, then closed, and he could feel a wall of anguish settling down around her. A visceral sensation washed over him. Her fingers tightened even more around his. She bowed her head, eyes closed and still hidden beneath her hand. She wanted to cry and she was fighting it. Why? He'd cried upon occasion himself, and it had been cleansing, lifting the weight of the trauma or grief, making him feel marginally better afterward. So often, it was drilled in to the military that crying was a sign of weakness. But it wasn't. He thought it was a brave thing to do.

Before he could say anything else, he saw two silvery paths escape from beneath her hand and trickle down her taut face. She was still fighting them, but her emotions were stronger than her will. How often had he seen his buddies do the same thing? Far too many times. Pain wrenched across his chest as he sat in the semidarkness with Sarah. She was using every vestige of her strength to combat releasing those stored-up feelings.

He ached for her, wishing he could cajole her into allowing herself to really cry. Understanding that Sarah probably felt if she invested in her tears, she would lose control of herself.

"Sarah, it's okay to cry. Come on, let those tears flow. I'll be here . . . I'll hold you if you want . . ." He was speaking from his heart now, not his head. The room felt so tight and knotted up that Dawson could feel the explosiveness of the atmosphere surrounding them. He saw a nearly imperceptible quiver flow through her. What inner strength she had! He marveled at her ability to continue not to give in to the ravaging emotions kicked up by that nightmare.

There was a low whine from King, his entire being focused on Sarah.

Dawson barely flicked a glance to the dog when he heard a terrible, tearing sound pulling so deep from within Sarah, it sounded like a wounded animal moaning. She yanked her hand out of his, both hands across her mouth as if to stop that tortured sound from clawing up and out. All he could do was sit there watching her begin to crumble inwardly.

Without thinking, he moved closer to her, wrapping his arms around her shoulders, urging her to lean on him. It was instinctive and had had nothing to do with any thought process. At that moment, she was a human being who was hurting terribly, and he wanted to somehow give her the strength and support to work through it. Her features tightened, eyes squeezed shut, tears splashing fiercely down her cheeks. Easing her forward, guiding her brow against his shoulder and jaw, he felt Sarah collapse against him, wrenching sobs making her shake and tremble. The sounds made him wince as he rested his head against hers, his palm moving slowly down her spine, and his other arm wrapping around her shaking shoulders as the sobs continued.

He absorbed her cries, his T-shirt quickly dampening with the flood of tears that were finally released. How he wished he could absorb the endless anguish that came with those tearing sounds, but he couldn't. All he could do was give her support and, maybe, a little sense of safety. Hopefully enough for her to surrender her pain, loss or grief instead of continuing to carry it so deeply within her. Her hair smelled faintly fragrant, the silky strands cool against his sandpapery jaw. Gown damp and sticking to her back, he continued to slowly ease his hand up and down her spine, silently encouraging her to allow the weeping to continue. He kept murmuring soft words of encouragement, cradling her, feeling her lean fully against him. Sweetness filled him; never had he wanted more than at that moment to make a positive difference in Sarah's life.

His mind tumbled over the possibility that this reaction was due to her nearly being killed. He'd seen other Marines who'd been hit by a bullet and, days later, hit a wall and break down just as she was right now. What bothered him, was the big question mark: Who was Lane? Unable to make sense of why Sarah was sobbing her heart out in huge, tearing gulps, he had no answer. When she placed one hand against his T-shirt, her palm connecting with his flesh beneath the fabric, his whole body tightened. No, this wasn't sexual or anything near it. Tempering himself as her hand ranged over this chest, across his shoulder, curving around his neck, he was once more totaled by her trust in him. His heart, bruised and wounded by his failed marriage years earlier, opened up. Dawson was stunned by the sensation, the heady, almost euphoric joy threading through him as Sarah wept without reserve in his arms.

Sarah hiccupped, embarrassed by it as she

slowly eased out of Dawson's protective, wonderful arms. His face was deeply etched and shadowed, the glitter in his eyes filled with concern for her. He opened his arms, allowing her to sit up. Wiping her wet face, her fingers trembling, she choked out, "I-I'm sorry. I don't know what happened . . ." She felt his roughened fingers moving lightly down her arm, feeling the peace he was feeding her.

Leaning over, he picked up a box of tissues from the bed stand and placed them between himself and her. "You were having a flashback or something," he offered quietly, handing her a couple of tissues. "King came into the kitchen and whined at me and then ran back into your room. That was unusual behavior for him, so I came in here to see if you were all right."

"A dream? I had a dream?" she managed, dabbing her eyes repeatedly, tears still falling, although at a much slower rate. Inwardly, she felt as if someone had taken a wire bottlebrush and viciously scrubbed her stomach and chest until they both hurt. She watched Dawson nod. Wanting his hand to remain on her arm, she felt alone when he removed it. Being in his arms was like being in a cozy nest. Maybe a cradle. He was a tall, strong man, but he hadn't used his strength against her. Instead, he'd shown his softer side, the one she needed so desperately.

"Yes. You were muttering. I think if your leg wasn't wounded, you'd have been tossing and turning, too." He motioned to the messy sheet and blanket beside her. "You kept gripping and loosening your hands on the bedding. I couldn't hear what you were saying because I was near the door. I was afraid if you woke and saw me there, I might scare the hell out of you, on top of whatever you were experiencing." He managed a one-cornered twitch of his mouth. "It looked like you were in a flashback or maybe a nightmare. At first, I thought it might be a reaction to you being shot and nearly dying. Everyone has those kinds of flashbacks days or even weeks after an event like that." Sighing, he said in a low tone, "The only words I could understand were about someone named Lane."

It felt as if the floor had dropped out of the center of her body. The hollowness that had been there for so long ramped up. She stared at him, aware of the sudden silence cloaking them. Searching his eyes, which looked sad and caring, she croaked, "Lane? I called for Lane?"

Giving her a confused look, he said,

"When I went over to your bedside, you eventually woke up. I asked you who Lane was, and you looked like an IED had exploded next to you."

"I-I don't remember. . . ."

"You were half asleep, so I'm not surprised. But it triggered your crying."

Rubbing her face wearily, she said, "I don't remember."

"Do you remember the dream?"

"No." She tucked her lower lip between her teeth, looking into the darkness. "I'm a mess . . ."

"I don't think so," he said, taking the damp tissues from her and dropping them in a wastebasket. Pulling two more tissues from the box, he eased them into her hand. "I don't know of anyone who doesn't hit the wall and break down after an experience like the one you had. You're only human, Sarah. And it's a good thing you can cry. You can't hold that stuff inside you. I've seen others try, and it never works."

Dawson's words hurt, but she knew he was right. Deep down, he was right. "Did I say anything else?"

"No, that was it." Cocking his head, he asked, "So? You weren't dreaming? You weren't caught in a flashback?"

"I don't remember anything." She grimaced.

"Who's Lane?"

It felt as if he'd just stabbed her in the heart. Catching her breath, fresh tears trailing down her cheeks, she wobbled. "My younger sister by two years." And a fresh round of tears came. Dawson kept handing her wads of tissue, throwing away the ones that were damp with spent tears. Why couldn't she stop crying? What was going on? Desperation clawed through her as she felt the ongoing, almost volcanic eruption of missing Lane, of never seeing her again, and it was so hard to bear.

Her head hurt from crying so much. At least this time, the tears were not wrenching, loud, desperate. This time they were a warm river flowing down her cheeks, so much old, buried grief oozing to the surface. She had no way to control or stop it. The tears just kept coming.

Finally, they stopped again. Dawson got up, went to the bathroom across the hall, got her a glass of water and brought it back. He handed it to her. Their fingers met. She was ravenous for any kind of connection with him.

"Thank you," she offered brokenly, holding the glass with both hands, sipping the water. She watched as he sat down on the bed once more, his hip almost touching her blanketed right leg. "I wish . . . I wish I had the serenity I see in your face and eyes, Dawson."

"I'm sure you feel anything but serene right now. Lane was your sister? She was two years younger than you?"

Frowning, she set the glass on the bed stand. "Yes." The word stuck in her throat and she gulped. For whatever reason, she did feel more settled inwardly. Maybe crying for a good, long time had freed some of the terrible glue that seemed to stick to her heart and mind, never allowing her to forget Lane or that day that had ended their lives with each other.

"Look, you don't need to say anything more if you don't want to. You're looking really exhausted. Maybe going to bed and trying to sleep will help?"

Tilting her head, her vision blurring for a moment, Sarah whispered unsteadily, "Dawson, for so long I've wanted to unload a horrible time in my life to someone. But I never found anyone I guess I could trust. Being around you is like me walking out of a blast furnace into a boat that's on a smooth lake instead."

"That's a nice compliment. Probably my

medic side showing. We have to project calm during a calamity," and he managed a slight twist of his mouth.

"It's more than that," she said, clearing her throat, wiping her eyes. "I feel like there's an invisible fist pushing slowly up through me. And I feel like if I don't talk about Lane, I'll die. I've known you long enough to know you don't judge others, and that you're a keen listener. You bear witness to other people's tragedies all the time."

"Yes," he rasped, "that's what I've done in the past, Sarah. If you want? Tell me about Lane. I'll just sit and listen. Maybe it's time for you to release your grief about her . . ."

# CHAPTER FIFTEEN

*June 23*

The anguish written across Sarah's face ripped him up inside. He'd only seen such pain when one of his team lost someone they loved. Automatically, his hands moved into fists, and he forced himself to open them. Dawson understood body language better than most. He needed to appear relaxed to silently broadcast that to Sarah. She gripped the covers, took a deep, shaky breath, avoiding his gaze. Finally, he saw her hands loosen a little on the bedding, forcing herself to make eye contact with him once more. He could feel her struggle between running and staying. She moved a pillow behind her back on the headboard and then leaned against it, drawing up her good leg.

The words came out slowly. "Lane was seven years old. We were walking home from school one afternoon in late September, only four blocks away. I was nine." Her fingers tightened on the bedspread. Shakily, she wiped her brow.

"We always took back ways home because it was faster. We were walking on one side of the alley and I heard a truck roaring up behind us. I automatically pressed Lane against the brick wall of a building, standing in front of her. It was a black pickup truck. I recognized the driver, Jethro Elson." She gave Dawson a significant look and saw shock ripple across his face. And then she saw rage in his eyes, though he struggled to get hold of his escaping emotions.

"Jethro Elson?" he growled.

"Brian's father. He slammed on the brakes, leaped out and grabbed Lane's shoulder, yanking her out from behind me." She swallowed and scrunched her eyes closed for a moment. "I grabbed Lane's arm as he pulled her toward the open door of the truck. I was screaming for help; so was Lane. I was so afraid. I saw the crazed look in his eyes and I was so frightened. I'd never been around that kind of violence. Lane was shrieking, beating at him with her small fists, digging her heels into the dirt and trying to get away. I grabbed Jethro's other arm. He shook me off. I fell to the ground, then scrambled to my feet, yelling at him to let my sister go. By the time I reached the door of the truck, he'd thrown Lane into the passenger-side seat. He turned around, balled his fist and hit me as hard as he could in the face."

She halted and touched the bridge of her nose. "He broke my nose and cracked my cheekbone, plus blacked my eye. But it was nothing in comparison to what he was going to do to my sister. I was knocked unconscious. I don't know how long I was out, only that when I got up, the truck was gone and so was Lane. My parents had given me a cell phone, so I sat in the alley, my hands shaking so bad I could barely dial my dad, who was at work. I told him what happened. I told him it was Jethro Elson. He immediately got every deputy on duty and called in those who weren't to help him find Elson."

"My God," Dawson rasped, "that must have been a nightmare." He saw the sadness, the guilt in her teary eyes. "What happened then?"

"My mom drove to the alley about five minutes later and picked me up. She was so pale it scared me. Dad had called her and told her to find me immediately. My poor mom. She saw me and started to cry, kneeling down, holding me. I was a bloody mess.

My nose was bleeding, and I didn't realize it, but he'd knocked out two of my teeth and I was bleeding from that, plus there was a cut to the corner of my mouth. I guess my eyes were already swelling shut and Mom told me later the left side of my face looked like a swollen pumpkin because of my broken cheekbone."

Reaching out, Dawson gripped the hand that lay across her stomach on top of the bedclothes. "Did she take you to the hospital?"

"Yes. And Mom was in touch with Dad via cell phone. I was shaking so badly, Dawson. I was so scared. I couldn't stop crying because I blamed myself for letting go of Lane. But Jethro was strong as a bull and I weighed all of sixty pounds."

"You were no match for him."

She clung to his hand. "They searched through the late afternoon. And all through the night. Everyone in Wind River was stunned. So many people came over to our house, where Mom and I waited for word about Lane. They comforted us. They stayed with us. The church formed a prayer circle for Lane. There were so many wonderful people who came to help us . . ."

"Did they find Jethro? Lane?"

Grimacing, Sarah whispered brokenly, "A

rancher, Roy Collins — his land was about twenty miles south of Wind River — found Lane's body thrown along the side of the dirt road leading to his property. He'd heard on TV and the internet about Lane being abducted. Roy was in his eighties, and a wonderful man. She was dead. He called my dad and gave him the bad news. He dispatched a forensics team and followed them out to where she lay in that ditch."

"When did you get the news, Sarah?"

"Shortly after Roy called Dad. It was horrible. Mom screamed and sobbed. I cried, wrapping myself into a little ball in the corner of the kitchen, feeling so guilty that I couldn't save my little sister."

Dawson smoothed his other hand over the back of the one he held. "That wasn't your fault. You were badly hurt trying to save her, Sarah." He saw her lift her head, her eyes wounded holes of grief.

"I was her big sister. My parents said I was always to take care of her. It was my duty to do that and I failed."

He continued to stroke her hand, seeing it gave her a small amount of relief. "We'll talk about that later. Did they capture Elson?"

"Yes, a week later." She lifted her hand. "He escaped up into the Salt River Range.

310

My dad had the best trackers in Wyoming working with him to find the bastard. And they did."

"In the meantime, your family was burying a daughter," he rasped, shaking his head.

"Yes," she uttered wearily. "It was a nightmare for all of us."

"And you were only nine? A child. It must have seemed surreal to you."

She tilted her head and gave him a long, searching look. "Why . . . yes, that's exactly how I felt. It was as if I were living in a nightmare that would never end. My parents were grief-stricken. I've never seen my mom cry so hard, so long and so much in my entire life. I can see the wounds it left in both of them to this day. That's something you never forget, when a child dies. You take it to your grave. . . ."

"And you suffered equally," he counseled gently. Sarah was trying to distance herself from it, and Dawson understood. "Who took care of you during that chaotic time?"

"Gertie and Nell were with my mom and me the entire time. They cooked for us, held us, listened to us when we needed to talk or cry, kept the house going. Dad was away for all but the hours of Lane's funeral. He was out hunting Jethro with a vengeance."

"Probably wanted to kill the sick bastard."

"I'm sure. He's never spoken or opened up about Lane's death since it happened."

"What about your mother?"

"Shortly after Jethro was caught and taken to jail, charged with kidnapping, rape and second-degree murder, she had a nervous breakdown." Giving a painful shrug, she choked out, "Who could blame her? Lane was . . . well . . . the opposite of me. She was like a sunbeam lighting up everyone's life. She made people smile and laugh. She loved all things, animals, insects . . . everything. I was the serious one. I didn't have that effect on my parents or people around me."

"Because you were given the responsibility as the oldest, that's why."

Looking away, Sarah said, "I've turned this whole event over and over in my mind ten thousand times. I look at it daily. As I grew older, I'd look at it a little differently, and when I was mature, I realized the incredible destructive impact Lane's death had on all of us." She pressed her hand to her breast. "There isn't a day that goes by that I don't remember her, remember something she said, visualize her, all her expressions, what she loved to do . . ."

"It will always be that way," he said, squeezing her hand a little more, wanting to feed her something other than grief and sadness.

"Yes, it will. Sometimes I see a purple dress in the dressmaker's shop, and I think of Lane. That was her favorite color: a reddish violet color. Or I'll see a child go down that very same alley on a bike, and I get slammed with what happened that day to Lane."

"There's probably a lot of things that bring it all back to you. Much like our PTSD from having been in combat, seen our friends wounded or killed."

"Same thing," she said grimly. Tears tracked down her wan cheeks. "I-I'm so tired of it all, Dawson. I've never admitted this to anyone, not even my dad, who has been a rock since Lane was murdered."

He released her hand and stood, moving closer to her, his hip meeting hers as he settled down, facing her. Lifting his hand, he cupped her damp cheek, holding her stormy green eyes. "I can see that. And now? You're mired in Elson family drama once again."

She pressed her cheek into his roughened palm. "Yes."

"In a sick kind of way," he murmured, more to himself than her, "it's like payback. Jethro murdered your sister and now you

313

killed his son. There's irony in all this, Sarah, but damned if I know how to understand it."

He saw her eyes grow thoughtful. "I hadn't even thought of that."

"Now? Jethro is experiencing what your family went through years later."

"He's in a maximum-security prison in Montana. I'm sure he's been made aware of what happened." She lifted her head and gave him a grateful look as his hand fell away. "I wonder if it's hit my parents."

"I don't know. But your getting shot and almost killed by Brian, I'll bet that's raised the specter of this deadly pattern between the two families. It can't be lost on them. It certainly wasn't on you."

"You're right. I should call my parents, talk with them. But it's so hard to bring Lane up to them. I tried when I was younger, and they would always deflect my questions about how they were feeling."

"I would guess because they were both working on their own grief and loss."

"I'm sure." She frowned. "I don't know if I should try to broach this with them. They're reeling because I was wounded. I think they've had enough."

"They'd lost one daughter. And now? They almost lost their other daughter: you.

I'm sure they're hurting as much as you are right now."

"Yes, but they at least have each other to lean on, to cry in each other's arms and hold each other at night when they feel so damned fragile, as if they're going to break from the weight of all the emotions we carry since Lane's death. I've been thinking a lot about that," she said wearily. "Dad was shot at six times in the twenty years he was sheriff of this county but never received a wound, thank God. I saw something important leave him when Lane was murdered. He wasn't the same man ever again. Even at nine years old, I saw it, though I didn't understand it for a long, long time. And every time Dad was in a situation where his vest saved his life, I watched another little piece of my mom die. It was as if his being in law enforcement was draining the life out of her." She rubbed her eyes. "Now I was nearly killed. It has to be brutal for my folks, Dawson. And I don't know what to do to help them, comfort them."

"First, you have to care for yourself, not them. That will come later."

"With the Elson boys threatening revenge? It's sent my parents into a whole new world where they aren't sure if any of us will live or die. My dad knows the Elsons, know what they're capable of doing. I know he talked to my mom about leaving town until this is settled, to visit her sister in Arizona, but she refused to leave. She's become a fighter."

"Like her daughter."

"Right now? I feel like a doll filled with sawdust for stuffing. I don't feel strong or confident like I used to, Dawson. I know in part it's due to almost dying. I've seen military friends go through something similar."

"It's a process," he agreed. Getting up, he picked up the glass of water on the bed stand, handing it to her. She'd cried enough tears to dehydrate herself. He was heartened when she took the glass, draining it.

"I think you're a mind reader," she said, wiping her lips.

"Me? Oh, no. If I was? I wouldn't have made so many damn serious mistakes in my life, so don't put me on any pedestal, okay?" and he smiled a bit at her, seeing a slight flush to her cheeks.

"Yeah, none of us need a pedestal to stand on."

Silence settled over the room, except for the panting of King, who sat near his feet, all his attention devoted to Sarah. He, too, could feel how fragile she was. Dawson wished he had more experience, maybe a true mind-reading ability, to get inside her head and know exactly where she was. He was afraid to ask too many questions precisely because of the delicacy he felt around her.

"You said you've never talked to anyone like this since Lane's passing?"

"I tried talking to my parents. I was desperate to talk; I had so much fear, anger and grief inside me." Her voice grew hoarse. "At nine? You don't realize much. Now? I realize my parents were so devastated by what had happened to Lane they didn't have the strength to help me, too."

"What did you do?"

"The grannies would take me for a day, usually on weekends because of school. Gertie was always trying to get me to talk about the experience, but I couldn't do it. One thing I did ask her one day was why it had happened."

"Did she have an answer?"

"No. She said everything was in another's hands, far outside the reach and understanding of we humans. Gertie is very spiritual. From her perspective, things happen for a reason, even though we'll probably never know why until we start to die, and our life runs before our eyes before we pass. Then we'll have all the answers to our questions."

"Did her explanation comfort you?"

"I was too young to appreciate her wisdom. I do now. But she held me, rocked me to sleep on nights when I'd wake up screaming from nightmares of Lane's kidnapping."

"Was Nell able to help you through it, too?"

"Grandma Nell is the soul of warmth and kindness. Her father was a Methodist minister, and she has a deep, deep faith. She helped me by kneeling with me at my bed, saying prayers before she tucked me into bed. She urged me to create prayers that came from my heart for Lane. That helped me a lot at the time."

"If anyone ever thinks grandparents aren't important . . ." he agreed, emotion in his tone. "They each gave you a rock to cling to during that time."

Again, Sarah gave him a questioning look, opening her mouth to ask something but deciding against it.

"How else can I help you, Sarah?"

"What if I told you that all I wanted and needed right now was to be held?"

His heart pulsed powerfully as he held her pleading gaze. "I can do that for you."

"Are you sure?"

"Better than a cup of hot tea," and the corners of his mouth hooked upward as he saw a brief flitting of amusement come to her expression. He could feel just how tired she was. Now he understood why.

"I'm going to lay down here," she said, pulling her hand from his and smoothing her palm across the rumpled covers. "I just want to be held, but not tightly."

"Just keep talking and we'll figure it out together." His voice had grown deeper, all his emotions churning within him. Partly for Sarah; the rest, for himself. Looking at the clock on her bed stand, he said, "It's 0400."

"I'm feeling it," she said, slowly moving and settling on her back.

Understanding that she couldn't lay on either side because of the freshness of her leg wound, Dawson patiently waited until she seemed okay in the position she had taken. He wore a T-shirt and blue-and-white-striped pajama bottoms. At least he wasn't seminaked; Sarah didn't need to worry about him in that way. Sure, he wanted her. But he wanted a woman to want him as much as he wanted her. Nothing less would do. He'd learned well from his past. "Ready?"

"Yes," she said, pulling the covers aside.

"I'm nervous, though," she admitted, her gaze flitting to his.

"Me too," he teased. "Keep talking to me as I settle in?" The mistake he'd made in his first marriage was not communicating. It had been a brutally hard lesson, one Dawson wasn't about to repeat. He slid in beside her, on the right side, and pulled up the covers. There were several pillows on the bed and he took one, shaping it with his hand. He made sure there was at least six inches between them. "I'm going to slide my arm beneath your neck. Okay?"

"Yes, that would be nice."

*Sure would be nice.* But he kept that to himself as he eased his arm beneath her neck. Already, he could inhale her scent, that sweetness combined with whatever she washed her hair with. He saw her lashes drop as he laid down, his arm beneath her neck, curving lightly around her shoulder. All the tension she was holding seemed to dissolve with his contact. Damn, it felt so good to be with her in a bed, something he'd dreamed of ever since meeting her. Right now, Sarah was hurting deeply for so many reasons. "Okay?" he asked huskily.

"Yes, wonderful. . . . Thank you, Dawson. . . . I trust you . . ."

Her words were slurring, and he realized

just how exhausted she really was. "Go to sleep," he urged, his chest barely touching her right shoulder. Closing his own eyes, he released a held breath, his senses taking over, washing through him on every level. Feeling the natural heat of her body beneath that colorful summer nightgown, he could feel his body responding to her. Suppressing any sexual desire for her was impossible. He was glad there was some distance between them. The last thing Dawson wanted was for her to become aware of his sexual need for her as well.

Soon, he could hear her breath shallowing out, slowing, and felt the muscles in her neck relaxing. Her scent was intoxicating to him, exciting him and yet, he reined in his desire. Dawson had learned from the tragedy of his marriage that love was more than just about sex or lust. Sure, it was a part of it, especially the first year or two. But then it began to take a secondary place to other ways of showing his partner, his wife, that he loved her. Things like this: holding a woman, cradling her, feeding her a sense of his nearness, strength and calm, among so many others being shared right now.

His mind refused to settle down. How hard it must have been when Brian, Jethro's son, had come after her. Just as his father had murdered Lane. My God, what kind of sick pattern was at play here? Lane and Sarah were the innocent lambs in this sordid drama. Lambs led to slaughter by the violent, dysfunctional Elson family. Allowing all that to sink in, Dawson began to realize just how much danger Sarah remained in. Which one of the brothers would seek revenge? All of them? He had no knowledge of them himself.

It made him furious that Sarah and her family were once again being subjected to the Elsons' murderous ways. They were all sociopaths as far as he was concerned, and he'd treat them in that light. It made them capable of being predatory hunters of Sarah and relentless about their revenge. He kept his right arm lying along the line of his body, but how badly he wanted to lift and curve it around her hip, hold her close.

Sarah knew from the get-go just how much danger she was in, and Dawson now understood completely why she'd wanted to remove her family from their gun sights. She knew better than anyone to what lengths the Elsons would go to get what they wanted. He wondered how long Jethro had lusted after Lane. Probably a long time, would be his guess. The old man knew they went down a particular alley on their way home from school. He knew exactly where to entrap them, to grab Lane without anyone seeing it happen. Worse, he knew in his gut that when Jethro struck Sarah full force in the face with his fist, he'd wanted to kill her. He probably thought he had because he'd have heard the crunch of bones breaking in her nose and cheek.

That bothered Dawson deeply; if Jethro had realized Sarah wasn't lying dead on the ground, he'd have continued to pummel her until she was. He wouldn't want any survivor to name him. It was a nest of predators they were dealing with. The Elsons reminded him of the vengeful Taliban at its worst, wiping out any Afghan village that refused to go along with them. The enemy would amass enough soldiers to break down the gate, get inside the mud walls of the village and kill every man and woman. They'd take the children across the Pakistan border and sell them as sex slaves to the highest bidder.

Now, he couldn't sleep. At all. It was imperative he make this cabin a lot safer. Before Sarah's admission, he'd done some recon in protecting the outer area. But now? No fucking way was Dawson going to allow any Elson to sneak up on them. He'd go out tomorrow to buy motion sensor equipment, not caring how much it cost. And if he couldn't cover the expense of a tight security system? Well, he'd go to Gertie and explain it. Dawson knew she would cover the expenses without question.

The Teton County commander, Tom Franks, had already loaned deputies to follow the three Elson boys. Dawson had a sneaking suspicion Franks knew all about the kidnapping and murder of Lane; that was probably why he'd been so generous. Things were clearer for him now. As a recon Marine, he knew how to assess any land for its strengths and weaknesses. He could create an unbroken system at least half a mile from the cabin that would alert them of an intruder breaking through the invisible lines, giving them time to prepare for an attack.

The next thing he had to do was get the assistant commander, Cade Jameson, to give him all the intel on the Elsons. He knew he'd do it. The more Dawson knew about them, the better he could anticipate what kind of attack they might spring on them. The Taliban had an MO; he'd learned it quickly, and that had saved his life many times. But it had also helped him see where and when he could set up an attack among the groups, like the shadow he'd become, and take them out. The more he knew, the better. He knew Sarah wasn't ready to go there. She was just trying to survive the first couple of weeks after getting shot. Never mind she'd killed Brian. Even though he was scum, he knew no one in law enforcement wanted to pull a trigger unless it was absolutely necessary.

His heart turned to Sarah. She was sleeping deeply now, her breath shallow and slow. She was relaxed, and he felt good about that. Surprised that she'd asked him to sleep at her side, he smiled a little to himself. Sarah might be going through a helluva lot right now, but she was no wilting lily. It took a set of cojones to ask him for something like this. Yes, this woman was a real warrior, an equal, and she saw him as being trustworthy. That made his heart soar. Trust, he knew from the loss of his marriage, either was there or it wasn't.

Tiredness drizzled through him. It had been a rough day. And a rougher night, mostly for Sarah. Her nearness fed him, allowing him to relax to a point. They had King, who would be their alarm should he hear anything out of the ordinary. There was a pistol in his bed-stand drawer, a bullet in the chamber, the safety on. He had gone years with a pistol that had no safety on it, a SEAL weapon, and he was used to having one around. Sarah wasn't and didn't like the idea of the safety being off, and he honored her request. Dawson had no qualms about defending themselves. It was just a question of how many of the Elsons were coming.

Terror sizzled through him as he thought about attack strategies to get to this cabin. The Elson boys, as he'd heard Sarah say, were expert hunters and trackers. What he didn't know was how many brains they shared between them. They were known drug smugglers and addicts. Drugs ate away a person's brain over time. How many brain cells did they have left? They were like animals, stripped of their humanity, ruthless, with no morals or values except the ones they lived by. Was one of them kinder or more benevolent than the others? Or were they all cold, hard killers? He didn't know, and that bothered him greatly. Understanding he had a deep learning curve to catch up with, Dawson drew in a deep, ragged breath, trying to force himself to stop thinking.

Sympathy for David and Emily Carter drenched him. What must they be going through? Did fear for their remaining daughter eat them alive, keeping them awake at night, too? He couldn't begin to know what they were going through, but he was very sure Lane's murder was staring them in the eyes right now. And then, to know that the Elson boys would try to find Sarah, no matter how long it took? The Carter family lived in a special hell, gripped by terror for their only surviving daughter.

Life wasn't fair, he thought bitterly. Not at all. Good people had bad things happen to them, just as it was happening right now to the Carters. The grannies were probably equally upset, having lived through Lane's sudden loss. Sleep probably didn't come easily to them either. He was glad Gertie had hired a security firm; that's what it would take to be protected, because Lincoln County just didn't have the funds or the manpower to deal with something like this.

But through it all? Sarah was carrying all of it and then some on her proud shoulders. If he wanted to know how tough a woman could be, all he had to do was look at the way Sarah was handling all this shit. She blamed herself for letting go of Lane; Dawson understood that far too easily. How did she do it? He'd never seen anyone in a combat situation that carried the past, the present and the future threat within them like Sarah did.

In the days and weeks to come, Dawson knew she would probably talk here and there about what had happened to Lane. He understood the need to unload the terrifying moments and events in one's life. It was healing. And if nothing else, he'd be her touchstone; someone she could have near her who lent her an aura of healing and protection. A person who was a role model, someone she aspired to be like. Or someone who had a quality, such as his calmness amid calamity, she didn't have, but that she saw it in him and therefore helped her remain calmer. Knowing he helped her emotionally in ways, that she was coming to rely on him more and more, meant the world to him.

Dawson liked thinking of himself as Sarah's touchstone, but really, she was *his* touchstone. He wished with all his heart there would come a time when they'd have time to explore each other deeply. Instinctively, he knew it would bind them even more tightly together.

# CHAPTER SIXTEEN

*June 23*

Sarah drowsily opened her eyes. Sunlight was bright and slanting around the edges of the curtains at the window, telling her it was well past her normal time to wake up. The covers were tucked in around her and she felt warm and cozy, a wonderful sense of peace flowing through her. Pulling her arm from beneath the blanket and sheet, she pushed a few strands of hair from her brow and eye. What time was it?

On the heels of that question, she suddenly remembered her nightmare. Was everything that followed a dream? Unsure, she slowly sat up, the bedclothes settling around her hips as she looked around the room. King wasn't in the room either, and the door was shut. Glancing at the clock, she blinked, surprised. It was nine a.m. She never slept in that late!

Pulling the blankets aside, the lingering

scent of Dawson surrounded her. Had she dreamed it? Or was it real? She was so groggy, her brain misfiring as she struggled to get back online, she pulled herself over to the edge of the bed. Her crutches were within easy reach. Instinctively, she inhaled his unique male scent again, realizing it hadn't been a dream at all. That discovery stirred her body and her heart to life. Dawson had held her, slept with her. So many new signals raced through her, reminding her she was a woman with needs. Rubbing her hands across her face, her toes touching the braided rug, she remembered everything about their conversation. Her mind wasn't firing on all cylinders like it was supposed to since she'd been shot. She knew from her PTSD that there were days after a firefight when she wasn't completely together, her mind not working then either. Sarah had learned to respect the power of shock and how it snarled a person's mind, emotions and reality for days, weeks, sometimes, for years after the incident.

Getting shot put a whole new layer on her mind and emotions she hadn't anticipated. It was bringing lurid nightmares, of Brian Elson knocking the door open and her landing on her ass. He was a strong, bull-like male on drugs that had made him think he was superhuman. She sat there, allowing her hands to fall into her lap. When would she feel whole again? Would she ever? Was this what people struggled with when they'd been wounded? None of her friends in the military had spoken of such things; they probably thought it would make them seem weak if they revealed where they were in their healing process.

It was then, as she stared at the bed stand, that she spotted a handwritten note next to the clock. Why hadn't she seen it right away? That scared her; in her life as sheriff, so much depended upon her ability to absorb myriad details at a crime scene or a standoff in one sweeping gaze. Reaching out, she picked it up.

Sarah, King and I are out doing some recon within a mile of the cabin. I left some scrambled eggs and fresh-baked biscuits for you in the kitchen. You can warm them up in the microwave. We'll be gone at least two hours, so don't worry about us. Dawson.

She saw the heart he'd drawn in front of his scrawled name at the bottom of the note. *A heart.* What did that mean? What did she want it to mean? He'd also put the time he'd left: 7:30 a.m. They'd return to the cabin in another half hour or so.

Muddled, her emotions in disarray, she set the note aside and used her crutches to stand up. Time for a shower and some clean clothes. She had her work cut out for her, hating that she was so damned helpless. And as she swung toward the door, her heart took off with yearning. Wanting Dawson. But it wasn't about wanting safety. It was about her hormones, her heart confused since he'd lain beside her. There was no question he could be trusted. He'd never touched her inappropriately. He'd followed her instructions. Yes, he was a rare man among men nowadays, she acknowledged. Reaching for the doorknob, Sarah could hardly wait until he and King came back to the cabin.

Dawson turned off the alarm before opening the cabin door. He didn't know what to expect as he entered. King's paws clacked on the wooden floor, heading straight into the kitchen to the left of him.

"Hey," he greeted Sarah, not wanting to scare her. He knew silence could jolt her in a bad way. She was standing at the counter, putting the finishing touches on the breakfast he'd made for her much earlier. She looked like a civilian, dressed in dark green slacks that outlined her tall, firm body, not a sheriff. He was happy to see the brace on her leg. The pink T-shirt she wore, with capped sleeves, complemented the shining ginger hair framing her face. He saw her lift her chin and cut a look in his direction, her hands stilling over the plate of food for a moment.

"You're just in time, Dawson." She gestured to the coffeepot on the counter. "I just made fresh coffee. Want a cup?"

He ambled over after settling his baseball cap on a wooden peg near the door. "Sure. Let me pour the coffee and I'll take the mugs over to the table."

"That would be nice; thanks."

He watched her trying to decide what was the best way to take the plate over to the table, given she had two crutches. The consternation at her predicament was in her expression. This was a woman who didn't like being hobbled in any way, shape or form. He couldn't blame her. Moving to her side, he said, "I'll take the plate over for you. Go sit down and get comfy." She had just washed her hair, some of the strands golden, others crimson, all against a background of dark brunette. The lights above the sink made them stand out.

"Thanks. When do you think I can get off these crutches? I really detest them."

"Not soon enough, obviously," he teased, flashing her a grin. Sarah was getting better at turning around utilizing them. Practice made perfect. He noted the sour look on her face, knowing she was miserable.

At the table, he pulled the chair out for her and set the plate down. He took her crutches and leaned them against the wall after she sat down. "You're looking good this morning. Have a good night's sleep?" Then he brought over the creamer and sugar bowl to her and settled into the chair at her right elbow.

"I slept so deeply," she admitted, sliding the white linen napkin across her lap and then picking up her spoon. Slanting him a grateful glance, she added, "Thanks to you." The sugar and cream went into her coffee and she stirred it.

He sipped his steaming black brew, studying her over the top of his mug. Swallowing, he said, "I'm glad you asked me to stay with you, Sarah. That took guts. We haven't known each other very long, and the time we've shared has been nothing but high-stress, life-and-death situations."

"I know," she said between bites of the fluffy scrambled eggs. Shrugging lightly, she

334

said, "I guess I trusted you from the get-go."

"Your intuition about people leading you to that conclusion?"

Nodding, she picked up one of the large biscuits and pulled it open, steam escaping. "I know that was a pretty bold request on my part. You didn't even look shocked by it."

"You've always spoken what's on your mind. That's one of the many things I like about you." He saw her cheeks flush endearingly. The sheriff game face didn't exist between them right now, and he was glad. "Look," he said, his voice lowering, "I understood where you were at, Sarah. After you told me what happened to Lane, your request wasn't out of the ordinary. People who are traumatized need a little comforting. I was glad I could be there for you."

"I've never asked anyone to do something like that for me before, Dawson."

"You were fragile. We all get that way when shit happens. I saw it a lot in Afghanistan, and I'm sure you did, too. Sometimes, I could help a friend, sometimes I couldn't. Some people close up, bury their reactions to trauma. Others unload them, reach out and ask for help. That's what you did, as far as I'm concerned. You can tell me I'm off

335

on my assessment."

She opened a jar of apricot jam and covered her knife with it, then slathered it across the biscuit. "No, you're right on target. I've never opened up to anyone like I did to you last night. I think it's because we've had a good connection ever since we met. I asked you because I trusted you. I knew you'd do the right thing for the right reasons. I didn't have to explain myself because I knew how deeply intuitive you are. Plus, we share a common background in the military."

He watched her take a small bite of the biscuit. "Our connection has been there from the time we met, and it's gotten stronger with time. We're a lot alike in many ways. More than you realize. You almost died a few days ago, and that's what precipitated your finally telling someone what happened to your sister. No one knows the power of almost dying until it happens to them. And then skeletons from our closet come to the surface, whether we want them to or not."

"You're right," she rasped, setting the biscuit on her plate. "I didn't understand it. I mean, I've seen people killed. I saw my friends die or be wounded when I was in the military. But until it happened to me? I didn't understand the full ramifications of how it would affect me. I really didn't. And no one was telling me how they felt when they got hit over in Afghanistan. You know how closemouthed military people are. They're afraid they'll be seen as not being able to take it."

"Yeah," he groused. "And it wounds us all over again. We pay a double price for it."

She pushed her fork around in the eggs. "I'm not sorry I asked you to stay with me last night."

"Me neither."

"I felt like glass inside. Like I was going to shatter into a million pieces and never be able to put myself back together again. I've never felt that way before, except for when Lane was kidnapped."

"That's exactly what it feels like, Sarah."

"How do you know so much about it?" she demanded. "Sometimes I wonder if you read my mind. I really do. If it wasn't you, if I didn't trust you, Dawson, like I do? I'd run as far and fast away from you as I could get."

He gave her a nod. "Yeah, well, it looks like we both carry some heavy family secrets, Sarah. I wasn't intending on telling you, though. You've got enough to handle right now. You don't need my sad story on top of it."

Tilting her head, she whispered, "I need to know, Dawson."

The burning look in her green eyes told him of the solemn request she'd just made. "I can tell you at any time. Aren't you feeling a little fragile this morning?"

"No. I feel a lot stronger and more confident. I think in part because I finally vomited up all my feelings over losing Lane. How I blamed myself for it happening. Growing up afterward, I carried that heavy guilt around with me 24/7/365. I never talked about it to anyone. That grief takes all your energy, and you feel so crushed and weakened by what happened. When my parents didn't blame me for losing the fight with Jethro, it drove my feelings even more deeply inside, so that I never, until just now, spoke to anyone about it. I was just so ashamed of myself. I couldn't save Lane, as much as I wanted to. . . ."

"Yeah, shame is one of the most damaging emotions we own as human beings," he agreed, grim. "Look, I'd like to table this talk with you until later. At a better time? Right now, I have a lot of things I need to discuss with you," and he pulled a small notebook from the pocket of his chambray shirt.

"Sure, I'm up for it."

"Try to finish your breakfast," he urged, giving her a somewhat pleading look. Sarah was losing weight, which wasn't abnormal in this kind of situation, but he felt it was up to him to cajole her into getting back on her feed. "It'll give you more energy. Your brain will work better." He saw a flash of frustration come and go in her green eyes, knowing he'd hit the right words when she picked up her fork and ate whether she was hungry or not. She was a fighter.

He got up and walked to his bedroom, returning with a white poster board. After she'd eaten, he cleared the table and placed it in front of her. Leaning over, his shoulder close to hers, he used a black marker to draw in the cabin with a huge circle around it, plus the only entrance/exit point dirt road leading to it. Capping the marker, he placed it back in his pocket.

"I did some serious recon work this morning," and he ran his finger around the circle. "We both know one or more of the Elson boys will try to make good on their threat."

"Yes, and if he or all of them do? They'll kill me. I don't fool myself about this situation."

"Nor do I," he said heavily, seeing the darkness come to her eyes. "That's why

339

King and I did our walk this morning. As soon as it got light, we took off." He opened his small notebook. "I've made some notes, using my GPS, so I know where each area is. In recon work, you look at the geography and figure out where the enemy is most likely going to go. Every area has places that are hard to access: a hill, a lot of rocks or a cliff, for example. Even the enemy will look at the land and try to find the path of least resistance. What they're thinking is that once they find and kill you, they want a swift, easy way out of the area. They want to be able to run back to their vehicle and escape without being detected."

"I hadn't thought of that," Sarah admitted, eyeing his notebook with appreciation.

"You weren't a trained recon Marine," he said, giving her a tight smile. "But we're going to turn this land around the cabin into an advantage for us, not the Elsons."

"I don't think all three of them will attack us, Dawson."

"Why?"

"It's Hiram, the oldest, who'll probably take this revenge on himself. He's the oldest in the family and he'll take over where his father left off. He's the leader of a drug gang. The other two boys, Kaen and Elisha, work pretty independently of each other and avoid Hiram. There's some bad blood between him and the two younger boys. They got into continual fistfights as kids all the way through school. It looked like survival of the fittest, or maybe three junkyard dogs going at one another's throats to challenge the leader of the pack. My gut tells me it will be Hiram who'll try to find out where I am and then attack. He's got a gang he can call on to do just that."

"How many men?"

"Last count, which was last month? Ten men. All druggies. We've got criminal records on all of them."

"And Hiram can order them to do something like that?"

She snorted. "Oh, for sure. He's a monster, worse than his father, actually. Brian was more or less reining him in so he wouldn't stir up any trouble in Lincoln County. Brian once told me, 'A dog doesn't shit in its own backyard.' He thought about that, and made sure his sons, with the exception of Cree, didn't stir up law enforcement here. Hiram spreads destruction everywhere he goes. He thinks nothing of punching his soldiers. He's even more violent and unstable than Brian was. His favorite drug is cocaine, and he's jacked up on it more often than not."

"Maybe Cade can get me a file on him?"

"I'll Skype him as soon as we're done here, ask him to have it ready for you next time you go into town."

He saw the stubborn strength in her expression. Sarah was a warrior, no question. He had her full attention, her focus laserlike, which was something that always separated out the warriors from the peacemakers. She wanted to be a part of understanding what he'd seen this morning, and Dawson knew she'd be able to offer good suggestions to support his own ideas for a defense around the cabin. Bridled anger was palpable within her, and he knew she was not only fearful but also angry at becoming hunted by another Elson. Sarah's strength had been born of tragedy and the loss of her little sister, and it had welded strongly to her soul. He saw the bitterness and fortitude coupled with grit in her expression. She was going to fight back. She was no victim. And she knew how to use a weapon. All necessary skills when dealing with the vengeful Elson family.

Sarah was sitting at the computer in the electronics room after lunch when a Skype call pinged. Dawson had gone into town, wanting to take the plan they'd settled on earlier to her father for advice and ideas. She saw it was her Grandma Gertie and quickly connected them.

"Hi, Gertie. What a nice surprise!" She saw her grandmother's very somber expression. "Is everything all right?"

"No, things aren't," she said gruffly. "I was over at your parents' when Dawson dropped by."

"Oh, that's good. Did you stay to see the plan he's forming for us here at the cabin?"

"Yes," she muttered. "And we had a long, involved talk about it, Sarah. Further, Cade dropped by, and we all found out Hiram is gathering his gang again. That's not a good sign. Cade said someone overheard Hiram bragging at Kassie's Café that he was going to come hunting you."

Her heart tightened in her chest. "Dawson and I expected that."

"Cade told them the other two boys wouldn't have anything to do with it. They're backing off. Smart little bastards, for once."

Grinning unevenly, Sarah said, "That's one way of putting it. So? It's Hiram and his gang who are going to try to find me?"

Nodding, Gertie scowled deeply. "I listened to the plan Dawson drew up with your input. Your father added some good ideas to it, and Cade did, too." Opening her hands, Gertie growled, "The only thing missing from all of this is, you don't have two nickels to rub together to make it work. Cade said the budget for the sheriff's department was low and they couldn't afford to put money into it."

"Yes," Sarah said, "because we have people leaving the county. Our budget this year was ten percent less than last year's."

Testily, Gertie said, "I told all of 'em it's about time you let me help out."

Brows moving up, she said, "But we've always let you help us."

"No, no, I didn't mean in *that* way. Cade made a very good suggestion. He wants motion sensors put a mile away from the cabin. Anything that moves will be sent to a computer inside, so you know someone's approaching, as well as at a computer in the sheriff's department."

"We had that idea too, but it would be much too expensive to do, Gertie."

"That's what Dawson said, but I raised Cain. Cade told us there were several types of motion sensors on the market. Some had a light that would flash on if it detected movement, others just sent a silent alarm to the computer. The one I liked? It had a video chip in it, and not only would you be alerted that there was an intruder? You could see and identify them. And the video sent it immediately to the computers as well as law enforcement."

"Yes, but those are horribly expensive, Gertie. There's no way we could afford them."

Shaking her finger, Gertie bit out, "I'm worth millions, Sarah. I can afford however many of them you need." She leaned forward, her mouth set as she stared at Sarah. "You're going to let me make a donation to the sheriff's department for however many of these monitors you need to make that place safe for you to heal up in. I'm not takin' any guff from you or anyone on it either. I already had it out with David and Cade. Right now? Dawson is putting in the order via your department. The video motion sensors will be sent by courier to my ranch. I just got done talking to Ray Paulson, the Forest Service supervisor. He's going to loan us a USFS truck. He felt it would look less noticeable if it came and went from your cabin because everyone knows the forest service owns it. I donated a goodly sum to him for the use of it. We can haul those boxes to the cabin without raising any eyebrows or suspicion."

"Wow," she murmured, "you've been

moving at the speed of light, Gertie!"

Gertie's face wrinkled up, her eyes blazing. Lifting her finger, she waved it toward Sarah. "You listen here. We already lost Lane, and it's broken our family. We're not going to lose you, too, Sarah. It's just not gonna happen. Not as long as I breathe, it won't. I have the money. And I'm not taking it with me. So buying those monitors isn't a big deal for me. I don't want you worrying about this. Right now, you need all the help you can get. I know you get your dander up and you won't ask for help. But that's all changed now."

Sarah heard the pain in Gertie's voice and, as always when Lane was mentioned, it scored her heart once more, too. She saw tears in her grandmother's eyes and understood why she was weighing in on protecting her from Hiram Elson's gang. "Thank you," she whispered unsteadily. "You're right, and I appreciate whatever you can do to help us through this hell we're having to walk through. I'm not going to throw a temper tantrum over you donating those monitors. In fact, it relieves me. I have the dog, King, and Dawson. Both are the best at what they do. But they aren't perfect, and they aren't mind readers. Nor can we be sure they'll be aware of Hiram's coming until it's too late."

Grumpily, she stared at Sarah. "Well, it's gonna be my way this time."

"I hear you," she told her softly, her heart squeezing with old pain, memories and grief. "I truly appreciate what you're doing, Gertie."

"Well," she muttered, "if I had my way about it, I'd be putting you on an airplane for parts unknown, as far away from Wyoming as you could get to heal up and get back on your feet. And then, come home to deal with the Elsons once again."

She felt Gertie's anguish and worry. "You know I can't do that."

"I don't like it either, Sarah. You're in constant danger. This isn't gonna let up, and we all know the Elsons are filled with hatred. If I thought I could force you to go away, I would. The people of this county voted you in as their sheriff, and that's why you can't leave. You have a duty to run the department, regardless. I know that. I don't like it, but I accept it."

"Thanks for understanding. I wouldn't leave, that's true. I can't run a county I'm responsible for thousands of miles away from it. Cade is a great assistant commander, but there are decisions only I can make."

"Oh, I know," she repeated grumpily. "I get it. But I sure don't like it, Sarah. You're all we have left. I know David and Emily are beside themselves over what has happened. It's resurrected Lane's kidnapping and murder all over again. It's never gonna leave us, not any of us."

Gertie was trying to hide her grief, but Sarah knew how much her grandmother had loved her sister. "Well, it's six weeks before I'll be mobile again."

"I just don't see any end to this, Sarah."

The frustration curdled in her throat. "I don't either. We can't pick Hiram up just because we think we know what he's going to do. He has to do something illegal before we can take him in and throw the book at him."

"So that leaves you hanging, and I'm sure you're just as anxious as all of us about your welfare."

She managed a grudging smile. "Just a little, Gertie. Just a little."

"Are you getting sleep at night?"

"Some. I'm still processing so much. I've never killed anyone, and that's bothering me a lot."

"Yet in Afghanistan you were in firefights."

"Yes, but when you're up against a common foe, you don't know whose bullet killed the enemy."

"Oh, I never thought of it that way. I 'spose you're right. What else is ailin' you?"

"Getting shot and nearly dying. If I hadn't been wearing my Kevlar vest, I wouldn't be here."

"Your father was saying the same thing. I'm so glad you wear it. I know some of the deputies won't because it makes you sweaty or chaffs your skin, but they're lookin' for more trouble than they can handle."

"I'd say ninety percent of our people wear them religiously. I think the rest will be wearing them from now on, now that they realize my vest is the only reason I'm still alive."

"Cade was sayin' the whole department is on edge, but you can't blame them. The Elsons have been a thorn in law enforcement's side forever."

"They have," she agreed heavily. "There's just some people who get under our skin and we have to take it."

"There are days when it would be easier to get rat holes like them outta this county. I guess if we lived in a dictatorship, they could be gotten rid of, but in a democracy, that doesn't happen."

"No, it doesn't. Our hands are tied until and unless they break the law."

"Your father, who's one of the mildest, most easygoing people I know, with the exception of this Dawson fella, gets red-faced, angry and barely in control of himself when the name Elson comes up."

"Dad had twenty years of hell dealing with them, that's why. That one family has pulled more law enforcement resources than any thousand people who live in this county."

"They stir up trouble. That's all they know. They're always into creating or fomenting drama of some sort. And if it's too quiet, they start picking fights with their neighbors, just to keep everyone upset and on guard."

"I don't know if it will give you any relief," Sarah said, "to know that there are counties in every state in the Union that have people like the Elsons. We're not the only ones dealing with this type of individual."

"Hmph! Even my chickens and geese are better than they are. A deadbeat family that uses county funds, who are on welfare, and we all know they're probably making millions on the drugs they run."

Sarah laughed a little. "You have the happiest chickens and geese in the world, Gertie!"

Her mouth twitched. "Well, I oughta give you Two Guns Pete. He's the best antiburglar rooster in the world."

Groaning, Sarah sat back and laughed out loud. Holding up her hands, she giggled, "Oh, no! Not Two Guns Pete! Dawson would go crazy if that Rhode Island Red rooster was strutting his stuff around the cabin."

Giggling with her, Gertie said, "Yeah, he's a permanent fixture around here. He's four years old, the cock-of-the-walk and he knows it. But he's the best at alerting the keepers when a coyote, wolf, fox or grizzly is around. He's the first to crow and let everyone know."

Smiling, she said, "You're good for me, Gertie. Thanks for that laugh at Pete's expense. I really needed it."

"Better than cryin', that's for sure. And we've shed enough tears in our family." Gertie gave her a wicked smile. "Just remember, Pete's available in case you want him."

# CHAPTER SEVENTEEN

*July 19*

"Easy now; don't get in too much of a hurry," Dawson coaxed Sarah, amusement in his tone. He kept a hand lightly on her elbow as she walked without the crutches across the living room of the cabin. Several of the screened-in windows were open, and the warm scent of pine flowed in. He saw the determination in Sarah's eyes as she took each step. It was four weeks into her healing process. The doctors had wanted her to start walking at the four-week point, and he was more than glad to be a hand in case she needed one. "Any pain?"

"No . . . just tender," she said in a soft voice. "It just feels good to walk without crutches, believe me."

"The doc's prescription is for you to walk around as much as you want in the cabin. He doesn't want you outside yet on uneven ground." In truth, Sarah had been walking since the third week because she had been going bonkers on those hated crutches. She was like a Thoroughbred horse that had been hitched up to a plow, hating having to remain less than active. He moved to her side and said, "Okay, you're free of me. You walk, and I'll be your shadow if you need support." Dawson understood how important it was to her to be under her own power. Her full lips were compressed, her focus on walking, which everyone took for granted.

Sarah took three more circles around the cabin, even slowly climbing the two stairs that led into the kitchen. She halted after her rounds and sat down on a chair in the living room. "That felt good, but my leg is feeling weak and wobbly now."

Dawson retrieved a glass of ice water from the counter and brought it to her. "You're doing great, but that leg has lost muscle mass and you're going to have to walk to start getting more circulation to start building it back up."

She continued to gently massage her leg beneath the jean fabric. "It's getting stronger every day."

Grinning, he said, "That's because you jumped the gun at three weeks, Ms. Carter. I've been good and not told your doc anything about your decision. Your secrets are safe with me." He saw her cheeks color. Saw the warmth banked in her eyes for him alone. Dawson no longer questioned the building desire percolating daily between them. He saw it in small but significant ways.

"Yeah, well, I want to get out of here, Dawson. I'm going crazy."

"Cabin fever." He looked toward the door. "If you'll wear your brace tomorrow? I'll take you outside. There's a nice, pretty even path that leads to the garage out back. Maybe we can start doing that and get you feeling like you're no longer in a prison." Relief came to her expression, and his heart instantly expanded with a wealth of need for her in every possible way. Despite the threat of Hiram and his gang finding them, he was contending with his own growing feelings for her. The last weeks had allowed them to acknowledge their relationship, although they'd never talked about it directly. Sarah was the kind of person who never made a move before thinking long and hard about it. Unlike him, which had gotten him into a quickie marriage, mistaking lust for love. He wouldn't make that mistake again, content to go at her pace, which was sane compared to his when he was twenty-two years old.

"That sounds so good," she murmured, leaning back in the chair, drinking deeply of the ice water.

Nothing Sarah did was wasted on him. Since the night he'd lain in her bed, she'd not asked him to do it again. Considering the vice in which they were held by Hiram Elson, he wasn't surprised. The talk and tears about Lane had given Sarah a belated gift. Now she had started sleeping better and longer. A sign that what they'd shared that night was healing for her. It made him feel a silent euphoria that warmed his heart. Their growing intimacy was leading them more closely together. Besides, even if they both wanted to make love, it couldn't be done due to her leg. Waiting, in an interesting way to Dawson, was worth it. They each savored the small things between them, the touch of a hand, an embrace and, sometimes, her softened look that shook him to his soul, letting him know just how much he was falling in love with Sarah. But that awareness wasn't spoken out loud. Understanding the threat, that would become a distraction. No, he wouldn't jeopardize themselves for the sake of what his heart already knew. In the future, somewhere, he could share it with Sarah.

"How about I get a tub of water ready and you can soak? That always helps your leg loosen up after these walking sessions."

"Thanks, that sounds good."

"You still thirsty?" and he went over to retrieve the emptied glass.

"No." She gave him an appreciative look. "Can you stay a minute before you go get my bath ready for me? I need to say something to you."

Hesitating, he heard that low, husky tone of hers, realizing whatever it was, was personal. "Sure," and he placed the glass down on the lamp table next to where he sat.

Sarah inhaled a deep breath and let it go as she held his gaze. She unclasped her hands in her lap. "These last weeks here with you have been a gift to me in every way, Dawson. There's something truly good between us." She pushed strands away from her cheek. "Maybe I'm being too bold, but I like what we have. What we're building toward. I just need to know how you feel about us."

He didn't smile, maintained a serious face. "I've always liked your boldness. And it's not one-sided, Sarah. It never has been. I like where we are with each other despite Elson and his gang threatening you."

"Then? It's mutual?"

Shrugging, he said, "Do you want to go for the long run and see where it goes between us?" Dawson knew now that Sarah wasn't one to pussyfoot around anything. She was strong on communication, and he was learning to be, having lost a marriage to being a clam.

"Yes. But I don't know what that end will be."

"I don't either, but I'm willing to find out. How about you?"

She gave him a worried look. "This is all happening at the wrong time."

"I don't know about that. When two people are drawn to each other, it might be the best thing possible, even if there's a threat surrounding them." He halted and searched her green eyes that reminded him of the forest trees. "This situation has pushed us together, but I don't read that as bad."

"You've been babysitting me."

"I haven't minded, Sarah, because I've always liked you." Her eyes widened a bit, and she sat back, seeming to assess his answer. She had a habit, he'd discovered, of absorbing the other person's communication, digesting it before responding. He waited, seeing tumult in her expression.

"What if . . . what if we're drawn to each other just because of the threat? That after it's over, we won't have that special connection I always feel when you're around me?"

"I'm game to find out if you are." He gestured toward the door. "This threat isn't going to last forever. Are you willing?"

"Yes . . ." and her mouth crooked. "I have another confession to make, and it's one you should know about. I don't believe in not coming clean with a partner who's investing his time and care in me."

Dawson heard the regret and apology in her husky tone. "We haven't exactly gotten to do much talking on a personal level. It took two weeks to install all those monitors around the cabin."

"I know, and you were working from sunrise to sundown." She gave him a fond look. "We're both walking on eggshells every day. But I wanted to let you know about my past. I fell in love at twenty-five with Steve Coris. He was a deputy here in Lincoln County. My dad ran the department and I was learning how to take over from him someday if the voters would have me. He'd already put in for retirement and I wanted to try to take his place." She leaned forward, gently massaging her thigh for a moment. Lifting her hands, she sat back, staring at

Dawson for a long moment. "I'd sworn never to fall in love with a military man because I saw so many of them killed or wounded. I made a real effort to stay clear of any serious relationships while in the Marine Corps."

"But things changed when you got out and came home?"

"Yes . . . yes, they did. I guess I was a lot lonelier, without a partner in my life, than I realized. I wasn't interested in a man who wanted me to stay home and cook and housekeep. I wasn't that woman. And while I felt it was important to have a family, it just didn't fit into the life and career I wanted in law enforcement."

"How did you and Steve meet?" he asked gently, seeing the strain around her mouth, the sadness in her eyes.

"At a Fourth of July dance over at Maud and Steve Whitcomb's ranch. They always throw a countywide celebration, and it was my first year home from the Corps." She smiled hesitantly, her gaze shifting off into space. "I was up at the bar and he turned and had a mug of beer in his hand. I was standing too close and the beer went all over me." She laughed softly. "Steve turned red as a beet. He was so stunned, and then apologetic. He offered to drive me home to get cleaned up, which I thought was sweet. He didn't know who I was because I'd just come onto the force."

"Helluva meeting," Dawson noted drily. Sarah looked happy in that moment, girlish almost. There was no question she'd fallen in love with Steve. So what had happened? He stilled his impatience.

"It was. I drove home, and he followed me in his truck. I was touched by his sensitivity and caring. That's important to me in a man, Dawson." She studied him for a long moment and finally said, "Steve was killed a year from our first meeting on a domestic argument call."

Brows dipping, he murmured, "I'm sorry, Sarah."

"It totaled me in a new way. He was my first serious relationship. We'd just gotten engaged when it happened. After that, I threw myself into shadowing my father's duties and lost myself in the politics of running for sheriff a couple of years later."

"That had to be rough on you."

"I worked twelve to fourteen hours a day, exhausted myself and dropped into bed to sleep. I guess I ran from the grief; tried to outrun it, maybe." She grew silent. "I'm drawn to you, Dawson. It just happened. I wasn't looking to get into another relationship at all. This scares the hell out of me."

"Why?"

"Because of Hiram and his gang. He could come find us, shoot up this cabin with AK-47s, kill one or both of us."

"That's made you afraid to reach out for another potential relationship?"

Nodding, she opened her hands and met his gaze. "Yes, it has. I guess I've learned so often that life is tenuous at best. That you can lose people you love in the blink of an eye."

"Life isn't for the faint of heart," he agreed. "Let me tell you a true story. I guess it's confession time between us."

"Okay," she ventured, tilting her head, curious. "Tell me."

"I fell in love with Lucia Steward when I was twenty-two. We had a whirlwind romance and married a month later. Then I got deployed to Afghanistan for three years in a row, with three months stateside with her and then got redeployed once more. I was acquiring PTSD at the time, but I didn't realize it. I'd come home to Camp Pendleton in Southern California and I couldn't talk to Lucia. We got into terrible fights all the time. She accused me of not loving her, because if I did, I'd talk with her, share what was bothering me, stuff like that."

"So many marriages break up over the man or woman coming home with PTSD," she said sadly.

"Mine was one of them. We divorced when I was twenty-five. It was an awful time for both of us. I realized later how my inability to talk to her, to let her into what I'd seen and done in Afghanistan, had been the reason. But I couldn't open up. I knew she wouldn't understand and God, I had no way of trying to tell her about it because you can't." With a one-shouldered shrug, he muttered, "At least I couldn't. So it was my failure and my fault. It wasn't Lucia's because she was hurt and angry. But at that time, I was beyond helping her or myself."

"That's so sad."

"The other part of it was that I was confused about lust and love."

"None of us are mind readers and most of us aren't self-aware enough to realize something like that in our early twenties."

He smiled a little, meeting her gaze. "My parents were right: age would give me maturity. I look back on that time in my life and realize it wasn't really love I was feeling for Lucia. I saw real love between some of my friends and their wives when we came off deployment and went back to Camp Pendleton. My parents had that same kind of love, too." He opened his hands and stared down at them for a moment. "A lot of little things tell me the difference between lust and love. I know the difference now . . ." And he loved Sarah but withheld the words. She wasn't ready for it, although he suspected she already knew how he felt toward her. Neither of them wanted to cross that bridge right now. But life was nebulous, in the moment. It seemed there was nothing they could count on from one hour to the next. All that stood between them and death was King and those monitors. It was a tenuous life they were living, and because of their military background, they remained silent.

*July 29*
Dawson's gaze swept around the area as Sarah walked with renewed confidence on her wounded leg. She still wore the brace but from the third week onward threw away the crutches and forced her weakened leg to get stronger every day. Sunlight slanted here and there down on the forest floor as she walked to the garage and then followed another trail back toward the cabin. Neither of them wanted to leave the safety of the

immediate area. Of late, according to Cade, the Elson gang had seemed to disappear from the county radar. No one knew where they'd gone. It had been a quiet week, and he wasn't feeling good about it.

Trying to put the threat aside, he followed Sarah, who was going at a good, fast hiking walk. She walked once every hour outdoors, and he could see the positive change in her as a result. An epiphany of sorts. Sweeping the tree-studded area, he watched for anything out of place, any unusual movement, but saw nothing. King was walking alongside Sarah, happily panting, glad to be taking these hourly circuits. Both dog and woman were type As who breathed in movement, action and forward motion. Smiling a little, he hung back, wearing a pistol on his belt. Dawson never went outside without it.

He had a go-bag stashed just inside the door of the cabin, should they be attacked or if the monitors went off and they had to make a run for it. There wasn't a night that went by, as he lay in his bed, hands behind his head, that he didn't consider escape routes should Hiram and his men attack them. Fortunately, there were two doors to the cabin, and the windows were large and opened. His mind went over these routes until he had them memorized. He didn't tell Sarah about them because he wanted her to focus on getting well. She had enough to do, working with Cade, overseeing many different aspects that needed her attention. No, better he do it, because he was recon. There were days when he left the cabin and King with Sarah and jogged up and down the slope, searching for points where they could run to escape if necessary. If she knew how much work he'd done in that arena, she'd probably have stressed out over it. He had planned a number of different escape points and trails to take if they were attacked.

There wasn't a night that went by when he didn't hear Sarah get up, go to the bathroom down the hall, then walk out to the kitchen. King would follow her wherever she went. Once he'd realized who it was, he'd remained in his bedroom. Sarah needed time to herself. Time to think, to feel and to heal. King was with her, so he fought the urge to get up and go out there, too. If Sarah wanted to talk with him, she would have knocked on his door and asked to come in. But she hadn't.

He looked down at the watch in his hand, timing her circuits. She was really pushing herself now. Although her femur had healed, it still wasn't solid. But she insisted, every time she did her rounds, she'd do an extra one, push herself faster and farther. Dawson cautioned her about wanting to jog instead of walk. Her bone wasn't strong enough yet to deal with the jarring impact of running; there was no sense in possibly fracturing it again. It was just too soon, he told her. Then he'd see the flash of anger and her impatience, walking around to blow off her emotions. Sarah wanted out of this self-imposed hiding, wanted to go back home, but she couldn't. Not yet. Cade had told her it was too dangerous. They were trying to find Hiram breaking the law so they could incarcerate him.

Frustration curdled in his throat as he watched Sarah and the dog round the corner of the cabin. He felt as if everything was in suspended animation. Cade was cautioning her to remain at the cabin another two weeks. He wanted her at 100 percent when returning to her job. Further, he voiced his trepidation over Hiram's disappearance. No one had seen him, and it wasn't as if the deputies and others hadn't scouted all of his known hidey-holes. Elson had vanished and so had his gang, and Dawson was damned uneasy. Constantly scanning the area, the cabin entirely enclosed by thick forest, he keyed his hearing.

The use of the Forest Service truck had been a godsend, camouflaging their whereabouts. Where had the bastard gone? Where?

*July 30*
The beep, beep, beeping of the monitor picking up movement, cut through Dawson's sleep. Instantly, he jerked upward, and yanked the bedroom door open and hurried down the hall to the office. Opening it, he wiped his eyes of sleep, staring hard at the computer screen. His heart banged once. It revealed Hiram Elson and at least eight men in militia-style guerilla clothing, skulking through the dark. They all wore night vision goggles.

He heard Sarah opening the door to her room across from the office. Turning, he saw her in the soft lighting, torn from sleep, wiping her eyes.

"Is it Elson?" she demanded huskily, peering at the screen, standing next to him.

"Yeah. I can see nine of them."

"How far away?"

He looked at the monitor that was taping them. "That's the farthest out. I'd say a mile from our cabin."

She let out a rough sigh. "Then we have time to get out."

Turning, he said, "Yes. Get dressed. Get

your go-bag. I'm going to harness King. I'll get our weapons from my bedroom locker."

Nodding, she turned carefully, not wanting to put too many demands on her just-healed leg. "Okay. I'll see you in a few minutes."

Dawson heard the concealed terror in her voice, saw her wrestling with the fact that Elson was so near and with the intent of killing her. He quickly hit an alert switch on the keyboard that connected him directly with Dispatch at the sheriff's office. In as few words as he could, he gave the GPS coordinates where Elson was, and the direction he was heading. The video feed was also going directly into Dispatch. There had been plans in place from the get-go, with not only the sheriff's office in Lincoln being alerted, but also the Teton office as well. They had a SWAT team that would deploy immediately. They were going to need every bit of manpower they could gather, going up against AK-47s and eight or more men who would fight back, wanting to kill everyone they could. Grimly, he signed off, hurrying out into his bedroom.

Sarah and he had practiced this egress every day. They had special clothing and boots, along with holsters holding Glock 18s with the safety off and a bullet in the chamber. Their go-bags were camouflaged knapsacks they'd wear. Most important, they each had level 2 Kevlar vests they'd wear. He even had a vest to protect King. His hands moved with muscle memory as he hauled on a black T-shirt, his vest, and the camouflaged twill shirt with long sleeves. Next came the trousers, the dark green thick socks and his boots. Turning, he went to the weapons closet and opened it. Inside were AR-15s with two vests that held the extra ammo magazines. Shouldering them, he hurried down the hall, knocking briefly on Sarah's partly opened door.

She was sitting on the bed, swiftly lacing up her boots. Her hair was in a ponytail and she was wearing a floppy bucket hat, infrared goggles hanging around her neck. Dawson was glad Sarah had been trained in combat in the Corps; she wasn't going to be some frightened, hysterical, out-of-her-mind civilian who wasn't used to this kind of threat or stress. She would be steady and reliable.

He set the rifles near the door, butts resting on the floor. Affixing his earpiece, the mic close to his lips, he made sure it was snapped onto the epaulet on his left shoulder. Turning it on, he saw Sarah stand.

"Radio check," he told her.

Nodding, her radio and mic already in place, she said, "Test . . . test."

"Copy that. We're good to go." He saw the holster around her waist, the Glock in the black nylon holster, a strap around her upper thigh to keep it in the position she needed for a fast draw.

"Help me on with the knapsack?" and she hauled it off the bed where she'd thrown it earlier. Every minute was precious. Sarah knew Elson would move as fast as he could. They didn't have time for anything but getting out of the cabin.

"Yeah," Dawson said, coming over and lifting it from her hands. "Turn around . . ." and he quickly slid it up and settled it on her shoulders and back. She was just as fast at buckling the nylon across the top of her breasts and around her waist, stabilizing the go-bag so it wouldn't flop around and make noise. He worried about her leg. They couldn't walk; they'd have to run. Would her leg stand up to such a beating? Would it fracture again, leaving her helpless and unable to escape? The dark possibilities surged through him. As he settled his own go-bag into place on his back, rapidly tightening and locking the straps into place, he saw her shadowed face, the set of her lips, the narrowing of her eyes. She was all business.

It gave him hope.

King was sitting nearby. He had placed the Kevlar body vest on the dog earlier, had a six-foot leash and he was ready, ears standing up, eyes glinting. At that moment, Dawson thought he looked more like a hound from hell than a Belgian Malinois. He felt good about having King with them.

"I'm ready," Sarah said into the mic.

"Let's go," he said, gesturing for her to follow him. He wasn't about to let her out the door first. And he didn't care if she got pissed or not. As they moved swiftly across the living room, Dawson felt his heart contract with terror and something else he'd never thought he'd feel again: love. What a hell of a time to feel it. He pushed the brim of his baseball cap up and settled his night vision goggles into place over his eyes. The infrared set would hang around his neck, should he need them instead. Sarah halted and did the same. They had two sets on them. One was the grainy green NVG to see through the night so they wouldn't trip and fall over anything. But it would allow them to see anything moving, too. They both flicked a small switch that turned them on. He'd used them as a recon with success. Everything would show green, and he allowed his eyes to adjust for a few moments before pulling the door quietly open. Sarah and the dog hugged the wall next to the exit. She had her pistol drawn, just in case. And so did he.

Slipping out into the cold night air, he halted and listened, scenting the night, peering into the darkness, looking for unusual movement. Look for what was out of place; it was a recon's mantra.

"Clear." Dawson had filled Sarah in on recon speak between them. It was short, terse, usually of one syllable. She also knew the silent hand signals they used. When she brought out King, he took the dog's leash, wrapping the leather around his left wrist. Moving down the porch to the corner, he heard Sarah close the door as quietly as possible behind them.

His heart was doing a slow pound. He felt as if he was back in Afghanistan. The stakes were high: life or death. Feeling Sarah's approach behind him, he gave her a hand signal: follow me. And then said, "Seven." He heard her click her radio, meaning she copied. Talk would be held to a bare minimum from here on out.

Leaping off the porch, he headed opposite the way Elson and his men were coming toward them. He'd scouted ten different exit points around the cabin and had familiarized Sarah with them, although she'd never walked them. The direction he was heading was a slope, the ground littered with dry pine needles, which hid the rocks below, a tripping hazard. Hoping she had memorized the trails, he took off at a swift stride.

There really wasn't a path or trail, although Dawson had given each exit point a number. Each headed in a different compass direction. The wind bit at his exposed ears as he forced himself to walk slower for a few minutes. Worried that Sarah's wounded leg would require a warm-up period so she could use it better, he cautioned himself not to jog yet. King strained at his leash, his ears flicking around like radar online. Most of the time, the dog's ears were oriented behind them, and he knew King was picking up on Elson's advance.

How far away were they? How fast were they traveling? He lengthened his stride, the gradient becoming steeper. They were at eight thousand feet, the slope of the mountain cresting at eleven thousand feet. Trees would grow to the ten-thousand-foot line, the last thousand feet nothing but rock and some leftover snow, plus deadly, undetectable ice. Dawson wanted to avoid the ice. One slip from Sarah and she could go down. *Not good.* Keying his hearing, he could hear her mouth breathing. She wasn't far behind him.

They crested a small knoll and Dawson halted, pulling Sarah into him. He could see her concentration, the warrior look in her eyes as she settled beneath his arm around her shoulder.

"I want you to go in front of me." He pressed the radium dials on the GPS he held in his hand. "The trail direction has been set into it. Just keep following it. I'm going to have your six and keep King with me." She was breathing harder now. For six weeks, she hadn't been able to exercise, lift weights or do anything, so she was going to be out of condition. He tightened his arm around her for a moment. "How are you doing?"

"Okay. I'm fine."

"Leg?"

"No issues. I'm warmed up now. I'm going to try to jog. We have to put daylight between us and them."

Dawson couldn't agree more. "I've walked this trail. There's lots of thick pine-needle carpet in this area, and limbs and rocks hidden beneath it. Just do a very slow jog. Lift your boots higher than normal. Nothing fancy. Okay?"

She gazed up at him. "Okay."

The words *I love you* nearly sprang out from between his thinned, tightened lips. They might be killed. Never had Dawson wanted to live more than now. Sarah was leaning into him, trusting him. He couldn't lose her this way. He just couldn't. He released her, and she reached out, grazing his chin with her gloved hand, then moved around him.

For a moment, Dawson stood there, listening. King had turned around, nose pointed up in the air, sniffing in the direction from which Elson was coming. Below him, he could see the cabin surrounded by the trees. There was no movement around it.

*Yet.*

# CHAPTER EIGHTEEN

*July 30*

Sarah lunged up the slope, the pine needles slippery, threatening her balance. They were nearly a half a mile up the slope from the cabin. She had switched the leash from King's collar to his vest. He was pulling her along with his eighty-pound body, helping her with every scrambling step he took. Fearful of falling behind, the terror of knowing Elson was hunting them, had shot adrenaline into her. She knew from combat that adrenaline would shield her from pain, but it wasn't necessarily a good thing with her just-healed femur. Other fears jammed into her mind: slowing Dawson down, leaving them open to Elson's swift-moving gang coming after them. She wasn't keeping up, no matter how much her heart was in it. Her body had six weeks of complacency. Every other day she'd worked out at a gym, and she ran two to three miles at least three times a week to keep in shape. But six weeks off had made her body lax, coupled with that damned broken bone. Feeling the jab of pain every now and then from the bullet wound, Sarah expected to feel that and much more later as they ran for their lives.

King raced forward, tugging her along, his hind legs like steel pistons, digging in. His large paws and claws dug deep into the pine needles, scattering them upward like small explosions with each lunge forward. Without King's support and forward motion, Sarah knew she'd be even further behind Dawson than she already was.

Knowing that the SWAT team from Teton County, and fifteen deputies from there as well, were speeding toward them right now gave her something to grab on to, and hope didn't completely dissipate. Ten of her deputies were heading their way, too. All deputies from both counties would be combat armed, wearing protective vests and Kevlar helmets. Three weeks ago, Teton County had loaned her deputies night vision goggles; her county couldn't afford such a thing. Clinging to hope, knowing it was a race to either die or live, Sarah dug the toes of her boots into the ground, gasping harshly for breath.

Every now and then, Dawson would slow

down and look over his shoulder. But he said nothing. Sarah knew she was slowing him down. *Far too slow.* She was making them an easy target to track. Elson would be able to follow them once he discovered which way they'd gone. It would give them time. How much, she didn't know.

Finally, they came to a stop about ten feet from the crest of the rocky top of the slope. Dawson came back, placing his hand around her right arm. Gasping, she sobbed for breath. He led her over to a grove of evergreens where they could hide while they rested up. Her knees were shaking. Leaning down, hands upon them once they were hidden, she hung her head, trying to catch her breath. Lungs burning, her heart crashing against her ribs like a wild thing that wanted to rip out of it and fly free, she fought to regain her strength.

"How are you doing?" he asked, placing his hand on her shoulder, leaning over, studying her with intensity and missing nothing.

Sarah removed the goggles, allowing them to hang around her neck. "Not as good as I want to be," she managed between gasps. His hand felt comforting and warm. Protective. "I'm sorry, Dawson. . . ."

"It's all right. I think you did a helluva job

climbing that slope. How's your leg feeling?"

"My legs feel really weak. The bullet wound jabs me with pain, but it's bearable. Adrenaline is in play."

Removing his canteen from the side of his waist, he unscrewed it. "Here, drink up. You can't dehydrate now. I'm going to check your wound. I want to make sure it's not bleeding."

Knowing he was right, she straightened, took the aluminum canteen and drank sips between gasps of air. Adrenaline did amazing things for a person's body, increasing their strength, but there was a price to pay for it. Dawson was right to check her wound. The puncture hole was healing from the bottom up, and he had to clean it out every day. It was damned painful every morning, and Sarah hadn't looked forward to it. Puncture wounds would quickly scab over the top, leaving a dark, airless space below it, and bacteria could blossom. Every morning, Dawson had to remove the scab across the top, clean down into the wound hole. If the scab at the top wasn't removed daily so oxygen could get into the wound to allow it to heal, bacteria would set in and the area could become infected.

She felt his hands moving knowingly, carefully, around her wound, gently probing here and there. He then slid his hands below the wound. Drinking more water, she let it nourish her, and she felt steadier. King sat at her side, panting heavily, always alert. She leaned over, cupped her hand so he could lick water from it. Afterward, she patted his broad skull, silently thanking him for his amazing strength.

Dawson straightened and stood. He placed his hand on her shoulder. "Your wound's bleeding, Sarah."

Terror pulsed through her. "How bad?" She hadn't felt the blood running down her thigh at all, thanks to the numbing effects of adrenaline.

"Your trouser is soaked with it down below your knee. You probably tore it open on that climb."

Hearing the heaviness, the concern in his soft voice, she handed him back the canteen. "But it's not hemorrhaging?"

"No, but it's not a good sign." He caressed her shoulder. "Stay where you are. I'm going to put an Ace bandage above it to slow the bleeding."

Wanting to groan with despair, she swallowed the sound. The tension was thick around them. She knew the score. If it continued to bleed, she could lose enough blood that, over time, it would weaken her to the point of her being unable to escape Elson. "I slipped a couple of times," she admitted as he opened his pack on the ground in front of her. "I probably tore it open then, but I didn't feel it."

"The beauty of adrenaline," he remarked, kneeling. "Hold on to that tree trunk next to you. This isn't going to be pleasant."

Her breathing had finally slowed. She gripped the trunk, the bark knobby against her palm. "Go ahead . . ."

Dawson tightened the bandage.

Sarah tried to remain silent. Gritting her teeth, fingers digging into the bark of the tree, she inhaled sharply.

"There," he muttered, standing. "How does it feel now?"

"It feels tight, but I'm not feeling much pain either."

Looking around, he said, "Let me check in with Cade to find out where they are."

"Yes." Sarah knew it was a matter of time. Who would get to them first? Elson or the deputies? Elson's men were armed with AK-47s. They had two M4s. Two against eight. It wasn't good odds. She listened to Dawson calling Cade, and although she couldn't hear her assistant commander, she could hear Dawson's end of the conversation. He ended the call and came back to where she was standing.

"How close are they to us?"

"Thirty minutes out." He pulled the NVGs off, allowing them to hang around his neck. "I'm sure Elson is at or very near the cabin right now. There's a half mile between us and them. Even though I've given Cade the GPS of our position, they'll have to run into Elson, who might have left a few men behind at intervals to act as his rear guard. We don't know if he's that strategic or not."

Shaking her head, Sarah muttered, "And half a mile is nothing. If they find our egress point and start tracking us, they can be here in twenty or thirty minutes."

"Yeah, not good." He gave her a long, hard look. "We're initiating plan B."

"What's that?" She saw the grim look in his shadowed eyes. As he placed his hand on her shoulder, she felt that powerful sense of protection emanating from him to her. It fed her, made her feel less terrified.

"A few days ago, I scouted along this ridge." He gestured toward the rocky spine that curved upward from where they stood. "There's a group of Douglas fir not far from here. They've grown together, their branches interlacing one another. If you could climb into that group of trees, you could easily make your way up at least fifty feet above the ground and remain completely hidden. There's plenty of branches to hide you, and to support you. That way? King and I could lead them away from there, create another tracking trail for them to follow. About two hundred feet from that grove is another similar grouping. There's also a small cave about ten feet away from it. I can put King into that cave and give him the command to stay, then, run back up to that grove, climb into it and wait for Elson and his gang to pass right under me without him realizing we're there."

"And what will you do? Pick them off like a sniper?"

He pulled off the baseball cap, running his fingers through his damp hair. "We have muzzle suppressors on our M4s. They won't be able to find me. I can keep them pinned down until help arrives if they suspect something and stop to look around. If they move on? I won't fire a shot."

"Maybe I can still be of help, though. If any of Elson's men loiter between the two stands of trees, we have them bracketed; we can pin them down." She saw Dawson give her a wolfish grin, his eyes glittering.

"You're right. It's only two hundred feet

from where you'll be hidden. The possibility of them retreating from where I am could drive them your way. A pincer's movement. Good thinking, if we have to use it as plan C. I'd prefer they don't get wind of us at all and they move on by us, though."

She felt slightly better. "Okay, let's get going. I've got a tree to climb." Pulling up her NVGs, she followed Dawson. He deliberately picked the rocky summit of the ridge for a good reason: they couldn't be tracked across rocks. Oh, she knew some Taliban trackers who could, but she was betting Elson and his group weren't nearly that good. Her boots slipped every now and then, and she was forced to focus entirely on not falling and watching where she placed her feet. She could see the white vapor coming out of her mouth. They were at nine thousand feet by now, judging by her labored breathing. King remained at her side, most of his attention downslope and in the direction of their cabin far below. Sarah would bet anything that Elson had located their trail and was tracking them. It scared the hell out of her.

Dawson halted and then led her down a steep slope. She saw a thick stand of fir. The closer she got, looking up in the tangle of branches, she could see it was like a thick latticework. Dawson drew to a halt at the middle tree in the group of ten trees.

"This is the one," and he patted a low-hanging branch about three feet off the ground. "The heavy snow up on this ridge bent a lot of these limbs toward one another when they were young trees. Sling the rifle across your back. I'll help you up."

Sarah nodded. She loosened the sling, allowing Dawson to place it diagonally across her back so it wouldn't slip off during her climb.

"How's the leg feeling?"

"Same." She moved forward, standing close to him and the trunk of the tree. Lifting her gloved hand, she placed it against his broad shoulder. "Be careful, Dawson." The words came out low, filled with emotion. She saw him nod. He grazed her neck with his thumb.

"When we get out of this? Things are going to change between us, Sarah. Good changes. We deserve quality time with each other."

Tears jammed suddenly into her eyes and she made an unhappy sound, blinking rapidly, forcing them back. "We might not get out of this. You know that as well as I do." She tightened her hand on him. "I'm falling in love with you, Dawson. And there's no guarantee we'll live through this. . . ." She saw his mouth flex, his hand caressing her nape.

"And I started loving you from the day I met you, sweetheart. Don't give up on us just yet," he rasped. "You're mine and I'm yours. We just need a clear spot in our lives to explore what we have. Come on; I'll help you start your climb," and he cupped his hands so she could place her boot into them.

Swallowing hard, pushing her love for him aside, she gave a jerky nod. It was the first time he'd used an endearment, and it coated her wildly beating heart with hope, the adrenaline starting to crash through her again. Grabbing one of the lower-hanging branches, she saw a pathway up the tree, much like climbing a spiral staircase. Dawson lifted her. With a grunt, she guided her left foot onto the limb, placing it next to the trunk, utilizing the strongest part of the branch. Dawson got behind her, hand on the small of her back, steadying her as she caught and regained her balance. With each lift of her wounded right leg, pain shot up into it. Taking one branch after another, gritting her teeth, Sarah didn't groan. Instead, she kept on climbing. Soon enough, Dawson was far below her. The branches overlapping from the other trees began to swat and blind her temporarily as she moved up through them.

"You're doing fine," he told her from below, speaking softly into his mic. "You're roughly twenty feet from that spot I saw. Can you see it above and to the right of you?"

Sarah craned her neck upward, staring hard through the grainy green of her NVGs, spotting the area Dawson had wanted her to go. It was an amazing tangle of branches, some interwoven, the large, fanlike greenery covering it almost like half an eggshell below it.

"Yeah, see it." Huffing, her grip sure on each branch she grabbed, straining upward, she pushed off strongly with her good leg. Finally, she made it up into the spot.

"I'm here," she gasped, and pulled her M4 off, settling the sling over a short, broken-off branch. Next, she slid out of her knapsack, hanging it on another nearby limb. She leaned back on the steadying trunk of the fir, settling her butt into a slight, cuplike depression of sturdy limbs beneath her.

"What do you think of your new perch?"

"Great. Comfortable. I can see the other grove two hundred feet down the slope from me."

"That's where I'll eventually go. Right

now, I'm going to backtrack and make a new trail for Elson to follow. Once I'm up in my tree, I'll contact you."

"Copy that. Be careful." She saw a couple of good openings in the fir branches to take a good, clean shot in several directions. With a muzzle suppressor on her rifle, the fir a second wall that would hide a flash from eyes below, it was almost a perfect hide for a sniper. Further, she could settle her boots on other limbs in several directions and not fall down. She was at least fifty feet off the ground. Above her, through the latticework of fir, she could see the top of this old tree soaring into the starlit sky sparkling above her. The wind was buffeting the area because she was just below the ridge. Sometimes, the wind howled. The trees would rock slightly, the outer branches a lot more active from the cold gusts whipping across the ridge, than the inner, more protected ones.

Sarah moved quickly to lay out extra clips from her vest so she could easily reach them. She began to relax in the cradlelike arms of the fir, her gaze continuously sweeping the area. Her M4 had an infrared scope, and she flipped it from the side of her weapon up onto the rail for use. Taking off her NVGs, she turned it on and peered through the scope that was designed to pick up body heat. A man would appear as a bright red body in her scope. She wouldn't see details, just a blur of red for his shape. She'd utilized this scope many times in Afghanistan, so it was known and familiar to her.

Her wounded thigh ached, and she gently laid her rifle against the inside of her left leg and pulled off her glove, feeling the fabric of her trousers below where Dawson had placed the tight bandage. It was wet with her blood, but it wasn't warm, which would indicate she was still bleeding. The tightness made her leg throb, but it was nothing compared to the alternative of slowly bleeding out over time.

She wanted to hear from Dawson. Two hundred feet wasn't that far away from her hiding spot. She knew he had to first create a different trail away from her. Then he had to take King to that small cave. Lastly, he had to run to his grove of trees and begin his climb after creating a backtrack. Looking at the radium dials on her wristwatch, she saw that only ten minutes had passed. Keying her hearing, she heard nothing but the wind sifting through the evergreens across the slope. It was a soothing sound to her, but she didn't want to get too relaxed.

Elson was coming. It was just a question of when and from what direction he would appear. She slowly moved her rifle, scope to her eye, slowly panning from right to left, trying to pick up a heat signature that would let her know it was Elson's gang coming for them.

Nothing so far.

"I'm treed," Dawson said into her earpiece.

Her heart leaped at the husky sound of his low voice. Despite the danger, just having him nearby fed her a sense of protection. "Copy that."

"Our rescue team has arrived. They're suiting up and preparing to drive the dirt road to the cabin. They're going to be cautious about coming in."

Relief poured through her. "Thank God."

"I ran my infrared scope around the area and found nothing. Maybe if we get lucky, they won't locate our trail at all."

"Don't count on it. Elson is a consummate hunter."

"You doing okay, Sarah?"

"I'm settled in and fine. You?"

"Same. If you see something? Click the radio once. That will alert me Elson is coming from your direction. If I see them first? I'll click once and you can assume he's either coming up the slope near me or he's to the east of where I'm located."

"Copy." How much more she wanted to say! Swallowing, she said nothing. Radio speak was kept to a bare minimum in circumstances like this. "Is King safe?"

"Roger that. I just hope he remembers the Stay command. If there's gunfire, I don't know what he'll do without a handler present."

"I worry about that, too."

"Best we can do."

"Copy that."

"No more talk. We're switching to clicks."

"Roger. Out." Sarah released the tab and, without making a sound, lifted her M4, starting to the west of her position and slowly scanning. She wasn't expecting Elson to come up the other side of this nine-thousand-foot ridge, the wind howling over the spine of it. If he were the hunter she knew him to be, sooner or later he'd find their tracks. And then the hunt would be on.

The snap of a branch being cracked instantly alerted Dawson. He sat up, away from his comfortable trunk, head tilted, listening hard. Someone had stepped on a branch south of his grove. His heart remained a slow pound as he slowly lifted the M4 and switched on the infrared scope. He heard nothing else but panned the area in a hundred-and-eighty-degree sweep.

*Movement!*

Dawson saw a bright red blob outline of a human being slipping between two trees at two hundred yards from where he sat. And then another, and another. He counted eight men in all. Elson hadn't left a rear guard. That was good news for the sheriff's team coming up that road. He quickly radioed Cade and signed off. Watching the enemy advance, he clicked the radio once, alerting Sarah. Then, he turned the frequency to the team, giving them the approximate GPS of Elson's gang surging toward them. A returning click meant Cade had received his message. Urgency thrummed through him. He needed the sheriff's team up on this slope pronto. There was no way to win this firefight with two against eight. It would be different if he had a sniper position without a lot of fanlike fir branches making a bead hard to take out the enemy. The gusts of wind kept moving the fir branches, making it impossible for him to draw a steady bead.

It was as if he was back in Afghanistan, hunting Taliban at night, alone and surviving with his years of experience and his sniper rifle. It was biting cold, the wind whipping across the backbone of the ridge. It made hearing hard. Keeping a scope on them, he saw a big man at the lead of the straggling group of men. That had to be Hiram Elson. They were now coming up the trail he'd backtracked on. *Good!*

Dawson needed luck to break in their direction. More than anything else, he wanted the enemy to come to him, not blunder into where Sarah was hidden. Worry ate at him. Had the bleeding stopped on her thigh? His heart contracted. He loved her. He wanted to pursue what they had. Dammit, he wanted a life with her. But would fate give it to them? Lips thinning, he kept his scope trained on the group. He had deliberately created a path for them to follow that would lead them right past his hiding place. From where he sat, he had an angle to shoot cleanly and reach his target, if it came to that.

The infrared scope didn't give distinct facial features. As they drew within fifty yards of his position, Dawson set the M4 aside and pulled up his NVGs. He wanted to make damn sure he identified Elson, that it wasn't some group of innocent hikers. Now he could see each man wore a Kevlar vest, carried an AK-47 and a cartridge vest jammed with extra clips. He distinctly saw Elson in the lead. His face was sweaty, he looked angry and there was no doubt he wanted to find and kill them. Even from this distance, the energy surrounding Elson was like a slap in his face. He was relieved he'd scouted this area earlier and found Sarah a much safer place to hide.

Elson was the first to pass beneath the branches of his hide. The men were obviously not military trained. As they straggled along in a tight group, they made for easy shooting. Dawson didn't want to have to kill anyone, but he knew from the looks of them, the weapons they carried, that he'd have one chance to get them and that was all. These were hardened drug soldiers. They took no prisoners.

The second man passed beneath him.

Then the third, fourth and fifth.

Dawson waited patiently. He had curved the path slightly upward between the two trees, knowing Sarah would have a shot at them, too.

Suddenly, he heard noise below him. Was it the sheriff's party? What the hell!

Elson spun around, jerking to a halt.

Cursing to himself, Dawson saw the other men run up and encircle their leader. They were all looking down the slope, readying their weapons. His finger brushed the trigger, but he waited. What was Elson going to do? Who had caused the commotion below him? He couldn't see if it was the team because they were too far away and too many trees stood between them.

And then . . . a bark.

Oh, hell; it was King. The dog must have run down toward the advancing sheriff's team.

His finger became firmer on the trigger, sighting on Elson. All the men were frozen, their attention downslope. Had King smelled the sheriff's men? Maybe his handler was with them? Dawson didn't know. But at least the dog would be safer with them than up here with him and Sarah. He'd worried that the Belgian Malinois might take things into his own paws and charged into Elson's group. They'd kill King without a second thought.

The enemy huddled below where he sat, at least twenty feet away. Unable to hear them, he knew Sarah had sighted them and was waiting, too.

Suddenly, a man's voice boomed out over a megaphone: "Elson! Freeze! You're surrounded! Drop your weapons *now!*"

Dawson recognized Cade's voice. Mystified, he heard the voice drifting from the other side of the ridge. Had part of the team come around the area and climbed up the backside of the slope? His mind whirled. They could have divided the group, half coming up this side of the ridge, the other half from the back of it. It was a genius plan. Another pincers movement.

Elson jerked around. The men jumped as the megaphone boomed again. It was darker than hell itself, but everyone had NVGs on.

Dawson heard Elson curse loudly and yell at his men to return fire.

Eight AK-47s fired toward the ridgeline.

Squeezing the trigger, Dawson sighted on Elson. He aimed for his knee and caressed the trigger. The M4 jerked hard against his shoulder.

Elson screamed, the AK-47 flying out of his hands as he landed hard on the ground, rolling several feet.

A roar of weapons discharging from several directions sounded around the area, echoing several times, adding to the ear-battering noise. Dawson knew the sheriff's team had trapped Elson's gang. And because Cade knew where he and Sarah were, he'd planned the takedown perfectly.

More drug soldiers fell. The *chut-chut-chut* of the throaty AK-47s continued.

The smell of gunfire burned Dawson's nostrils as he took down two more soldiers, wounding them.

In less than a minute, Elson's team had been decimated. Two appeared dead to Dawson, but the others were writhing on the ground. He grinned darkly. Sarah had joined the fray as well. Between them, they'd taken down five of the eight tangos. Keeping his M4 sighted on the druggies, he wanted to make sure none of them tried to go for their AK-47s.

"Stay down," the megaphone blared. "Do not try to pick up your weapon. If you do, you will die."

Bright lights suddenly flashed on, blinding the group from three different directions. The light was so intense, many of the men who were down covered their eyes. Dawson pulled his NVGs off, seeing the scene through the glare of the lamps carried by a number of deputies. He was proud of all the men and women below him who had planned this mission. It had been brilliantly executed. He saw King with his dog handler, Jasmine Delano, leashed and tense, ready to attack if given the signal. He was glad the dog was back with her; that took a load off his mind.

Cade appeared below his tree, dropping

the megaphone for his pistol. The SWAT team from Teton County surrounded the moaning, groaning men writhing in excruciating pain, unable to fight, much less get up and run. He waited and watched as Cade, who was the commander of the raid, had his men disarm each of the druggies, then cuff them. Pistols were thrown to one area, AK-47s to another. All the while, Elson was screaming and yelling obscenities.

To his surprise, he saw Sarah appear at the edge of where the SWAT team had encircled Elson's men. He saw the grim look in her eyes as she walked with a confidence he'd seen before she'd been wounded. On her left shoulder was slung the M4. Her NVGs were hanging around her neck. The SWAT team leader went to her and shook her hand, then had a short conversation with her. Dawson didn't know what was said, but he led Sarah into the circle. She came to a halt in front of Elson, who was sitting up, glaring at her with hatred.

Sarah stood there, returning his look, calm and unaffected by him. She was a warrior now, and he was getting to see her in that mode. Pride flowed through him. She was one of four women in the group, but she was the only one with a bloodied pant leg and a bandage around her wounded thigh. There was nothing weak or fragile about her. He smiled a little, watching her focus on Hiram, staring him down until he looked away, spat and deliberately ignored her.

*Yeah, you don't mess with Sarah Carter.*

Dawson called Cade on the radio, letting him know he was going to climb down out of his tree. He, in turn, told the rest of his crew, so no one would mistake him for a druggie. In no time, he was back on the ground. Shaking Cade's hand, he nodded to everyone and then left the circle, heading to where Sarah was standing. He saw her lift her head, that stubborn chin of hers, her eyes shadowed but narrowed, every inch the Marine she'd once been. He loved her. He couldn't conceive of life without her.

Halting in front of her, he smiled down into her eyes, seeing her flattened lips barely curving, the tension leaving her features. Her hair was mussed, she was sweaty and yet she looked beautiful to him. "All right?" he asked her.

She reached out, sliding her gloved hand around his. "I couldn't be better. You?" and she flashed a glinting look up and down him.

"I'm fine. Are you ready to head down the hill?" he asked.

Cade came over to them. "We've got three Teton helicopters coming our way. All Black Hawks. Sarah? I'd like you and Dawson, plus your deputies, to take the first one that lands on the ridge over there," and he pointed in that direction.

Sarah turned, looking into the darkness. She could see the flashing lights of a helo rapidly heading their way in the night sky. "Sounds good, Cade."

"They're going to take you to the Wind River Hospital so a doc can look at that leg of yours."

"That's fine. As soon as I get it cleaned up and bandaged up, I'll be over to the office. I'll meet you there after you fly down with this crew."

"First, we're going to have to take the wounded to the Jackson Hole Hospital. It's a much larger ER, and they've already given us permission to fly all of Elson's men to it for medical help. Some may need surgery." Cade gave her a tired smile. "Tell you what, boss. How about when you get out of the ER and your leg is patched up, you go home with that hombre?" and he gestured toward Dawson. "You look exhausted. We've got this handled, so go rest. Besides, I think you two deserve a time-out after all this."

Sarah gave her assistant a sheepish grin.

"Can't keep any secrets from you, can I, Cade?"

"No, you can't, boss." He clapped her gently on the shoulder. "The helo's going to land in about five minutes. Make your way up to where the Teton deputies are standing with landing lights in their hands."

Dawson nodded his thanks to Cade. It was obvious he'd been the right choice to run the department in Sarah's absence.

She turned toward him, slipped her hand into his. "Ready, partner?"

A good feeling wound through him. "Yeah, let's go, sweetheart. First, a visit to the ER and then I want to have you in my arms. Where you belong."

## CHAPTER NINETEEN

Sarah emerged from the hot, life-giving shower feeling utterly spent. It was nearly 0400 and she felt woozy. The doctor had estimated she'd lost half a pint of blood from her healing bullet wound, and that was a tiny part of why she felt this way. With a waterproof dressing around her thigh, she could shower and still keep the wound dry. Ruffling her just-washed hair, she pulled another towel off the rack to dry herself. She loved her small home, never more than now, having been away from it for so long. Dawson was in the other bathroom taking a well-deserved shower himself. How much she wanted to join him, but now wasn't the time.

Later, after donning a knee-length cotton nightgown, she padded out to the kitchen, her ears picking up sounds that Dawson was there already. It sounded like he was making something, and she halted at the end of the hall. There, in a pair of clean jeans and a body-hugging tan T-shirt, barefoot, he was busily stirring something in a pan on the stove.

"What are you making?" she asked as she moved into the kitchen, halting a few feet away from him. His hair was still wet, but combed, his beard darkening his face, making him even more desirable.

Glancing over at her, he said, "Hot chocolate. Want some?"

Her stomach growled. She laughed a little, placing her hand against it. "I guess I do."

"We've been on the run, burning up all our sugar energy, and I figure milk has a calming effect on the nervous system. Might help us come down off that cliff we were on."

"Or the trees we were hanging out in?" She went to the cupboard and brought down two large red ceramic mugs.

Chuckling, he nodded. "That, too. How are you doing?"

She put down the mugs, then leaned her hips against the counter, absorbing his shadowy countenance because the only light was from the stove. Dawson was all male and hard muscle, and he hid so much of himself from her, but eventually, she'd been able to see much more of him at the cabin.

"Whipped. My mind's muddled. I can barely lift my feet to walk. How about you?"

"Same. It's going to crash down on us in about half an hour, I would guess."

"The adrenaline crash. You're right."

He lifted the pan off the stove and carefully poured the steamy, rich chocolate into the mugs. "Thought we could sit down on your couch, sip this and just be. How does that sound?"

"A man after my own heart." She picked up her mug, seeing the glint in Dawson's eyes. Now, she understood what it meant: that he wanted her. Right now, sex wasn't on the table for her, but being held by him, sleeping with him at her side, was. They were too exhausted to do anything else but that. "Come on," she urged, walking into the carpeted living room. There was one lamp on in the corner, and it shed enough light not to stub one's toe on something. Sarah waited until he sat down in one corner.

"I want to sit beside you."

Dawson lifted his arm. "Come on."

It felt so right as she nestled herself next to his lean, hard body, his arm falling around her shoulders, drawing her gently against him. She balanced the mug on her knees where she'd drawn them up against his legs. "This feels so good," she whispered, giving him a look of thanks. There was a predatory look in his darkened eyes, but it didn't scare her off. She knew that look. He needed her. And she needed him.

"Sure does." He leaned over, placing a light kiss on the damp hair she'd brushed into place. "I sat up in that tree wondering if we would ever be given a chance to know each other on a personal level, when there wasn't a threat constantly surrounding us."

"I was thinking the same thing, Dawson. Even with Hiram Elson going to jail and then prison for a long, long time, it still leaves two other brothers in this valley." She sipped her chocolate, the mug warming both her scratched and bruised hands.

"We'll worry about that tomorrow. Right now, all I want is you next to me, enjoying this peace and quiet."

She nodded and relished the dark chocolate taste. Licking her lower lip, she said, "Time hasn't been on our side, has it?"

"No. But I want to build more time for us after things calm down around here. Is that what you want?" and she lifted her lashes, holding his smoldering gaze.

"Yes. It's easy enough helping Gertie, and she's been good about giving me time off to be with you when I asked."

"It's my career that's making it tough to be with you." She said it more to herself than him, feeling his fingers move in a slow pattern on her right upper arm. His touch was evocative, making her want to be with him more than ever. "I liked staying in the cabin with you, Dawson. It was the first time we'd been in tight quarters together."

His mouth lifted. "Yeah, and we didn't mind it, did we?"

"No. I wanted that time alone with you. Helluva way to get it, but that six weeks with you showed me who you really were."

"Same here. No regrets, Sarah. Only question is: do you still want to move forward with me?"

"You know I do. That's never been a question."

He gazed deeply into her eyes. "Good. I didn't think it was an issue, but I learned from my marriage to never assume a thing. Asking is always a good thing."

She smiled a little. "We've always been that way with each other." She reached out, sliding her hand across his hard thigh, the jean material taut and rough, much like him. "Here's want I want," she began softly, moving her fingers slowly down his hard thigh. "I want you to sleep with me tonight, Dawson."

He took her hand on his thigh, wrapping it in his, holding her upturned gaze. "We want the same thing."

"All bets are off when I wake up," she warned him throatily. She saw his lips quirk, deviltry dancing in his eyes, his hand tightening around her shoulder momentarily.

"Yes, they are. Let's finish our hot chocolate, then go to bed."

Dawson lay awake for another hour, his mind not shutting down, thanks to the adrenaline still swirling in his bloodstream. Absorbing Sarah's body heat, her long, shapely body against his, her leg thrown over one of his, her head nestled in the crook of his shoulder, sleeping deeply, he never wanted anything more. How close they had come to dying out there. His mind skipped over how many things could have gone wrong tonight. Sarah could have been killed. Or him. Or both of them. A shudder worked deeply through him, and he understood once more the fragility of life, how tenuous it really was. It was all brought home to him tonight.

Inhaling deeply, he smelled her dried hair tickling his jaw, the scent of what she said was guava, a tropical fruit shampoo. Even better, he could inhale the scent of *her*. It was a heady aphrodisiac. He would never tire of breathing in her fragrance. Or feeling her leaning against him in sleep, that shallow breath slow, telling him she trusted him enough to let go, let him take care of her. Never able to get rid of wanting to protect her, he knew she was a woman who really knew how to take care of herself. They had a relationship of equals. Smiling tiredly, closing his eyes, he slid his arm around her back, holding her lightly, not wanting to awaken her.

In another half hour, he was sure the dawn would begin to crawl up on the night horizon. Holding Sarah was like holding the life he had been searching for but had never found. His marriage had faltered for many reasons, and he was going to make sure he didn't make the same mistakes twice. The differences between Lucia and Sarah were vast. Lucia had been eighteen years old when he'd married her. Neither had had the maturity needed to keep a long-term relationship going. How well he could see it now but hadn't when so much younger. Sarah was twenty-nine years old, had been in love and lost Steve Coris. Each of them had been wounded in different ways, but it seemed to him those events had served to help them draw toward each other, not away. And right after that thought, he fell into a dreamless sleep, the woman he loved fiercely in his arms, at his side.

Sarah awoke slowly, barely lifting her lashes. Becoming aware that she lay sprawled across Dawson, her one arm across his narrow waist, her nose tickled by the dark hair on his chest, the slow up-and-down movement of his breathing brought her heart in sync with his. She felt the expansion of a love that was endless, that moved like silken bonds around her exploding heart, pulsing with quiet joy.

At last . . . at last, they were together. Barely turning her cheek, which lay against his flesh, she pressed her lips to his chest. His male scent entered her nostrils, part soap and part him. Beneath her lips, she felt his muscles tighten. She continued to place soft, slow kisses on him, becoming lost in who he was to her. Pulling her arm across his waist, she could feel his growing erection and spread her fingers upward to feel the slab hardness of his abdomen, exploring the silky sprinkle of black hair. Dawson was awake, and her kiss turned into a smile as she nuzzled him.

She felt a fine tension sheeting through him, felt him coming alive from the depths of his own healing sleep. Eyes closed, she felt his fingers tunnel slowly into the strands of her clean hair, memorizing every inch of her. Fingertips massaging her scalp, the wild little electric jolts racing down her skull to her neck, spreading into her upper body, she felt her nipples harden instantly beneath his caring exploration. She felt cherished. Loved. Needed.

Slowly, she eased away from him, opening her lashes, seeing his gray, stormy eyes studying her with hunger. Her lips parted, and she got to her hands and knees, keeping contact with him. Leaning forward, one hand near his left shoulder, her hair tumbling forward, she leaned over him, seeking his mouth, gliding her lips across him, feeling his hands curve around her back and hip, holding her so he could return her kiss. His mouth met hers with a burning urgency, drawing her down on him, easing her across him so that she lay on top of him, her legs coming to rest between his.

A low hum of pleasure rose in her throat as he caressed her hip, curving across her rounded cheeks, adoration in his touch. Heat bubbled within her lower body, and she could feel the dampness of need collecting rapidly between her legs. All the while, his mouth was moving across hers, tasting her, matching her eagerness to continue to kiss him, to celebrate their coming together in the most intimate and wonderful ways. She shivered from the way he built a brighter, hotter fire within her. He was in no hurry, sampling her deeply, wanting her against him, wanting her joyous response as well as wanting his. Celebrating together.

With her eyes closed, she felt all her senses shift to him, to a man who had always treated her as an equal, never less. Dawson had never tried the tired old Neanderthal tactics that so many men still practiced. Instead, he invited her to continue to kiss him at a leisurely pace. It built the coals that had been ignited into burning new life. She had never met a man quite like him. He seemed like an easygoing type B male, but last night, she'd seen the warrior in him come out, and the confidence that came with it. He had saved her life and she knew it. She could never have made it out alive if Dawson hadn't been there to lead her, show her the escape, have a plan B, helping her climb up into that tree to hide. There was such a celebration going on inside her heart, the love that had grown between them, with the small but oh, so meaningful things he did for her every day. All of them, she realized, sinking against him, his arms wrapping warmly about her, were acts of love.

She felt him roll her onto her back, and she barely opened her eyes, meeting his intense gray gaze and smiling, sliding her hands down across his taut body. As he eased her thighs open, she closed her eyes, mentally welcoming him to enter her. Sarah wanted . . . needed . . . this fusion with Dawson. Nothing else would bind them as the act of fierce mutual love. Last night, before they slept, they'd talked about this possibility. Each was free of disease. And no, Sarah didn't like condoms. And yes, she was in a clear space and wouldn't get pregnant. She disdained birth control pills and any other device altering the natural environment and rhythm of her body. As he framed her face with his hands, looking down into her barely open eyes, she smiled once more, encouraging him to enter her, to make them one.

As he tipped his head, his mouth crushing hers with breathtaking command, he slipped inside her, moving gently, allowing her body to acclimate to his girth. Just as hungry, Sarah lifted her hands, framing his face, kissing him as eagerly as he was kissing her. She became lost in the beauty of his mouth worshipping hers, moving into her, asking

412

her to participate, and she did. The ancient, rocking movement, the heat and wetness of her body enclosing him, providing that slick and incredible sensation that made her moan with pleasure, was unending, echoing through her body like an ancient song once more joyously remembered.

Lost in his strong mouth on hers, he slid one hand beneath her hips, lifting her slightly as he moved fully and completely into her. Nothing had ever felt so good, so wonderfully intimate as that one movement. A low moan tore from her lips as he broke the kiss, lifting his head. And as he sampled first one nipple and then the other, a building orgasm was triggered and she cried out, gripping his shoulders, frozen with the ripplelike circles that enlarged throughout her lower body and engulfing her like a wild tsunami.

It had been so long since she'd had an orgasm, she nearly fainted from the powerful intensity of it rolling through her. Was it possible to faint from too much pleasure? That one thought flitted across her blown mind as she drifted into white light, consumed and surrounded by it. And then, moments later, Dawson released within her, his low growl, his freezing upon her, his hands on either side of her head all occurring at once. She lay there feeling as if she was floating in a whole new world, but Dawson was with her. He collapsed seconds later atop her, their brows touching each other, their breathing more like animals in rutting season, harsh and explosive.

How long they lay together, fused, each breathing raggedly in the aftermath, their arms wrapped around each other, she didn't know. Nor did she care. The lean, tough muscling of Dawson complemented her softer, rounded form. Together, they were one in the best of ways. Slowly, she moved her opened hands, palm down, across his broad, thick back, covered with perspiration. Now she wanted to memorize him, and she did, skimming his waist, narrow hips, taut buttocks and hard, thick thighs. He was beautiful. Utterly beautiful to her.

He eased out of her, lying beside her, gently gathering her into his arms, one roughened hand splayed across her hips, drawing her against his weakened erection. A pool of heat, of glowing coals, burst back to life within her. She rested her head on his shoulder, content to be cherished by him, his fingers moving through the silky strands of her ginger-colored hair. Soft kisses fell on her hair, her temple and cheek, his breath warm and moist. He moved strands between his thumb and index finger. Kissing her throat, and then her sensitive collarbones, and he made her melt into him in a new and wonderful way. He lavished her with his touch and his mouth, and his callused fingers elicited delightful surges of pleasure across her skin. And somewhere in that world of only feeling good, she drifted off to sleep once again. Only this time, as she felt herself falling into the darkness, she felt safe and loved.

Dawson watched Sarah sleeping. Propped up on one elbow, he kept his arm across her abdomen and hips, wanting to keep in contact with her. He had sensed that even one orgasm would spin her off into another few hours of the sleep she so desperately needed. Sleep was restorative; no one was more aware of that than him. He wanted her whole. And she'd lost so much the past month and a half, that true healing could begin on the deeper levels that flesh couldn't fix. The woman he loved so much carried other wounds Dawson knew only love could correct over time. And maybe not heal her completely, but to a large extent, Lane would no longer be an anchor she carried on her capable shoulders. Rather, what Dawson hoped for her was that her baby sister would begin to be a warm, fuzzy fluttering in Sarah's heart and the guilt she carried would dissolve, with only the wonderful memories left instead.

Wanting to kiss her but knowing it would wake her, he was content to lie beside her and watch the summer sun climbing in the sky, the light leaking in around the drapes across the eastern window. The soft light accented Sarah's broad forehead, her clean nose, high cheekbones and those luscious lips that fit his mouth so perfectly. Dawson gazed across the landscape of her face, watching how the light caressed her slender neck, her shoulder and collarbone. There was nothing but her beauty wrapping around his heart, in awe that she was perfect for him.

Sleep was imperative for Sarah. With slow movements designed not to disturb her, Dawson eased out of bed and picked up his clothes, leaving the room. He quietly closed the door and tread down the hallway to the bathroom. A hot shower would revive him. He'd make a large pot of coffee, call Cade at the sheriff's department to check in, let him know Sarah was exhausted. Dawson knew Cade would ask him to tell her to come in tomorrow. That would be soon enough. There were a lot of details to tie up regarding the capture of Hiram Elson and his bloodthirsty gang.

He decided to make them pancakes after he'd had a shower and gotten dressed in jeans, a light blue chambray work shirt and cowboy boots. That had been his uniform of the day since starting to work for Gertie. He'd called her, too, and let her know Sarah was fine and sleeping. Gertie would call the rest of the family, letting them know how she was doing.

Two hours later, Sarah emerged from the bedroom in her wrinkled nightgown, her hair mussed, looking sweetly drowsy. Dawson had just gotten off the phone from an update on the Elson gang.

"Hey," he called, standing up, "how are you feeling?"

Sarah halted and slowly turned to her right. "Oh . . . I woke up and I was alone." She pushed her hair off her cheek. "I missed you."

Those words meant the world to him. He walked over and pulled her into his arms, and she laid her head against his chest, her arms going around his waist. "I missed you too, but I woke up two hours ago and I wanted to let you sleep." He kissed her hair, feeling her arms tighten around him. Easing some strands of hair away, he cocked his head, seeing her eyes were closed. She was so vulnerable right now. It was a new level of trust she was establishing with him. Tucking the hair behind her ear, he leaned down and kissed her temple. "Are you hungry?"

"Yes," she murmured, her voice hoarse with sleep. "What time is it?"

He looked up at the clock in the kitchen. "Ten o'clock."

Gasping, Sarah pulled away enough to look up at him. "You're kidding me!"

"No," he said. "Hey, you've been through a lot, sweetheart. Your body is begging you to rest, to get that deep sleep. It's the best thing for you."

She pouted and held his amused gaze. "I need to get to work."

"Uh-uh; Cade said to take the day off. I just got off the phone with him and he gave me a detailed update on what was going on. How about you go get a shower, get dressed and I'll make us some buttermilk pancakes for breakfast? I'll give you his report then. How does that sound?"

Sighing, she kissed him lightly and then stepped out of his arms and rubbed her face with her hands. "Cade's right," she managed. "I feel whipped even now." Her hands fell away. "And that was the best orgasm I've ever had, Dawson Callahan. I want many, many more of them. Hear me?"

Sponging in her husky tone, her green eyes lighting up, he laughed. "That's good to know. I was thinking us making love probably tired you out."

She playfully hit his arm. "That would *never* happen, cowboy. Pancakes sound great. See you in about half an hour. Okay?"

He patted her rear. "Sounds good to me. How many?"

"Three. A short stack, please," she called over her shoulder. "And you for dessert . . ."

# CHAPTER TWENTY

*August 15*

"You takin' Dawson away from me?" Gertie demanded of Sarah. The three of them sat around the kitchen table, having coffee and dessert after their meal.

"Only at night, Gertie. You get him five days a week," Sarah said, spooning in some homemade peach cobbler her grandmother had made earlier in the day. She saw a merry twinkle in the old woman's eyes.

"Well," she said, aiming a dark look at Dawson, who sat to her right, "I need him. He's really been of great help."

"And I like helping you, Gertie," Dawson said, scraping the bowl clean with his spoon. "Sarah lives five miles away from here. I can always come up here if you need me. It's a short trip."

"Except in winter," she pointed out smartly, wagging her finger in his direction. "Want second helpings on that cobbler? A little more vanilla ice cream with it?"

He grinned. "Naw, better stop now. Can I have some tomorrow for lunch?"

She snickered. "We'll see. I can't say there will or won't be any left by that time. Everyone who lives in the house loves this cobbler."

"How about we take a piece for him when we go?" Sarah suggested. She saw Dawson give her a wink.

"Well . . . yes . . . that would work."

Sarah blotted her lips with a bright orange linen napkin and set it beside her emptied bowl. "That was delicious. I always look forward to the organic peaches down in Salt Lake City becoming ripe."

"A shame we can't have fruit trees and gardens here," Gertie grumped. "This place only has a sixty-day growing season and nothing' gets ripe in that time frame."

"Nell has a couple of huge greenhouses and she's able to keep all of us well supplied with organic veggies," Sarah noted.

"Yeah, well, I asked her why she didn't grow some trees inside there. She keeps it heated for eight months outta the year. Fruit trees would grow well in there."

"I think I did ask her that," Sarah murmured, "and she said the greenhouses aren't big enough to accommodate their size, that

421

the leaf cover would throw shade on the veggies she had growing nearby. And veggies don't like a lot of shade because it squelches their growth."

Rubbing her jaw, Gertie said, "Hmmm, maybe I should have some built that could accommodate fruit trees." She slanted a look at Dawson. "Is it possible?"

"Sure, but it would have to be a customized greenhouse."

"In your spare time? Could you go check it out online and find out what the costs will be?"

"I'll do it first thing tomorrow morning," Dawson promised.

Sarah rose and picked up the empty bowls and flatware. "Thanks for the wonderful meal, Gertie. You're *such* a great cook!"

Gertie sat there staring at Sarah, who was still in her sheriff's uniform, her hair caught up in a ponytail. When she returned to the table, she asked, "Have you two thought about gettin' hitched?"

Sarah sat down and picked up her mug of coffee, taking a sip. "We haven't really talked about it yet, Gertie. Why?"

" 'Cause," she said, "I have a wedding gift if you can get together and agree to get married."

Surprised, Sarah looked across the table

at Dawson. "Did you know about this?"

"Me? No." He glanced at Gertie. "This is all her doing," and a grin leaked out the corners of his mouth.

Flourishing her hand and waving it in Dawson's direction, Gertie said, "Sarah, you know that two-story Victorian house half a mile to the south of here? You should, because you played often enough in that house as a child."

"Oh, that pretty yellow Victorian?" Gertie had three such homes on her property that had belonged to other family members until they passed on. All were well cared for, the 1900s' furniture covered in white sheets to protect them but standing empty. "The one with the white trim and that huge wrap-around porch?"

"Yep, same one. Now, if you two decided to get married? I'd like to give you that home, deed and all. A wedding gift. I like having our family living close to one another. Besides? Dawson works here. All he'd have to do is walk half a mile to work or drive up here in snowy times. What do you think?"

Sarah's heart opened with love for her grannie. "That's a stunning offer." She looked at Dawson. "What do you think?"

Opening his hands, he said, "That would

be a wonderful gift, Gertie. But Sarah and I haven't lived together that long. We're still working out things between us, and I want to make sure when I do ask her to marry me, she'll say yes."

"Well," Gertie growled, giving them both a dark look, "you need to get married before I kick the bucket. How long do I know I have left? Sarah, I want to see you happy. You deserve it. And Dawson? You're special. You're not like most wranglers. You're different, and you seem to fit each other like missing puzzle pieces. Ain't that so?"

Sarah saw Dawson's cheeks redden and realized Gertie was embarrassing him. Placing her hand on her grandmother's arm, she said, "I promise, we'll discuss it. Okay?"

"How soon will I know?" Gertie demanded. "I might stroke out tomorrow or have the big one come along. You wouldn't want me to go to my grave without knowing, would you?"

Sarah swallowed her smile. Gertie was known to manipulate. Oh, she wasn't mean or selfish about it, but if she wanted something, she was like a chess player, planning strategically so she could get what she wanted. Patting her arm, she said, "Soon. We'll talk about it tonight. I promise."

■ ■ ■ ■

Sarah slid into Dawson's arms, and he tucked her in beside him. They were naked, a light sheet pulled up to their waists as soon as she got settled.

"Mmm, you smell good," he said, kissing her shoulder, inhaling the lemony fragrance of the soap she'd used earlier.

Snuggling, she nestled her head below his jaw, spreading her fingers across the outline of his left shoulder. "You feel good." She was aware of his erection, knew they would make love, but before that, she wanted to talk with him. His hand skimmed her spine, and her skin reacted to the roughness of his fingertips, tiny sparks of pleasure dissolving her mind, making her smile softly. "I like coming home and having you here at night. Did you know that?"

"No, but it's nice to hear," he teased, sliding his fingers through her hair, smoothing it away from her face. "And I like it, too." He slid his hairy leg across hers, keeping her close to him.

"That was sweet of Gertie to make dinner for us tonight."

"Because she knows how busy and stressed for time you are."

Groaning, she closed her eyes, content to be in the safety of his arms. "Cade and I just finished a huge amount of paperwork on Hiram Elson and his gang. We've got everything legally recorded."

"Are all of those men still going to stay in the county jail?"

"No. We don't have that kind of room. I've gotten the judge to allow us to move all of them to Salt Lake City until their trial date can be set here."

"I don't imagine the Elson family is in favor of that."

She snorted. "They don't visit Hiram anyway."

"No? Why am I not surprised? Are the other two Elson boys continuing to keep a low profile?"

"Yes. Roberta hired an attorney outside of the county and she's suing the sheriff's department for her husband's death." Her voice turned dark. "That won't get anywhere in a court of law."

"She's pissed and, like her sons, wants retribution."

"Like all the rest of the vengeful Elsons. Nothing new."

"Hey, let's stop talking shop. Okay? You have no idea how much I look forward to this time of night when you're in my arms.

Everything else in the world goes away."

She pulled back just enough, her head resting on his shoulder, to fall into his shadowed gaze. "I've become addicted to it." Caressing his sandpapery jaw, she whispered, "I love you so much, Dawson. You complete me, my life. I was thinking today that you were the man I'd always been unconsciously searching for."

"And there I was," he said, amused, smiling into her eyes.

"Yes, there you were." She trailed her fingertips across his smiling mouth, watching that hungry look come to his face. There was no question they would love each other tonight. It didn't happen all the time, but on the hard, stressful days she sometimes had, it was as if Dawson intuitively knew and became more protective and caring of her. She didn't know how he knew; he just did. Her heart flew open as he caught her hand, turning it over, licking her palm, sending heat and the promise of things to come up her wrist and into her lower arm.

He released her hand and settled her on her back, studying her. She could feel the intensity of his gaze, felt his need of her pressed against her hip. Caressing her cheek, he leaned down, capturing her lips, moving his slowly across hers, engaging her, pleasing her, his breath moist and warm against her cheek.

Wrapped in the warmth and tenderness of his kiss, she languished within that cocoon that made her feel so loved. Never had Sarah felt this deep, ongoing emotion that smothered her with such happiness as with Dawson. He was so right for her in every possible way. Slowly, his mouth left hers.

"Mmm, I love what we share," she whispered, giving him a quick kiss.

He studied her in the darkness of the room relieved only by a small nightlight near the closed door. Threading his fingers through her hair, he said, "Want to make it permanent?"

Her heart banged once. Blinking, she stared up at him, his nose an inch from her own, his breath caressing her cheek. "As in marriage?"

Nodding, he gave her a boyish smile. "Stay where you are," and he rolled away from her and pulled open the top drawer of the bed stand.

Mystified, she sat up, barely able to see what he was doing. The sheet pooled around her hips and she leaned against the headboard after placing her pillow between it and her back. The drawer closed and Dawson turned, beautifully naked, darkly shadowed and all male. He held something in his hand as he came back to her side. He settled next to her, back against the headboard.

"Come here," he urged gruffly, placing his arm behind her shoulders, bringing her into the curve of his arm.

Sarah said nothing, melting against his hard body, absorbing the heat of his skin against her own. He lifted the box and held it out to her.

"Open it?"

She took it. "Is this what I think it is?" she asked him, looking up into his hooded eyes.

"Probably so," he answered, amused.

"How long have you been hiding this from me, Dawson?"

He shrugged and chuckled. "A month after I met you, I knew you were the woman I wanted in my life for the rest of it." He grew somber as she opened the black velvet box and heard her gasp. "It's a funny thing," he told her as she touched the set. "These are my great-grandmother's set of rings she wore for fifty years before she passed away at the age of ninety. Her name was Mary. My mother held them since she passed. I knew she had them because when I was a teen, she'd shown them to me. Mary was well known to be clairvoyant. She'd written down on a piece of paper tucked inside the box, 'Give this set to Dawson when he's found the woman who will live with him the rest of his life. She will have red hair.' "

Sarah gasped. "Really?"

"Yes." Shaking his head, he said, "When I met Lucia, who had blond hair, my mother didn't say anything to me about the rings. She wasn't going to give them to me even if I remembered them."

Giving him a pensive look, she moved her finger across the engagement ring, which had three gold roses, a small diamond in the center of each. The wedding band was a simple gold without any designs on it. She pulled the engagement ring from the box. "This is so beautiful. Who would have thought to create gold roses and then put a diamond in each one? I love that it lays flat across the finger, not high. I would worry while I was wearing it that it might get caught on something and either take my finger with it or maybe lose one of the diamonds."

She handed Dawson the ring. "Will you put this on my finger?" She saw him relax, and then realized he was probably holding his breath on her answer. She sat up, and so did he. Taking her left hand, he slid the ring on her finger.

Dawson held her watery gaze. He wasn't too steady himself. "You mean the world to me, sweetheart. You always did and always will. Marry me? Be my best friend? My partner? My life?"

Whispering his name, she said, "You know I will. . . ." And Sarah wrapped her arms around him, kissing him long and deeply, wanting nothing more than this quiet man who always brought calm to her hectic world, allowing her to relax. As their mouths met and slid wetly against each other, she immersed herself in his strength, his care and that special tenderness she'd rarely seen in men. Never once had he disrespected her but had always held her up as equal to him. From the beginning, they had worked off their strengths, not their weaknesses. They had long, searching conversations she fed on, grateful he trusted her fully.

Finally, she separated reluctantly from his mouth, eyes barely opening, drowning in his stormy gray ones. Their breathing had heightened, and she absorbed how good he felt against her. "I'm going to love wearing your great-grandmother's rings, Dawson. They're precious."

"Because family has always meant so much to you." He cradled her in his arms, their heads against each other as he held her. "Since we met, you've gone through so much. Are you sure this decision isn't being pushed by all of it, Sarah?"

He was concerned, hearing it in his rasping voice. "No. Am I still struggling with nearly being killed by Brian? And then having to shoot him? Sure, I'm wrestling with it, Dawson. Any human being would. I didn't become a law-enforcement officer to kill people. I want to help them, not hurt them." Drawing in a ragged breath, her eyes tearing up, she whispered, "There are good days and bad."

He squeezed her gently. "The military taught us that."

"And it will always be with us. Having been in combat helps in a strange kind of way."

"Killing a human being changes you forever."

She pressed her face against the column of his neck, her arms around his torso. "My dad told me there would be times like that."

"I'll be here for you, Sarah. The job you chose isn't lightweight. It's one of the most responsible ones on the planet. I don't think you ever have an easy day."

"Oh," she muttered, lifting her hand, wiping her eyes, "we do have good days, too.

The program I put into place for the children of the county, so they won't fear our uniform or fear us, is always a high for me. To give children a chance to see all our gear, to ride in a cruiser. With the way it is these days, there are people who hate and fear us. I'm going to continue to try to get the people of our country to trust and like us."

"You're one of the most grounded, sensible people I've ever met. There's still a lot for you to work through, but I'll be at your side. I'll listen to you. We'll hash things out. You're not alone on this journey anymore, sweetheart." He caressed her hair, leaning back a bit to meet her glistening eyes. "I'll walk with you. Always . . ."

She sniffed, a trembling smile touching her lips. "I always felt so confident until I got shot. And then I felt myself shriveling up, wanting to hide, scared and out of control."

"I saw that," he said heavily, sliding his arm across her shoulder. "It's going to take time, Sarah. And everyone is different about it." He moved his hand slowly up and down her arm. "Maybe now? We'll get a window where peace will reign in the county and the Elsons won't be stirring things up like they always do."

"I could use some quiet. Just today, we

finished all the reports to all the agencies. I'm glad this is off my back, even though I'm not sure what the Elsons are going to do now."

"Cade said with Hiram, who was most like his father, being out of the picture, the other two boys might settle down. They're followers, not leaders."

"I hope you're right, Dawson. I really do. I need that window of quiet just to get myself together. I put on a brave face out there for my people, to the public, but inside I cringle like a frightened little girl at times. It just hits me in waves, out of the blue, and then it disappears as quickly as it came." She grazed his cheek. "I'm so glad, every night when I leave the office, I have you to come home to."

He caught her fingers and pressed them against his heart, his hand over hers. "And no one's happier than me to see you walk through that door, Sarah."

She sat up and looked down at the engagement ring, tiny sparkles of light shooting through the facets as she slowly turned it. Her voice became soft. "I feel as if I've come home to you," and she lifted her lashes, meeting and holding his warm gaze. "I think I've loved you all my life, even though we hadn't met yet. Maybe a dream I had, never believing it would come true." She pressed her hand to her lips. "When Steve was killed, I thought I'd died with him. I was slowly falling in love him. It was the first time I'd opened my heart to the possibility of loving someone and having that love returned." Wiping the tears streaming down her cheeks, her voice wobbly with emotion, she added hoarsely, "And then you walked into my life. I tried to ignore you, Dawson. You scared me. I wanted my hurting heart to remain hidden, not react when you came near me, or I listened to your voice, or I saw your gentleness and understanding with others. I didn't want to. . . ." and she shook her head.

"I could feel something going on within you," he admitted quietly, reaching over, sliding his hand down her arm, and enclosing her right hand. "I couldn't understand it, of course. I just felt this tug-of-war going on inside you. At first? I thought it was me. I thought you were having a pretty negative reaction to me being in your space." He sighed. "Instead? It was that invisible thread pulling us closer to each other. And I was resisting it, too, Sarah. I'd made a mess of my marriage; I knew I was to blame for it falling apart. I didn't feel ready to look at any woman, even you, because I lacked the confidence to try again."

"But you did try, and I'm so glad you did. I was scared, too. More scared than you, because you reached out to me in large and small ways. I guess I knew I had to cash my hand in when Gertie hired you and you lived at her home. I knew I'd be seeing you a lot because I always dropped over there once or twice, sometimes three times a week."

Mouth quirking, Dawson admitted, "And I was jumping up and down for joy that I knew I'd be seeing you. I could hardly wait, and that shocked the hell out of me." He pulled his hand away and studied her in the lulling silence strung between them. "I was shocked because my head had already decided not to pursue you. That you would have to show me you were interested in me before I'd take that step toward you." His mouth grew wry. "But my heart? Well, it had other ideas. It was celebrating, and I began counting the hours until you'd show up at Gertie's. I needed to see you, Sarah. I needed to hear your voice. Hear what you thought and hear your laughter. I wanted to know the woman who hid behind that uniform."

"It happened, didn't it?" and she managed a short laugh, looking up toward the darkened ceiling and then down at him. "I felt the same way. I knew Gertie needed someone like you, an organized, disciplined assistant who could help her run her company in a leaner, better way. I tried to tell myself that." She wiped the tears from her eyes. "Seeing you there, in her house the first time, I just melted like a marshmallow. I didn't realize how hungry I'd become for you, your presence, your voice. . . . It was then I realized I was falling in love with you."

"I guess we kinda admitted it to ourselves about the same time. I got so I'd ask Gertie when you would visit again. She always gave me that look that told me she knew what was behind me asking her that question."

"Isn't that interesting? Gertie began calling me, making excuses for me to drop over more often. Now I know why," and she reached out, slipping her hand into his. "She knew."

"Don't grannies always know?"

Laughing, Sarah admitted, "You don't get anything past Gertie or Nell."

He enclosed her hand with his, holding her gaze. "Tell me what you want to do now? Gertie's about bursting at the seams wanting to hear from us."

"I wanted to talk to you about it, Dawson. Are you comfortable marrying sooner rather than later? Or do you want the time we thought we had here at my place to settle down and get to know each other thoroughly?"

"I'm fine with whatever you need, sweetheart. I caved in and admitted not only that I loved you months ago, but I also, if things went good between us, was going to ask you to marry me at that time."

"Leave it to Gertie to upend the apple cart," she groused, amusement and fondness in her voice. She laid her left hand over his. "I know Gertie and Nell are up there in age and no one knows when we're leaving this planet. What would you think of getting married in mid-September? The colors of the fall leaves will be so beautiful around here. And it's my favorite month of the year. We'd have a month to plan the wedding. Would your parents be able to come?"

"They'd drop everything to see me married," he teased. "That sounds good."

"I'm going to ask Gertie and Nell to work with Mom on all the wedding plans. With my job, I won't have that luxury, and I trust those three to do everything that's needed. Sound okay with you?"

"I don't think a team of horses could pull Gertie away from heading up this mission to marry us," and he chuckled.

Sarah laughed softly, scooting over to where he sat and pulling her hand from his. Framing his face, she leaned forward, her lips caressing his. Feeling his hands fall over her shoulders made her feel so loved. Their noses touched, and she slid her lips more fully against his mouth. There was a warrior inside this man who matched the warrior within her. And maybe that was what attracted them so undeniably to each other; that recognition of spirit, of bravery even if they were scared witless. This was the man she wanted as her husband, her confidant, her best friend and someone she could fully entrust her heart and soul to. "I love you, Dawson," she whispered against his mouth.

Her drew her ever close to him. "And I'll love you forever, Sarah. Forever. . . ."

# ABOUT THE AUTHOR

*New York Times* and *USA Today* bestselling author **Lindsay McKenna** is the pseudonym of award-winning author Eileen Nauman. With more than 185 titles to her credit and approximately 23 million books sold in 33 countries worldwide, Lindsay is one of the most distinguished authors in the women's fiction genre. She is the recipient of many awards, including six *RT Book Reviews* awards (including best military romance author) and an *RT Book Reviews* Career Achievement Award. In 1999, foreseeing the emergence of ebooks, she became the first bestselling women's fiction author to exclusively release a new title digitally. In recognition of her status as one of the originators of the military adventure/romance genre, Lindsay is affectionately known as "The Top Gun of Women's Military Fiction." Lindsay comes by her military knowledge and interest honestly — by continuing a family tradition of serving in the U.S. Navy. Her father, who served on a destroyer in the Pacific theater during World War II, instilled a strong sense of patriotism and duty in his daughter. Visit Lindsay at lindsaymckenna .com.

The employees of Thorndike Press hope you have enjoyed this Large Print book. All our Thorndike, Wheeler, and Kennebec Large Print titles are designed for easy reading, and all our books are made to last. Other Thorndike Press Large Print books are available at your library, through selected bookstores, or directly from us.

For information about titles, please call:
(800) 223-1244

or visit our website at:
gale.com/thorndike

To share your comments, please write:
Publisher
Thorndike Press
10 Water St., Suite 310
Waterville, ME 04901